"Would you like to dance?"

Abby's heartbeat quickened. It would be very strange to be held in the arms of a man so like the one who'd entranced and ruined her Aunt Lydia. However, if she agreed, it would be a chance to recreate a little bit of history. Even the music the band was playing hinted at the days of rebels and belles.

"I'd love to," she agreed, getting up. Gallantly Carter led her out to the dance floor. Then, with a courtly bow, he took her in his arms.

As Carter held her, Abby felt somewhat overwhelmed by his closeness. It was one thing to admire a man like him from a distance; it was quite another to be caught up in the orbit of his physical presence.

ABOUT THE AUTHOR

Clare Richmond lives in Maryland with her husband, three children, two youthful german shepherds and her maine coon cat. She writes nonfiction, mysteries, and poetry as well as romances. *Pirate's Legacy* was inspired by a recent riverboat trip she took while researching a travel article. When she's not at her typewriter she can be found pursuing her various hobbies: swimming, snorkling, reading, taking photographs, and ice skating.

Books by Clare Richmond

HARLEQUIN AMERICAN ROMANCE

174–RUNAWAY HEART
215–BRIDE'S INN

CLARE RICHMOND

PIRATE'S LEGACY

Harlequin Books

TORONTO • NEW YORK • LONDON
AMSTERDAM • PARIS • SYDNEY • HAMBURG
STOCKHOLM • ATHENS • TOKYO • MILAN

To Linda and Jake

Published July 1990

ISBN 0-373-16352-5

Printed in U.S.A.

Chapter One

As the amber lights of New Orleans faded in the distance, the huge red paddle wheel of the *Mississippi Queen* churned up a moon rippled wake. The merry-go-round sounds of "Dixie," mixed with the excited chatter of the boat's passengers, filled the air.

Abby Heatherington watched the levee slide past her stateroom window. She'd been planning for this day for months and now that it was here she could hardly breathe. Somewhere in the festive crowd on board was the man she sought—the man who held the key that could undo a more than century-old injustice. But she knew that to manage that she'd have to play the hand fate had dealt her as carefully as a riverboat's gambler.

Turning away from the window, Abby lifted two scarred books out of the satchel she'd been carrying. She opened the smaller of the two, a diary, and her green eyes scanned the familiar faded handwriting.

> I know I shall never see my love again or walk the green fields of The Prize of India. My soul is heavy with the knowledge that my remaining years will be barren. I hardly know how I will bear such a cruel and unjust fate. But I believe that heaven will guide my steps and

reveal the truth someday. Until then my thoughts shall remain in Louisiana and my dreams harken back to my beloved Byron. For surely my poor heart will always ache for him.

Abby lifted her gaze from the page. Closing the diary, she placed it on the bed and picked up the second volume, a Civil War History. From long use it fell open to the page she wanted. For a moment she allowed herself to gaze on the dark-eyed man pictured there. Her nostrils flared and she shut the book with a snap.

After placing the two books in the dresser drawer, Abby checked her watch. It was almost time to begin. She picked up the colorful brochures that had been provided for the eight journalists on this press trip.

As she prepared to leave, she lifted a hand thoughtfully to one of her pearl-drop earrings. For several seconds she rolled the smooth orb between her fingers, enjoying the silky feel of it against her skin.

The earrings were special and symbolic—as if all the history of one hundred years could be distilled into the two round opalescent beads that peeked from behind Abby's shoulder-length brown hair. Over a century ago, they had belonged to the tragic diarist, Abby's ancestor, Lydia Stewart.

Normally Abby would not have brought anything so valuable along on a press trip, but for her this was no ordinary jaunt. True, she was on assignment for *Southern Pursuit*, an upscale magazine directed at the affluent traveller venturing below the Mason-Dixon line. But she also had a personal agenda. She was stalking Carter Forbes, the owner of The Prize of India plantation, the place where a century ago her Great-great-great-aunt Lydia met her doom.

Squaring her shoulders, Abby walked out of the room to make her way upstairs for the orientation that was to kick off both the trip and her secret mission.

"There you are," Denise Markham cried out as Abby walked into the riverboat's lounge. Dressed in a well-cut yellow suit, the ship's public relations representative came forward and took Abby's small hand. "How nice you look. Let me take you around and introduce you to your fellow writers."

"I'm anxious to meet them," Abby replied with a smile. As she spoke she looked beyond Denise's auburn mane to the circle of men and women chatting with the paddle wheeler's captain. She was disappointed that none of the men looked the way she expected Carter Forbes did. But she expected she'd be meeting him soon.

She took a mint julep from a waiter and stood sipping it while Denise began to make introductions.

"This is Ordell Bradley," the public relations woman said as she tapped the shoulder of a short, rotund man with a blond handlebar mustache and receding hairline. "He's our culinary expert. Ordell has his own cable television show, *The Bon Vivant*, up in New York and has written several best-selling regional cookbooks."

"Pleased to meet you," Ordell told Abby, holding out a soft but capable-looking hand. "I fully plan to expand my boyish waistline on this trip. And judging from the hors d'oeuvres I've been testing," he added, eyeing a passing tray of spicy popcorn shrimp, "it's a good thing I packed my elastic waistbands."

Abby had to laugh. Obviously this was a man who enjoyed his work.

"Don't worry," a tall, thin woman added, "everything is no calorie on this trip. That's right, isn't it, Denise?"

The redhead laughed. "But of course. By the way, Abby, have you met Joanna Hudson, the food writer for Baseline News Service?"

"No, I haven't had the pleasure."

"Well, I'm pleased to meet you. We'll be next-door neighbors on the cruise," Joanna said, shaking Abby's hand.

Abby's green eyes crinkled at the corners as she smiled at the attractive gray-haired woman. The journalist was probably in her late fifties but she had an air of vitality that made her seem ageless.

"I hear you're from Baltimore," Joanna went on. "I'm heading that way next month to do a restaurant feature on your Inner Harbor."

"Mmmmmm, the Chesapeake Bay," Ordell exclaimed, "Soft shell crabs, hard shells, oysters, clams, crab fluff."

"Yes, we've got great seafood."

"Could you fill me in on the best places to eat?" Joanna asked.

"Better yet, I'll take you around when you come into town," Abby volunteered.

The older woman's blue eyes sparkled. "Oh, I'd love that, but I know you must be pretty busy."

Abby shrugged. "Well I do juggle two jobs," she conceded. "I do free-lance articles for *Southern Pursuit* magazine, and I teach history at Catonsville Community College. But really, I'd love to show you the Inner Harbor."

Joanna looked wistful. "You teach history? That was my favorite subject in college. What period do you specialize in?"

"The Civil War," Abby answered.

"Well," Denise exclaimed. "This is the right place for you. The area is bursting with Civil War atmosphere."

"And sometimes," Ordell put in with a wink, "I think the battle is still being fought."

Little did he know, Abby thought, how true that was. As she took another sip of her julep, she looked around again. Was her quarry here yet? She had done some research on Carter Forbes before she'd left Baltimore, and she knew that he was thirty-nine and lived on his ancestral estate. She'd also learned he was a filmmaker and had won several awards for his travelogues.

Though Abby had never seen a photograph of Forbes, she had found the one of his great-great-grandfather Byron in an old history book. She could still remember the thrill that had shot through her when she'd first flipped open the book and thumbed through the inset of old portraits. Byron's face had seemed to reach out to her, stopping her cold.

Abby, normally sensible to a fault, had grown obsessed with the picture. No wonder poor Aunt Lydia had forsaken her home and heritage and had fallen under the spell of that man. Even a century later with nothing more than an antique photo to look at, Abby had felt the pull of Byron Forbes's attraction. But paradoxically that had only made her all the more determined to investigate the wrong he had done to Lydia.

Meanwhile Abby had lost the thread of the others' conversation, but no one had noticed. Ordell and Joanna seemed to be discussing dim sum in Hong Kong and Denise's attention was on someone who was signaling her from a far corner.

"Time to go in for the presentation," Denise said. "Then we'll have dinner."

On the way to the library, Abby chatted with her new acquaintances, striving to keep up with her companions' light banter. But her gaze kept straying to corners and doorways.

Several minutes later Abby, Joanna and Ordell joined the five other writers already ensconced in the boat's small library. Abby settled into a seat and looked around expectantly. There was still no sign of anyone who might be Carter Forbes.

Then the door swung open and a tall man strode into the room, waved to Denise and found a spot by the back wall. Abby's hand jerked up to her throat. Those dark mesmeric eyes, the same that she'd seen in that old photograph, left no doubt. This, indeed, was Carter Forbes, Byron Forbes's descendant.

"Everybody," Denise announced with a wave of her hand, "we're ready to begin now. First let me make a few introductions. This is Captain Ritchie."

After the captain had smiled and greeted them, Denise turned and put her hand out toward the handsome newcomer at the back of the room. "Now it's my great pleasure to introduce Carter Forbes, travelogue maker extraordinaire and master of one of Louisiana's finest plantations, The Prize of India. As you all know, starting this year, The Prize is opening its doors to visitors in a big way. The Forbes family will be hosting overnight guests at the plantation, and will be wining and dining fans of Creole and Cajun cuisine in their new restaurant, The Ruby."

"Here, here!" said Ordell, and several of the other writers began to clap. Abby glanced back at Carter who, grinning, acknowledged the applause.

Denise continued, "In addition, The Prize will be the setting for the Louisiana Heritage Festival and Pageant." She looked down at her notes. "Ordell, Joanna and Abby, you all are scheduled to stay at The Prize for the festival while the rest of us journey upriver to Natchez."

Abby hid a smile. When Denise had first gone over the proposed itinerary with Abby, the public relations woman had mentioned that two food writers were planning to stay on at The Prize of India to review its new restaurant and guest quarters. Snatching at what seemed like a heaven-sent opportunity, Abby had managed to get herself included with the shore-bound group. Hopefully that would give her the opportunity to investigate the scene of the crime firsthand, and maybe even find some local records that would help her research.

As Abby silently congratulated herself, Denise went over the other writers' schedules and, that done, launched into a brief orientation lecture about the boat. Abby, along with the others, took out a notebook and dutifully scribbled down facts about paddle wheelers, but she was having trouble concentrating. Ever since Carter Forbes had walked in, he'd been all she could think of.

He certainly looked every inch the true descendant of the Byron Forbes she'd discovered in that photograph. Tall, athletically built with a broad-shouldered, narrow-waisted figure, the latter-day Mr. Forbes was romantically handsome. With his thick, wavy black hair and muscular physique he would have looked right at home in a Confederate gray uniform, atop a charging steed or in a ballroom filled with crinoline-skirted belles, fluttering fans as they vied for his attention.

"Now let me review what will happen tomorrow," Denise was saying. "We'll tour Houmas House, a pre-Civil War plantation home—that's where *Hush Hush Sweet Charlotte* was filmed. We'll be on the river again that afternoon and the following day we'll tour Baton Rouge and enjoy a banquet together before we go our separate ways."

There were murmurs of approval from the writers.

Abby told herself she should try to get a seat next to Carter for the buffet dinner that followed the orientation. But she wasn't aggressive enough and was outmaneuvered by the recreation columnist for *Waterways Magazine* and the travel editor from the *Gator Gazette*. Instead Abby wound up at a table with Ordell, Denise and a writer from *Senior Traveler*. The conversation was interesting, hopscotching from war correspondent experiences, to skydiving, to Moroccan cuisine. But Abby's mind kept slipping back again and again to the subject of Carter Forbes. Tomorrow she'd have to make an opportunity to approach him.

Early the following morning the press group walked down the plank to the levee where a crinoline-skirted young woman waited to take them through Houmas House. While the guide shepherded everyone else, including Abby, through the antique-filled rooms, Carter filmed the manicured grounds and took shots of the interior for his travelogue. It wasn't until later as some of the writers plopped down beneath the moss-draped live oaks on the mansion's lawn to sip glasses of cool lemonade that Abby got close enough to Carter to speak to him directly.

"I'm so looking forward to our stay at The Prize of India," she ventured as she gazed into his fine, chiseled features and acknowledged to herself that he had to be one of the most attractive men she'd ever met.

Carter's warm gaze lingered on Abby's piquant face with its vivid green eyes and frame of curly light brown hair, and slowly he gave her an appreciative smile as if noticing her for the first time. "I'm looking forward to it myself. For months we've been working on the cottages, getting them ready for guests. You, Joanna and Ordell will be our first overnight visitors as well as the first to dine in our new restaurant."

"You're a brave man, opening your house and restaurant to food critics and travel writers," Abby replied.

"Brave or foolhardy." Carter favored Abby with another knee-weakening smile.

Abby laughed. "Well, I feel quite honored to help inaugurate The Prize," she added, fingering the pearl-drop earrings she had donned again. They served to remind Abby why she had initiated this conversation with Carter. She was here to learn from him, not to be bowled over by him.

"Indeed," he drawled, "it will be a pleasure to play host to a lovely lady from the North."

Abby smiled and then let her gaze drop to her glass of lemonade. I certainly hope with better results than Aunt Lydia experienced, she thought.

"The Prize of India," Joanna interjected. "What an unusual name for a plantation. How in the world did you come up with it?"

Carter laughed. "Believe me, I'm not the one responsible."

"Ah, pray tell. Who was?" Ordell chimed in.

Carter stretched his legs and leaned back on his elbows. "It's a long story."

"Well, we've got the time," Joanna persisted. Several others seconded her motion.

Carter sat up, shrugged and grinned. "All right. If y'all are willing to listen, I'm willing to tell the tale."

Under her lashes, Abby's green eyes were alert. She knew the story well, but it would be interesting to hear it from the lips of a Forbes.

"The plantation was named after a family treasure," Carter began. "Back in 1720 the original Forbes, Warrick Forbes, that is, was part of a pirate expedition that plundered a grand mogul's treasure ship in the Red Sea."

"Pirates! How romantic!" Joanna gazed at Carter with starry eyes.

"Bad food on those ships, though. Nothing but wormy hardtack and salt pork," Ordell commented between sips of lemonade.

Abby laughed and set her own glass down on the ground. Her gaze fell on Carter's strong tanned hand, which was angled to support part of his weight. An expensive-looking gold watch circled his sinewy wrist, but he wore no rings on his long, well-shaped fingers.

"I don't know about romantic," Carter said. "There was more than a bit of larceny in old Warrick's heart. In addition to his share of the loot, he made off with a priceless ruby the size of a robin's egg, which he called The Prize of India." Carter locked his fingers together and cradled them at the back of his head. "Now, with his ill-gotten riches the pirate came to New Orleans—along with a lot of other thieves and rascals, I might add."

"What did this piratical forebear of yours do with all his ill-gotten riches?" Denise queried.

"Started a sugar plantation near Baton Rouge on the banks of the Mississippi River."

Joanna clapped her hands. "Aha! And named it after the jewel he'd absconded with," Joanna finished.

Carter nodded, and his gaze flicked to Abby and then away. Was it her imagination, or every time he looked her way did she feel a little jolt of electricity between them?

"I'll bet Warrick got a mint for that ruby," Ordell interjected as he wiped his sweaty forehead with a large white handkerchief.

Abby remained quiet. She knew better.

"Actually," Carter said, "he sold the rest of the plunder and kept the jewel. He felt it was his lucky piece. As long as he held on to the ruby, good fortune would smile on him."

"Quite a costly rabbit's foot," Abby commented. "And did it work?"

"Yes, in the decades that followed the family did very well and the region became so civilized that a few generations later my forebears even took the jewel from its hiding place and displayed it among the china, porcelain and other treasures once a year at Christmas."

"How marvelous! Just think, dragging out a mogul's ruby along with the holiday greenery," Joanna exclaimed.

"Unfortunately that's a custom long gone." Carter gazed out on the river, a grim expression settling around his mouth. "During the Civil War, the ruby disappeared."

"Disappeared!" Ordell exclaimed. "What happened? Did some damned Yankee make off with it?"

Abby braced herself. This was the part of the story that affected her most closely.

"You might say that," Carter replied, emptying his glass and shifting his position on the grass.

While she waited for his next words, Abby twisted a paper napkin.

At that moment Carter shot her such an engaging smile that suddenly she wished she could be open with him about the investigation she wanted to launch. Originally that had been her plan, but her father, who was also a historian, had talked her out of simply writing the Forbes family and asking to visit The Prize of India for her research.

"Believe me, Abigirl," he'd advised, "these southern aristocrats can be very touchy about the honor of their family patriarchs. If the Forbes's know that you're related to Lydia Stewart they probably won't let you anywhere near their estate. If you really want to clear your great-great-great-aunt's name and publish something in the process that will win you tenure, you'd better keep it under your hat until you've taken the lay of the land."

"But I only want to find out the truth," Abby had protested.

Peter Heatherington had shaken his head. "Take my word for it, in a case like this the truth can be buried in a field full of land mines."

Carter had continued his story while she'd been lost in memory. "The Forbes men have always had a weakness for a pretty face. And I'm afraid my great-great-grandfather, Byron Forbes, was no exception."

Joanna smacked her palms together. "Ah, the plot thickens. Sounds like a woman had something to do with the ruby's disappearance."

"A female Yankee spy, I'll wager," said Ordell, obviously entranced by his theory.

"As a matter of fact, yes."

Guilt forgotten, Abby forced herself to repress the protest that sprang to her lips. Since reading and rereading her aunt's diary, she'd come to feel very close to her ancestor. And now that she was in the part of the country where Lydia had met her doom, Abby's protective feelings toward that unfortunate woman, who'd died in her thirties forlorn and disgraced, seemed to be intensifying by the minute.

"Go on, go on," Ordell and Joanna chorused.

"It was one Lydia Stewart." Carter glanced over at Abby, wrinkled his brow, and then went on. "As a matter of fact, Lydia was from your neck of the woods, Abby. Didn't I hear you say you came from Baltimore?"

Abby nodded and tried to look as if she had only a passing interest in his tale.

"Well, so was the notorious Miss Stewart."

At that moment one of the young guides from Houmas House brought out a pitcher to refill their glasses, and for a moment conversation ceased as everyone savored the tart, icy drink.

"To continue," Carter finally said, "back in 1860 Lydia Stewart came south to visit a school friend who lived not far from The Prize of India. The friend brought Lydia to a ball and there the charming Miss Stewart met Byron Forbes."

In her mind's eye, Abby had imagined this affair many times. And once again it sprang to life. She knew from an old family album what Lydia had looked like, so it was easy to picture the petite, golden-haired beauty in a green satin gown. With her curls piled on the top of her head and a delicate pearl-drop in each ear—the very ones Abby was wearing—Lydia would have been a lovely vision. And when Byron Forbes in his frock coat and narrow-cut trousers saw her step down the grand staircase, their eyes would have met and locked.

In Abby's imagination, from that moment they'd danced every dance, whirling beneath candlelit chandeliers. And when the ball had ended they must have parted reluctantly, their hands lingering in each other's touch.

"They fell madly in love and soon became engaged," Carter was saying. "The wedding was planned for the following spring. But history intervened."

"The Civil War," Ordell muttered as he rearranged his bulk on the grass.

"Fort Sumpter," Abby said despite herself.

Denise turned toward her. "That's right. You're a historian. You know all about things like that."

Carter raised an eyebrow. "A historian?"

"The Civil War is Abby's specialty," Denise elaborated.

Abby shifted uncomfortably. "Yes, so I'm finding your story quite fascinating," she said to Carter, trying to turn the attention back to him.

"Well, then you've undoubtedly heard of my great-great-grandfather and his activities."

"I certainly have," Abby admitted, no longer able to contain her enthusiasm for the subject. "As I recall, Byron Forbes was a rather famous spymaster."

"Byron was skilled at cracking Union codes and ciphers and establishing new ones for the Confederacy."

Joanna smoothed her skirt and cradled her chin in her palms. "How exciting! But what about he and Lydia?"

"The marriage was postponed, but Lydia stayed on with her school friend. Back home, Baltimore was in chaos. Many of its citizens were pro-Confederacy, but because it was so close to Washington, D.C., the state went Union."

"But what about Lydia?" Joanna persisted. "Where did her sympathies lie?"

"Good question," Carter replied. "At the time, everyone thought she was on our side. But as events turned out, they were wrong."

Abby gritted her teeth. What an impossible situation it must have been for Lydia. Imagine, trapped behind enemy lines and in love with a man who was plotting against all her kin who'd donned the Union Blue. Worse than that, Lydia was probably an object of suspicion everywhere she went. How else could one explain the way all her Southern friends had turned against her in the end?

"Byron used a cipher disk that he had developed to crack enemy codes," Carter said.

"A cipher disk?" Joanna repeated.

"Nowadays codes are cracked with computers," he explained. "But back then spymasters developed devices that allowed them to decipher military messages about troop movements, supplies and battle plans." He explained how the inscribed letters and numbers on the disk were manipulated to work out secret messages.

"Anyhow," Carter went on, "at the height of the hostilities, the cipher disk was stolen along with the Forbes Ruby."

"You mean The Prize of India disappeared," Joanna exclaimed. "But who took it?"

"Lydia, of course," Ordell said. "Tell me, did she look like Mata Hari?" He batted his eyelashes in parody.

Carter smiled. "As a matter of fact, not at all. There's a portrait of her at the plantation. She was a very sweet and innocent-looking blonde, not at all the type one would suspect to be a spy."

"That must have made her all the more effective," Joanna commented.

Abby's blood was boiling, but she said nothing.

"The jewel and cipher disk disappeared just as Lydia was sneaking off to the North to rejoin her family in Baltimore."

That was too much for Abby. "I've read about the case and as far as I could tell there was no solid proof Lydia stole the ruby or the cipher," she blurted our. "The evidence was all circumstantial."

Carter regarded Abby with amazement. "It was obvious that Lydia was guilty, Madame Attorney," he countered with a shade of sarcasm that told Abby that she'd overstepped her bounds and that her father had been right about the Forbes family feeling. Immediately she realized her mistake. No matter how strongly she felt, it would be foolish at this stage to cast suspicions on his family honor in front of an audience.

But in a few short days, she hoped to be able to make Carter Forbes eat his words.

Chapter Two

Following Abby's outburst there was a moment of discomfort, which Carter smoothly dispelled. "Anyhow," he said with a forced laugh, "guilty or not, Lydia Stewart didn't pay the price of her treachery. Though she was actually sentenced to hang, she escaped and made her way back to Baltimore."

Yes, Abby thought, where her reputation had followed her. Lydia had been ostracized by Southern sympathizers there and had pined away from disgrace and heartbreak. She'd never married and had died young. Some escape.

"The jewel and the disk were never recovered," Carter said, finishing the story.

Ordell sucked his teeth. "This is quite a family you have, Forbes. Spymaster, smuggler, pirate—with all those roguish genes etched in your DNA, it's a wonder you're not on assignment for *Soldier of Fortune* magazine instead of just making tame travelogues."

Carter laughed. "Between traveling, filmmaking, running the plantation, arranging a festival complete with food and entertainment, not to mention bringing up my daughter, Callie, I have more than enough challenges to meet."

So Carter was married. The twinge of disappointment that Abby felt after hearing this information was much stronger than it had any right to be.

A puzzled look crossed Joanna's face. "Hmmm. Why did I have the idea you were single?"

"Probably because I am. I was divorced three years ago," Carter told her matter-of-factly.

"Sorry to hear that," Joanna replied.

Carter set his jaw. "Don't be. It happens."

Once again Abby's emotional barometer rose sharply. Yes, she admitted, Carter Forbes was one very attractive man. But she wasn't about to play Mata Hari, as Ordell suggested Lydia had done, to get what she needed.

Joanna opened her mouth to ask another question but Ordell beat her to it, hitting Carter with a barrage of queries about the festival and the regional specialties that would be served at it.

"These questions should wait until we arrive at The Prize," Carter protested. "My aunt Mary Lou, who lives with Callie and me, is really the one you should ask about the festival. It's her pet project."

"Hmmm," Ordell said. "I can't wait till we get there."

Abby was thinking exactly the same thing.

UNDERWAY AGAIN that afternoon, they flew kites from the stern of the *Mississippi Queen* as the big paddle wheeler glided past heavily laden barges. After they arrived at Baton Rouge, the writers climbed into a van for their tour of the Plantation Life Museum at Louisiana State University. The tour took all morning and was followed by a gourmet Creole lunch of blackened redfish and ratatouille.

"What are you going to do with your free afternoon," Denise asked as she pushed away her empty dish and turned toward Ordell.

"I've arranged to visit Chef John and trade some recipes with him," Ordell answered, patting his paunch.

"Oh, may I join you?" Joanna asked. "I've heard so many good things about his jambalaya."

"Ummmm, it's close to heaven." Ordell kissed his thumb and forefinger. "I should warn you," he added scanning Joanna's trim figure, "you'll come back looking like me."

Joanna dismissed his remark with a wave. "Don't worry. I've got a great metabolism. Years of writing about pasta, pork chops and pastries and I haven't put on a pound."

"There's no justice in this world," Ordell said. He turned to Abby. "How about you, Abigail? Are you willing to risk your waistline with us this afternoon?"

Abby smiled and shook her head. She had to think quickly. Her plans for the afternoon were ones she didn't care to divulge. "Actually I have a friend I want to look up," she replied cagily. It was the truth, sort of.

"I'm glad to hear that," Carter interjected, leaning forward from the end of the table where he was seated. He favored Abby with a warm smile. "I'd hate to see a figure like Ms. Heatherington's put in jeopardy."

Abby blushed and smoothed the skirt of the pink-and-white floral cotton dress she was wearing. She hadn't realized that Carter was listening to their conversation or that he'd been looking at her that closely.

While the dessert menus were being passed out, Abby excused herself and left. She was anxious to get started on her enterprise and she didn't want to have to do any more explaining.

"The Archives," she told the taxi driver as she slid into the back seat of a cab.

About an hour later Abby found what she'd been looking for. The trial transcript, in a tiny faded handwriting, covered several pages. Reverently Abby turned its yellowed leaves, her eyes glued to the drama unfolding on each line.

As she read, she pictured the scene. The time was August 1863 and it must have been a breathlessly hot day, the kind of muggy afternoon when people sat fanning themselves with folded newspapers. In the humidity, tempers would flash like heat lightning across a darkening sky. Clearly emotions had been running high during the testimony. Some of the accusations against Lydia Stewart sounded almost rabid.

"A pack of lies," she muttered to herself. What an ordeal it must have been for her aunt, trapped in that steamy courtroom, hearing those cruel words, surrounded by people who'd already condemned her to the hangman's noose.

Abby's hands clenched as if she were the one being accused. How could Byron Forbes, who'd loved her, have stood there and let his neighbors hurl such slander at Lydia? In her mind's eye, Abby pictured not Byron Forbes, but Carter, as she'd first seen him in the boat's library, standing against the wall with his arms folded across his broad chest. A wave of hostility swept over her. Then Abby brought herself up short and shook her head to clear it. That wasn't rational, she warned herself. Carter and Byron might share the same bloodline, but they were, after all, two different men, living in two different eras.

Pushing Carter's image away, Abby read on. After she'd finished the last page of transcript, she stared at the shadows on the floor, reflecting on the long-ago events that had touched so many lives. Everyone in that courtroom had condemned Lydia, but one person's testimony in particular seemed to have clinched her great-great-great-aunt's fate.

"That woman's a vicious Yankee schemer," Jerome Matthews had accused. "Who knows how many Confederate deaths she may be responsible for."

"Jerome Matthews," Abby muttered under her breath. Who had he been? And had he really overheard Lydia passing secret information to a Northern spy as he claimed? If he'd been lying, what might his motives have been? And would it even be possible after all these decades, Abby asked herself, to unlock the true story?

Thoughtfully she wrote down the man's name in round, neat script on the pad in front of her. She tapped her pencil against the edge of the pad. Maybe when she got to The Prize of India she'd be able to find out more about him.

BACK ON THE *MISSISSIPPI QUEEN* that evening, men in suits and women in cocktail dresses swirled around the wooden floor in the boat's main ballroom. Abby, along with the other writers, had gathered to sip after-dinner drinks and trade tall tales about their travel adventures. As she sat, dressed in a filmy white chiffon frock, in the plush cushioned chairs at the edge of the dance floor, she brushed back some strands of dark hair, revealing Lydia's pearl earrings. She was beginning to regard the antique jewels as if they were a rabbit's foot, or at the very least a talisman to propel her on.

During the conversation, Abby's eyes strayed to Carter who, handsome in his dark charcoal-gray suit, stood nearby talking to the boat's social director. Though she'd been seated diagonally across from him earlier at dinner, Carter's attention had been taken up by Denise who was making suggestions on new angles for his latest Mississippi River travelogue.

All evening Abby had been intensely aware of Carter. She couldn't help but be piqued that he seemed oblivious to her. She knew that her reaction was silly. But Carter was just so much a part of the family drama that she'd been researching that he'd already become the center of her world on this trip. Okay, Abby warned herself, move slowly and don't be so intense. But she knew she wasn't the only one depending on the outcome of this expedition. Back in Baltimore, her father would be waiting, hoping that she would right the ancient wrong. And she wouldn't have much time to do it in, so she'd better get started as soon as she reached the Prize.

"Oh, this afternoon with Chef John was culinary heaven," Joanna breathed. "He's so creative, not only with taste but with the way he blended the colors on the plate. It was like looking at an artist's palette."

"Only better," interjected Ordell. "You can eat his."

The group chuckled and then another writer began to describe an afternoon of garden tours. Yet another talked about visiting the Myrtles Plantation, a two-hundred-year-old haunted house.

Denise turned to Abby. "And how did you spend your time?"

"Very profitably," Abby replied.

"That depends on how you define the term," Ordell teased. "On our way back in the taxi, Joanna and I saw you coming out of the State Archives. How you could waste a glorious afternoon in a stuffy old library, I can't imagine."

"Not like us," Joanna said, poking her elbow into her plump companion. "We spent the glorious afternoon inside a steaming hot kitchen."

"That's different," Ordell insisted.

Abby laughed and wondered how much she should divulge. "I'm doing some research for a book I'm planning to write."

"A Civil War tome, naturally," Ordell said, taking a sip of club soda.

Abby searched for a way to tell the truth without revealing her purpose. "Yes, it will be a novel of plantation life."

Denise's eyebrows shot up. "Oh, you must tell Carter. I'm sure he'll want to help you. Your stay at The Prize of India will be a perfect opportunity to immerse yourself in the era."

"Yes, I'm sure it will," Abby said, nodding. In fact, she was counting on it.

"And your friend?" Joanna asked.

"Oh, she wasn't around," Abby replied. Inwardly she was groaning. What was that old saying? Something like "Oh, what a tangled web we weave when first we practice to deceive."

Their conversation was interrupted by the social director who announced the stage show, an old-time riverboat review featuring banjo players and a sultry singer. As the band assembled, Carter came over and took a seat behind Abby. She sat up very straight, conscious of his proximity.

"And now, let's hear it for Mimi Malone, the last of the red-hot mamas," the emcee blared, his lips to the microphone.

With a drum roll and a burst of applause, a buxom blonde in a slinky red floor-length dress that might have come from Mae West's closet strolled out on stage. Flinging her black feather boa over one white shoulder, she belted out, "One of these days..." The audience clapped wildly and she continued, booming out familiar song after song, many of them filled with coy innuendos.

After the singer finished her set and made her bows, the dance band took over, playing a dreamy waltz.

"I must get my beauty rest," Ordell announced after a bit. "We get off bright and early tomorrow morning."

"Party pooper," Joanna said as the portly gourmet got up to depart.

When he had disappeared, a couple of other writers stood to dance so there were only four left in their group—Abby,

Joanna, Carter and the columnist from *Senior Traveler*. He and Joanna quickly immersed themselves in a discussion about New Orleans. For a few minutes, Abby pretended to be listening but her real focus was still on Carter who now lounged comfortably a few feet away in the chair catercorner to hers. Once again their eyes met and he smiled.

"Would you like to dance," he asked.

Abby's heartbeat quickened. It would be very strange to be held in the arms of a man so like the one who'd entranced and ruined her Aunt Lydia. However, if she agreed, it would be a chance to recreate a little bit of history. Even the music the band was playing hinted at the mood of the days of rebels and belles.

"I'd love to," she agreed, getting up. Gallantly Carter touched her elbow and led her out to the dance floor. His firm hand was cool against her warm skin. Then with a courtly bow, he took her in his arms.

The music changed to another nostalgic melody that was slow and sensual. They glided effortlessly among the other couples. As Carter held her, Abby felt somewhat overwhelmed by his closeness. It was one thing to admire a man like him from a distance; it was quite another to be caught up in the orbit of his physical presence. The whole time they danced, she was very much aware of his tall, athletic body beneath the fine light wool of his jacket. He wore no aftershave but his skin emitted a healthy masculine scent that appealed to her own long-suppressed femininity.

It had been a while since Abby had been so attracted to a man. She'd had two serious relationships during her twenty-seven years but neither had worked out. Lately, encouraged by her father, a retired history professor, she'd been preoccupied with publishing enough professional articles so that she could get tenure at the college where she taught. And then her academician father had thrown another distraction in her path—Lydia Stewart's diary. Since he'd dusted it off and presented it to her more than a year ago, she'd dreamed of writing a book about Lydia Stewart and her times.

"You're a good dancer," Carter murmured.

"Well, I've a good partner," she replied. It was no exaggeration. Carter was light on his feet yet he guided her with authority.

Through the next four numbers, they lived up to each other's compliments as they swept through a waltz, two foxtrots and a long, exhausting jitterbug. So caught up were they in their dancing, that it wasn't until they stopped and walked back to their seats that they noticed the other writers had gone.

"Looks like we're the only ones with stamina," Carter said.

"I don't know about my stamina," Abby replied, still trying to catch her breath. "Ordell is right. We do have an early morning tomorrow. Maybe I should turn in."

"Surely you have enough strength for a nightcap or a stroll around the deck," Carter countered. "It would be a shame to waste all that Mississippi moonlight out there."

Abby glanced out the window at the lights of Baton Rouge. They glittered against the night sky like tiny bonfires. The cooler temperature outdoors would feel good after all their strenuous activity, and she had to admit that she didn't want to say goodbye to Carter yet. Wasn't this the perfect opportunity to get to know him better?

"I wouldn't mind a breath of fresh air," Abby heard herself saying.

"Good." He guided her through the dwindling crowd and out onto the observation deck. As the door closed behind them, the music became a muted backdrop to the warm breeze blowing gently off the river.

"Now isn't that better," Carter said as he stretched his arms over his head. He took off his jacket and draped it over one broad shoulder. Together they walked to the railing where they leaned over to look at the velvety dark water.

Suddenly Abby remembered a passage from Aunt Lydia's diary:

> It was when I saw Byron in the moonlight on the veranda that I knew our fates would be joined. He was standing there in his gray frock coat, leaning against the porch railing. He was watching the moonlight sparkle in the river but I was much more taken by the way it outlined his strong, chiseled profile.

Now Abby turned to glance at the outline of Carter's handsome features. A strange feeling of déjà vu rippled down her spine. Quickly she returned her gaze to the river.

"Is that the Old State Capitol over there?" she asked, using the question to divert her disturbing thoughts. She pointed to a strange castlelike building. On the tour today, she'd seen the statehouse but at night everything looked different—more mysterious.

"Yes," Carter told her. "And down in front of it is the Art and Science Center."

"This is such an interesting part of the country," Abby went on. The breeze lifted her hair off her forehead and her gauzy white skirt billowed out around her knees.

"Yes, but with the oil bust, we've had some hard times lately. However, we've survived worse."

"The Civil War?"

"Exactly." He turned toward her. "But you know all about that since it's your field."

"Not all about it. There's a lot I'm hoping to find out when I visit The Prize of India." Abby winced, hoping she hadn't given anything away. She'd phrased that last comment badly.

"The Prize certainly has its share of history," Carter continued. He paused for a moment and then looked at her quizzically. "Denise mentioned that you're writing a book. Just exactly what sort of book is it?"

Abby hesitated. If she were honest with herself she'd have to admit that what she'd seen of Carter Forbes so far, she liked. In fact, while they'd been dancing, she'd found his physical allure almost overpowering. Should she tell him exactly why she wanted to visit his plantation? It was difficult for her to be dishonest with anyone so she was tempted to tell him the truth. But she knew doing that might color anything he or his family told her about The Prize's history. No, she decided, she'd just have to stick to her original plans. And not, Abby thought, looking at her handsome escort, make the same foolish mistakes Lydia had.

"It's a novel about plantation life," she said finally. "But I want it to be as historically accurate as possible."

The corners of Carter's mouth lifted. "Is this novel of yours going to have a heroine as lovely as you?"

Abby felt herself flush. "I guess in some ways, she's going to be a lot like me."

"Oh, then she's going to be a Yankee," he queried.

"Well, sort of—really a woman from a border state. She'll be from Baltimore."

"And will the hero be a plantation owner?"

"Yes, I did have something like that in mind." Abby was getting uncomfortable. His guesses were too close to the truth.

"That's not an uncommon story down here." He took a step closer to her. She could see the starlight reflected in his eyes. "We southern gentlemen tend to be susceptible to the charms of pretty northerners."

He tipped her chin up and looked searchingly down into her face. Abby was sure he meant to kiss her and, despite all her strong resolve, she felt herself drawn to him. She leaned closer and her eyelids half closed as she gazed invitingly up at his strong features. But to her surprise and undeniable disappointment, instead of bending down to touch his lips to hers, he stood gazing at her for a moment. Then he let his hands drop and drew back.

"And," he said, turning back to the river, "sometimes mixing North and South even in this day and age isn't such a good idea."

"Oh? The Civil War's been over for more than a century." Abby's voice was shaky.

"Not down here. I think you'll discover that after you've been in these parts for a while. Anyhow, Abby, to be honest with you, I just fought one of the latest battles myself."

She studied the back of his head. "What do you mean?"

"When you come to The Prize of India tomorrow, you'll meet the real prize of the plantation, my daughter, Callie. She's twelve now but when her mother and I separated, a year before the divorce, Callie was only eight."

"That must have been very rough."

"Very."

Abby noted the way his broad shoulders had hunched. Obviously this was still a very sensitive subject and she decided it was best not to press him. For a while they were both silent. Only the quiet lap of the water against the hull of the boat and the occasional footsteps and conversation of fellow passengers as they walked by on the deck disturbed their solitude.

Finally Carter spoke. "My ex-wife was a New York City girl, a model who I'd worked with on a film. Diana was gorgeous—tall and blond. Callie looks a lot like her."

"Coming down here and living on an old plantation must have been quite a change for your wife after the hustle and bustle of New York."

"Indeed. Diana did try, though. As a matter of fact, she made a valiant effort the first couple of years we were together. Even after we had Callie, Diana would take the baby and travel with me while I did my films. But she missed New York and modeling. And she hated Louisiana."

Abby sensed the turmoil behind Carter's quiet voice. There was a lot of pain and unhappiness in this man's past. She wanted to reach up and touch his shoulder in sympathy but she restrained herself.

"Anyhow to make a long story short, Diana got herself a month-long modeling assignment in Paris. And never came back to The Prize. It was painful for me but it wounded Callie deeply."

"That explains your comment about the antagonism between North and South."

He smiled wryly and turned to Abby again. "Yes, that's what I meant when I said the two don't mix very well. With my failed marriage and, as you'll find out, with my family history, the Forbes family should probably just stay away from pretty Northerners." For a long moment, he looked at her regretfully and then he kissed her lightly on the cheek. "It's been a lovely evening but it's getting late. Maybe we'd both better turn in."

Abby took one last look at the moonlight rippling on the water and then looked back at Carter. She hoped she wasn't about to fire the first volley in a whole new war between North and South.

Chapter Three

"Well, Carter darling, where are they?" Mary Lou asked, looking up from the paper she was writing on. The slender, elegant grand dame of the Forbes family sat in her favorite blue velvet wing chair by the window, working on some last-minute changes for the pageant. The morning sun streamed in through the window haloing her bouffant silver-blond hair.

Carter smiled at the effect. "You look like an angel with your hair all lit up like that," he joked.

"Well, I'm certainly a candidate for sainthood after dealing with all these details," Mary Lou grumped good-naturedly as she placed her clipboard on the antique Pembroke table beside her and gazed expectantly at her handsome nephew.

"To answer your question, our three honored guests took a side trek out to Nottoway to sample an outdoor brunch," Carter said, striding across the polished wood floor of the ladies' parlor. He bent to give his aunt's powdered cheek an affectionate peck. Still a Southern belle at heart despite her sixty-five years, Aunt Mary Lou smelled of gardenias, as always.

"Nottoway," Mary Lou cried, "that's our competition."

"Oh, come now, Aunt Mary Lou," Carter replied with a chuckle. "There's enough tourists to keep all us plantation owners happy."

She sighed and rubbed her eyes. "You know how I am. I've been in such a dither what with The Ruby's opening and the festival next week. I swear if I survive all the politics, details and mix-ups, I really will have earned my spot in heaven."

Again her nephew laughed. "I'm sure when that day comes—and it's a long way away for sure—Saint Peter himself will escort you through the pearly gates."

"Oh, Carter," she said with a wave of her hand and a flirtatious smile. "You're incurable. Flattering an old lady like me." She pointed at the damask love seat that rested opposite her chair on the faded Persian rug. "Now, dear, why don't you sit down and tell me all about these Yankees who'll be invading us. By the way, when will they arrive?"

"Later this afternoon," Carter said as he sank his long body into the horsehair cushions and stretched out his legs.

"Uh, oh. I'm giving a house tour at three. If they come in around then can you take care of them?"

"No problem."

Mary Lou sat back and folded her hands across her lap. "Well, tell me about our guests," she repeated.

On his way to the plantation from the boat, Carter had been wondering just what to say to his aunt about the three travel writers. Joanna and Ordell would be easy enough to describe but Abby... He remembered last night, when they'd come so close to embracing in the moonlight. Abby was another matter. Where man-woman relationships were concerned Mary Lou had been born with high-tech radar and he knew she'd quickly detect any interest he had in the pretty young travel journalist.

Cautiously he recounted the riverboat trip to his aunt, giving thumbnail sketches of the entire cast of characters.

"This Ordell," Mary Lou exclaimed, "he sounds delightful. I can't wait to place a napkin under his chubby little chin and ply him with our blackened redfish. And Joanna with her round-the-world adventures sounds like a wonderful addition to any house party. But," she added narrowing her blue eyes as she studied her nephew's innocent expression, "you haven't said much about this Abby."

Carter tried to respond casually. "Well, she's a nice young lady."

"And?"

Carter shifted in the seat. "And what?" he said as if he were a teenager evading a curious parent's inquisition.

"Well, you've told me she writes for a magazine and teaches history in college, but what's she like? Is she tall, short, thin, fat, charming, dull, pretty as primrose or plain as skunk cabbage?"

Carter rolled his eyes and groaned. "Plain as skunk cabbage?"

"Are you admiring my poetic language or answering my question?"

"Recoiling from the image," Carter parried. "Miss Heatherington, for your information, is about the right height and about the right weight and she's more like a rose than a cabbage."

"Hmmm. Now there's an illuminating description. I suspect your wishy-washy adjectives are cloaking a secret attraction." She lifted a penciled eyebrow expectantly.

"Aunt Mary Lou, I just met the woman." So much for trying to be casual, Carter thought. Ever since his divorce three years ago, every time his matchmaking aunt had seen him in the vicinity of any remotely eligible female, she'd gone on the alert for wedding preparations.

"A very promising first step," she shot back.

"All right, Miss Abby Heatherington is a very attractive, smart and charming young lady and I like her, but you can forget picking out a dress to wear to the wedding. The last thing I need is an involvement with another impossible Yankee."

Mary Lou nodded. "Well, you do have a point, dear. It isn't as if there aren't plenty of eligible young ladies around here who'd trade in their mother's false teeth to get a second glance from you. Still, I'll be very interested to meet Miss Heatherington."

"Well, you will soon enough," Carter replied, dismissing the subject as he leaned forward and picked up the clipboard Mary Lou had set on the table when he'd walked in. He flipped through a few pages and stopped at one with a sketch on it. "Very nice," he said, studying the pencil drawing of a hoop-skirted antebellum ball dress. Then, still holding the clipboard, he walked over to the fireplace and looked up at the full-length portrait in the ornate gilt frame above the mantel. He stood, holding the sketch at arm's length, comparing the two.

"You've made some changes."

"Yes, the seamstress suggested that we add some lace to cover up the low neckline because, let's face it, Elaine lacks Lydia's voluptuousness."

Carter raised his eyes to the oval-faced beauty in the portrait and mentally compared it to his spinsterish neighbor, Elaine Matthews. She might be playing the part of Lydia Stewart in the pageant but she *was* a far cry from the curvaceous original.

"Lord knows, we tried stuffing her, fluffing her up with a lot of padding, but Elaine just looked like a stick wadded with cotton, so the seamstress came up with this little bit of froufrou. What do you think?"

"About Elaine or the lace?" Carter said, laying down the sketch.

Mary Lou gave her nephew a dismissive wave. "I already know what you think of Elaine. That woman is like a stuck record—caught in the same old song. Ever since Diana ran off with that horrible Frenchman, poor Elaine's been chasing after you as if she were an old hunting hound hot on the track of a prize jackrabbit. Anyhow, I was asking about the costume."

"Looks fine to me. How is everything else going with the festival?"

Mary Lou was in the middle of regaling Carter with an account of the latest dustup over the new version of the pageant script written by Elaine Matthews's brother, Prestwood, when the sound of a barking dog and slamming door put an end to their discussion.

"Daddy," a high-pitched girl's voice squealed in delight. "You're back!" The owner of the voice, a wiry, ponytailed blonde with a dirt-smeared face bounded through the room followed by a contingent of playful canines.

"Callie, those pesky dogs belong outside," Aunt Mary Lou cried as she jumped up and brushed away the lolling tongue of Barney, the big old hound dog who led the pack. "Just look, they've already shed a bale of hair on your father's pants' legs."

Carter, however, merely looked amused as he stroked the gleaming head of a golden retriever named, appropriately, Goldie.

"These pants are due for a trip to the cleaner's anyhow," he said as Callie competed with the affectionate dog by throwing herself into her father's open arms and giving him a big hug. "How's my girl?"

She pulled away and gave him a mischievous look. "In the doghouse."

"Where you, young lady, belong the way you look right now." Mary Lou scowled. "Just look at those jeans—they were clean and pressed this morning. And your shirt—it's smeared with mud. What have you been doing, child, rolling around in a pigpen?"

"Just playing."

"Playing where?" Mary Lou demanded. "Lord, you haven't been traipsing through the swamp again, have you?"

Guiltily Callie glanced from her father to her aunt. "Bobby and I wanted to catch bullfrogs. His cousin Dan's here from Arizona and he's never seen one. We caught a whole passel—big ones, too."

"I can imagine," Mary Lou replied testily. She eyed her nephew. "You're going to have to do something about this wild creature of yours."

"Oh, she's just young and full of high spirits," Carter drawled, gazing at his daughter fondly. "A few bullfrogs never did anyone any harm."

"Maybe not," Mary Lou said, "but there's a time and a place for them. Why just yesterday, Callie tore up her pageant gown. In the middle of the fitting, she upped and ran out of the room and climbed the old live oak tree."

"But I had to save Tiger," Callie protested. "She was stuck up there."

"That ridiculous old cat would have come down on her own when she was good and ready. But the rip on that beautiful dress will take Miss Belinda a good half day to repair—and it will never be the same." Mary Lou threw up her hands. "Being a tomboy is all well and good when you're a little tyke of seven or eight, but Callie Kleeson Forbes, you were twelve last month. It's high time you started acting like a proper young lady."

At this Callie pursed her face into a rebellious expression. The subject of Callie's rough-and-ready ways had become a sore point lately between her and Mary Lou. Realizing that another confrontation was brewing between his only child and his aunt, Carter interrupted and changed the subject. "Come on," he said, sliding Callie off his lap and standing. "Why don't you take me to see these new pets of yours? I haven't seen a passel of bullfrogs in a boll weevil's age." He shot his aunt a mischievous look.

"A boll weevil's age!" Mary Lou exclaimed, throwing up her hands in mock despair. "And you make fun of the way I talk!"

"ABIGIRL? Is that you?"

"Yes, Daddy. It's me," Abby told her father. She was standing by the telephone in Nottoway Plantation's restaurant. The rest of her party, Ordell and Joanna, were still outside at the checkered cloth covered tables with the Baton Rouge public relations reps, sipping wine and polishing off the last pieces of the pecan pie that had topped off their sumptuous brunch.

"Has my spy lady started the Second Civil War, yet?" Peter Heatherington asked.

Abby laughed. "Not yet. In fact so far my mission has gone quite well." Quickly she described her expedition to the Archives and gave an edited version of her meeting with Carter.

"Hmmph. Well, it sounds as if you've uncovered some interesting footnotes to history." Peter Heatherington had come out of retirement to teach Abby's classes so she could pursue her mission in Louisiana. In truth, he, too, had been intrigued with the idea of setting the record straight on Lydia Stewart.

"What do you make of this information about Jerome Matthews?" he asked.

"I don't know, but as soon as I get to The Prize of India, I intend to poke around. If Jerome Matthews played a part in Aunt Lydia's fate, there may be some information about him there."

"Any idea where you're going to start?"

"I don't know," Abby confessed. She glanced toward the open door and noted with alarm that her companions had gotten up from the table. She could see the skirt of Joanna's flowered dress fluttering in the warm breeze and Ordell's white linen suit was bright in the sunlight. They were heading her way. "Anyhow it's a lead. I've got to go, Daddy. There's someone coming and I don't want to blow my cover."

"Wait, Abigirl," Peter Heatherington said quickly. "One word of advice. When you get to The Prize of India be careful whose toes you tread on. Southerners, just like those of us a little farther north, can be very touchy about their families and their traditions. I'd hate to find you coming home dressed in tar and feathers."

"I'll be the soul of discretion," Abby promised. "I never did look good in feathers."

She said goodbye and hung up just as Ordell and Joanna stepped over the threshold. "Wasn't it a glorious brunch?" Joanna exclaimed.

"Terrific," Abby agreed.

Joanna smiled her satisfaction. "So far this has been a culinary fantasy come true. After this feast The Prize of India's new restaurant has its work cut out for it. I hope it can live up to the challenge."

"Well, we'll soon see," Joanna said, slipping her arms through Ordell's and Abby's.

AN HOUR LATER their rental car passed the massive wrought-iron gates of The Prize of India. A canopy of huge live oaks hung over the narrow lane making it seem as if they were riding through a gently curving green tunnel. At the end of the leafy underpass stood a handsome two-story brick mansion with a mellow slate roof broken by three dormers. Eight white columns supported the heavy overhang and a white railed gallery ran the length of the impressive facade.

"Oh, my, how marvelous!" Joanna exclaimed. "Look at those massive chimneys. They must have grand fireplaces inside."

"Yes," Abby agreed, peering through the frame of trees at the beautiful old home. So this was the place where it all happened. Once again that odd feeling of déjà vu swept over her and she felt as if she were returning after a long absence to a home she'd known and loved. The feeling was crazy, she told herself. She'd never even been to Louisiana before.

After Ordell had nosed the car into a gravel parking area to the left of the mansion, they got out and walked up a camellia-lined path to the carved front door with its antique brass knocker.

"What a heavenly smell," Joanna said as they stood waiting.

"We obviously have different ideas of heaven," Ordell replied. "Mine would smell like a pot of simmering cassoulet."

While Abby chuckled Joanna gave Ordell's shoulder a playful thwack. "The man is incorrigible."

A young redheaded woman in a maid's uniform opened the door, greeted them politely and showed them into the entry hall. While they waited beneath the crystal chandelier that was suspended from the two-story ceiling, the maid went through a nearby set of open double doors. She reemerged a few moments later. "Mr. Forbes should be returning at any moment and Miss Mary Lou is in the middle of giving a tour. You're welcome to join the tour group if you like," the maid said, gesturing through the entryway to the ladies' parlor. From the parlor they could hear the murmur of a genteel feminine voice.

"Not a bad idea," said Ordell. "It will give us the lay of the land, so to speak—an orientation to The Prize of India."

"Well, I'm game," Abby replied and the three writers followed the maid into a high-ceilinged room, elegantly furnished with brocaded chairs, mahogany tables and puddled draperies in shades of crème and blue. A small group of ladies stood listening to Mary Lou who was pointing to a large gilt-framed portrait that hung above the marble mantel. "Byron Forbes had this painting done when he and Lydia first became engaged."

"Ah, the notorious Civil War Mata Hari herself," Ordell commented sotto voce behind Abby.

Abby's hand flew to her heart and she suppressed a gasp. This was it—the famous portrait of Lydia Stewart. Abby's gaze traveled over her ancestor's delicate face to her full green gown and then to her pearl-drop earrings. Emotions, strong yet undefined, welled inside her and Abby felt her eyes fill with tears. She wiped them away before anyone could see them.

"Such a beautiful face," one of the elderly women in the group commented. "So sweet. You wouldn't think with an angel's face like that she'd be capable of such treachery."

"A pretty face can mask a barrelful of trouble," another woman answered.

"Lydia Stewart would have had to be beautiful, as well as clever, to blind an astute man like Byron Forbes," Mary Lou said.

The words of Mary Lou and the two visitors pierced Abby's concentration. A flame of anger burned in her throat, overwhelming her urge to cry. Tempted to snap a rebuke, she focused her attention on the speakers. But at that moment Mary Lou came forward to greet the writers and the moment to speak in Lydia's defense passed.

"Welcome to the Prize of India," the older woman said, extending her hand. "We're delighted to have all of you here." After shaking hands with her new guests, Mary Lou went on, "I must apologize. Carter was supposed to be here to greet you, but one of the cats, a very pregnant one, decided to have her litter in a trunk full of pageant props we have stored in the barn. Carter had to go shift her and her newborns into a more suitable maternity ward."

Ordell, Joanna and the women chuckled. Even Abby was able to manage a smile while she pulled herself back together. It had been such an emotional experience for her to be suddenly confronted with that portrait. Given the plantation's history, she hadn't expected to find Lydia's picture so prominently displayed. It gave her revived hope that her mission here would be successful and she'd find the evidence she needed to clear Lydia's name.

"After hearing your comments about the lady in the portrait, I'm surprised to see you have her portrait front stage, so to speak," Joanna commented, echoing Abby's thoughts.

"Actually the perfidious Miss Stewart had been tucked up under the attic rafters for over a century," Mary Lou replied. "We brought her out because of the pageant we're putting on at The Prize of India next week."

"So that means after the pageant it's up under the eaves with her again," Ordell exclaimed.

Mary Lou looked thoughtful. "I must admit that now that I've gotten used to seeing her there, she seems to fit somehow. My nephew will probably have the final word on her fate, but I have a mind to vote that she stay put. It's worth it just for the conversational value alone."

Suddenly, despite Mary Lou's description of Lydia as perfidious, Abby found herself liking Carter's aunt. "Lydia does look as if she belongs there," Abby blurted out.

"Indeed," Mary Lou agreed, studying the painting. "She seems to light up the room."

For the next half hour the little group followed Mary Lou around the big house. As she spoke in her soft southern drawl the plantation's long history came to life. It was almost as if the ghosts of decades of the house's residents had only left the rooms momentarily and might return in the blink of an eye. I'm a hopeless romantic, Abby said to herself as her fingers stroked the leather bindings of some of the old books in the dark cyprus paneled library.

The last stop on their tour was the dining room, and when Mary Lou opened the French doors to the large striped wallpapered space, Abby blinked. There on the wall behind the head of the long polished mahogany table was a large, full-length painting of Byron Forbes. As if hypnotized Abby made her way over to the portrait and, while the rest of her group admired the carved chairs, studied the curious glass fly catcher on the sideboard, and marveled at the unusual wooden overhead fan, Abby stood transfixed before the portrait of her great-great-great-aunt's lover and enemy.

Byron's dark compelling eyes were the focal point of the painting and she was drawn to their mesmerizing gaze. For a long while she stared into it then, forcing her eyes away, she noted the rest of the portrait—the fine cut of the suit he wore, his white linen shirt, gray vest with a dragon's head gold watch fob hanging from it, and the large ring on his finger—probably his wedding ring from his marriage to Carter's great-great-grandmother, Abby guessed.

Mary Lou, noting Abby's interest, came up behind her. "Quite a handsome devil, wasn't he?"

"Oh, yes," Abby agreed. "Those eyes—they're captivating."

Mary Lou looked up at her ancestor with pride. "I'm sure Byron was quite a charmer."

By now, the others had gathered in front of the portrait and Mary Lou began her speech. "This portrait was painted in 1868 after Byron's marriage to Emily Woods."

As her hostess spoke, Abby found herself only half listening. Byron's pull was too powerful and blocked out the words. No wonder Lydia had been so taken with him.

After the tour group left, Mary Lou showed the writers to their rooms. Suitcases in hand, Joanna, Abby and Ordell followed Mary Lou outside and down a gravel path to a row of low outbuildings. "We call this Rhett's Retreat," she said with a smile. Unlocking the door, she ushered Ordell, followed by a curious Abby and Joanna, into a brick-walled room with an enormous fireplace. Antique cast-iron utensils stood on the hearth and a large pot hung on a dark metal arm in the fireplace opening.

Ordell rubbed his hands and turned to Mary Lou. "This isn't, by any chance, an old kitchen?"

"Yes, this used to be a cook house," Mary Lou answered with an appreciative laugh.

"Well, you couldn't have chosen a more appropriate abode for yours truly," he said, putting his leather duffel bag on the pencil-post bed. "The ambience is perfect. I shall have marvelous dreams in this room. Who knows what culinary magic will seep into my sleeping subconscious."

Abby shook her head. "We'll expect to hear all about it at breakfast."

"Indeed, you will. Indeed, you will." When they left Mary Lou escorted Joanna to a cabin done up in country furniture. Then she led Abby two doors farther down, to a white cottage framed by ancient scarlet crepe myrtle. There was a little wooden porch with a hanging swing. Behind it a rosebush, budded out but not yet blooming, climbed a painted trellis.

"We call this Myrtle Cottage," Mary Lou announced as she opened the door. "I hope you'll be comfortable here. When we start taking regular guests, it's going to be our honeymoon suite."

"I can certainly see why," Abby said as she stepped over the threshold. Against the whitewashed wall the delightful pink-and-green flowered chintz made the room seem like perpetual April. A four-poster with a lacy white canopy dominated one wall and opposite it was a small white fireplace flanked by Spanish-moss-stuffed velvet chairs. Off to one side there was a pretty little bathroom with a claw-foot tub. "Oh, even on the worst day of a person's life a room like this would seem cheerful."

"That's exactly what we'd hoped for," Mary Lou told her. "I want my guests to leave the Prize with happy memories." She walked over to the dresser and held up a rose-colored tassel with two keys dangling from it. "This is your room key and there's also a key to the big house in case you want to go over late at night. We keep brandy in the parlor and you're welcome to sit and read there any time you want. And let's see..." Mary Lou tapped her brow. "Is there anything else I should tell you? If for some reason, the lights should go off, you know an electric storm or some such act of God, there's a flashlight in the dresser."

Abby smiled. "Thank you."

"Well, hopefully you won't need it but just in case, you know where it is. Now I'll go on my way so you can relax a bit before dinner. Is there anything I can get you?"

"No, thank you. I'll be just fine."

After Mary Lou shut the door, Abby unpacked her suitcase and shook out her clothes. Taking a surreptitious glance at the windows, she removed the diary and the old history book from her tote bag and fingered their pages. Where should she keep them, she wondered. They were too fragile to cart around with her. Yet she didn't want to leave the books where the maid might stumble upon them and get curious.

She was just checking out the top of the wardrobe next to the window, when she caught sight of a now-familiar figure. Carter was coming up the path with his arm around a young girl. That must be his daughter, she thought, noticing the resemblance as they came closer to her cottage. The light wind ruffled Carter's dark hair and he smiled down at his child. Abby was struck by the obvious warmth of their relationship. For a moment it made her feel guilty—almost as if she, like Lydia Stewart, was an invader about to wreak havoc on a strong and happy family. She sighed. She wasn't here to destroy anything but an untruth. Oh Lord, she thought as she stowed the diary and history book on the hollow top of the armoire, please, please, let me do what I need to do without hurting anyone.

Chapter Four

That evening, refreshed by a nap and a soak in the ivory claw-foot tub, Abby emerged from her cottage in a white gauzy dress with a rose-colored sash that accented her narrow waist and neat figure. When she knocked on Ordell's door, he greeted her with an enthusiastic "You look as scrumptious as a dollop of whipped cream, my dear."

"And you, good Sir, look quite dapper in your white linen suit."

Ordell held out a courtly elbow for her to link her arm around. "I'm honored to escort such a lovely young lady to what I hope is going to be an almost equally lovely dinner."

Chuckling, they walked up the path through the fragrant gardens to the back of the main house. There they met Joanna who was already drinking mint juleps with Mary Lou on the veranda.

"You two are just in time for a cool drink before we repair to The Ruby for dinner," their hostess declared. She craned her neck and looked toward the kitchen door. "Maria should be out here in a moment to get one for you."

"Ah, a tall glass of liquid refreshment would hit the spot," said Ordell as he took out a handkerchief and wiped a bead of perspiration from his mustache. Gallantly he pulled out a rocker for Abby before settling into the rush-bottomed seat of another. "Tell me about this marvelous new restaurant of yours."

"We're still putting the finishing touches on it," Mary Lou replied. "But everything," she added, crossing her fingers, "will be set for The Ruby's grand opening at the pageant next week. And we do have a marvelous new chef, Pierre. Carter found him working in a small restaurant down in New Orleans and snatched him up and brought him here." She patted her tummy. "And we've been eating right well ever since."

"Did I hear my name?" Carter asked as he opened the screen door and stepped out onto the veranda.

Abby turned in her seat at the sound of his voice and their gazes met momentarily. He was wearing slacks with a white-and-beige textured weave, topped by a an open-throat white cotton shirt and cream linen jacket. With his dark coloring framed by the porch's tall white pillars, he cut a romantic figure. Once again, Abby couldn't help thinking about Byron's photograph and how Carter could almost pass for his Civil War spymaster ancestor.

"Ladies, you all look like one of those soft-focus paintings," Carter said, his eyes going first to Abby in her gauzy white dress, then Joanna in pale blue silk, Mary Lou in pink cotton, and back to Abby again where they lingered. "Makes me wish I had my camera handy."

"Well, if you're nice to us and find Maria and ask her to get Abby and Ordell some drinks, we might agree to pose for you sometime," Mary Lou teased.

"Better yet I'll mix them myself," Carter answered. "Abby, Ordell, would mint juleps be okay, or would you prefer something else?"

"Mint julep, by all means," Ordell exclaimed.

"I couldn't think of anything more fitting," Abby seconded.

For the next forty minutes the five sat rocking on the porch, enjoying the balmy spring evening. As Carter and Mary Lou entertained their guests with anecdotes about growing up on the plantation, Abby sensed that taking either of the Forbeses away from The Prize of India would be like tearing a tree from its roots.

A little prick of jealousy hit Abby. Having such strong ties to a piece of land was so different from the way she and everyone else she knew had grown up. She and her father had lived in several different houses, trading up as they made their way in the world. And even now, though Abby was quite fond of her own little apartment in a restored Baltimore carriage house, giving it up for another would be no particular trauma.

Then a more disturbing thought struck Abby. Now that she was beginning to understand how attached the Forbeses were to The Prize and its history, she could also imagine that they were equally attached to its legends, whether those legends were true or not. Indeed, if Mary Lou and Carter discovered what she was up to, she would probably be a most unwelcome guest.

"Pierre's expecting us for dinner in ten minutes," Carter said, consulting his watch. He looked out over the gardens and then glanced over at his aunt. "Where do you think Callie is?"

Mary Lou threw up her hands. "Lord knows. I sent her up to bathe and change nearly an hour ago and told her to meet us down here when she was done." She stood and smoothed her dress. "I'll go check on her. You all go on ahead and I'll catch up in a minute." With that Mary Lou disappeared inside the mansion.

The four others got up and, leaving their empty glasses on the wicker tables, strolled up the path, veering off to the right toward the new restaurant. As they walked, Carter gave a brief history of The Ruby's construction. "Because of codes, we decided to go ahead and put up a new structure but we tried to keep the flavor of the rest of The Prize in mind when we designed it."

"Well, it looks as if you succeeded," Joanna commented as they came to the graceful white building with its tall Palladian windows and pillared veranda. Through the glass they could see the warm glow of candles.

"Oh," said Abby as they stepped through the door and looked around at the crisp white covered tables topped with fine china and polished cutlery. "The Prize would be a perfect setting for a romantic movie. Couldn't you just see the hero and heroine having a cozy tête-a-tête here?"

She turned and her gaze met Carter's. The amused look that danced in his eyes made her regret her impulsive words. An image of the night before when she and Carter had come so close to kissing fluttered through her mind. And she sensed that picture had flashed through Carter's mind as well.

Carter chuckled. "I hadn't thought of it that way but I believe you're right."

"Speaking of romance," Joanna added, turning to Abby, "I think Carter would make a good model for the hero, don't you think?"

As her face reddened, Abby really regretted bringing up the subject. At least the lighting was low enough to hide her embarrassment.

She was rescued by Carter who replied, "Thanks for the compliment but I'm not sure I could live up to the billing."

Much to Abby's relief, the conversation about romance was interrupted when Callie, freshly scrubbed and dressed in a pink skirt and matching blouse, bounded into the restaurant. Beaming, she made her way into the group with no sign of shyness. "Hi, Daddy. Hi, everyone," she said. "Sorry I'm late. A button on my other dress popped off and I couldn't find one to replace it with and my blue outfit had a stain on it—and I knew Aunt Mary Lou wouldn't like me showing up in that." She shot her aunt, who'd followed her in, a teasing look. "So," she said, turning back to the guests, "I had to change my clothes twice."

Behind Callie, Mary Lou rolled her eyes but held her tongue. Carter just nodded and began making the introductions. When Abby held out her hand and Callie took it, Abby was impressed by the girl's firm grip. Not only did Callie, with her dark eyes and regular features, look like her father, but she also had his same confident bearing and intelligent direct gaze.

"It feels so strange to have dinner in a big restaurant with no one else here," Abby said after they'd taken their seats. "I almost feel as if we're sneaking in."

"Just consider it a command performance," Carter said, ushering Abby to a seat between Mary Lou and Callie. Then after seating Joanna and Ordell, he took the chair opposite Abby.

The way Carter had placed them, Abby mused, made it seem as if he were trying to keep her at a distance. Any other man, with all the little currents of attraction that kept sparking between them, would have chosen a seat next to her. Was Carter merely playing the good host, sharing his attentions with all his guests, or was he really leery of developing a relationship with her? Well, if he was trying to keep his distance, she could relax and not worry about keeping her own guard up.

"If this is a command performance," said Ordell, shaking out his napkin and picking up a knife and fork, "I'm ready for the opening act."

As if on cue, the chef, wearing a tall white hat and big apron, came out and personally greeted the party. "I'm going to start you all off with a gumbo," he said. "After that I'll serve a sampling of the fare we'll be offering when The Ruby officially opens. I hope you don't mind passing the dishes around."

"As long as Ordell doesn't keep custody of any of them for too long," Joanna said.

"Hmmmph," Ordell replied with twinkling eyes.

A few minutes later, bowls of thick, steaming soup brimming with okra and rice were set at each place. "Superb," Ordell pronounced as he tasted the first spoonful. There were *oohs* and *ahs* of agreement from around the table and then the group fell silent as they savored the spicy mixture.

"This is great. It tastes just like Aunt Hat's gumbo," Callie said as her spoon scraped the empty bowl.

Mary Lou lifted her eyebrows and looked at her niece. "Callie, I told you to stay out of the swamp. You haven't been out to that conjure woman's house again, have you?"

Callie frowned. "Aunt Hat's my friend," she protested. "Anyhow, Dad doesn't mind, do you, Dad?"

At a look from Mary Lou, Carter cleared his throat. "I think being friends with Aunt Hat is just fine, Callie. She's a lovely old soul, but I don't like you going back into the swamp by yourself." He shook his head. "Too many things could happen—your boat's motor could conk out or get tangled in roots, you could fall overboard..."

Mary Lou turned to the others. "You must be wondering what we're talking about. Aunt Hat is an old woman who's been around here forever. I swear she was cooking up weird potions and powders back when I was a little tyke.

Anyhow she lives all by herself in this old shack way out in the bayou."

"Do you mean voodoo," Ordell exclaimed. "Good heavens, I thought that was only in old movies."

Carter waited until the soup dishes were cleared and then said, "Actually New Orleans was once a center of the practice of voodoo or hoodoo."

"Yes, wasn't Marie Laveau, the famous voodoo queen of the 1800s from New Orleans?" Abby offered.

"Absolutely." Carter gazed across the table at Abby with new interest. "I guess it shouldn't surprise me that a historian would know about the infamous Madame Laveau. Have you ever been down here before?"

"No, but when I knew I was coming to Louisiana, I did some research," Abby replied.

"Well, history is all well and good but I'm not sure I like all that black magic stuff going on so nearby, and I certainly don't like a member of our family taking it so seriously," Mary Lou declared, frowning at Callie.

"It's not fair to say that Aunt Hat does black magic," Callie blurted out.

Just then the waiter brought out a large tray of assorted delicacies. The chef identified each dish as the waiter placed a separate entrée in front of each diner who, amid exclamations of delight, took a serving and passed it on to his or her neighbor. Somehow all the plates seemed to wind up in front of Ordell where they came to rest. The group enjoyed each mouthful, listening while the chef explained the ingredients and method of preparation of each. As they ate, Ordell, Joanna and Abby pulled out pads and made notes for their articles.

After the chef returned to the kitchen, Callie brought the conversation back to its earlier topic. "Aunt Hat doesn't do bad voodoo. She only does white magic, which is good voodoo."

"Good voodoo, bad voodoo. What's the difference?" Joanna asked.

"A big one. Bad voodoo is casting evil spells and turning people into zombies," Callie informed the food writer. "But good voodoo," she said, pulling out the little cloth bag that hung from the chain around her neck, "keeps away evil."

Mary Lou gasped. "Callie Kleeson Forbes, what in the world is that thing you have hanging off you?"

Callie clasped the little sack tightly. "This is a gris-gris," she proclaimed. "It protects me against evil spirits."

Mary Lou looked genuinely horrified. "Callie, you take that disgusting old thing off this very minute."

"But, Aunt Mary Lou, what's going to protect me from evil spirits?"

"You're going to have more to worry about from me than any old evil spirit, Missy."

Reluctantly Callie removed the charm and mischievously passed it across the table to her aunt. Mary Lou held up her hands in horror. "Don't give it to me. I don't want to even touch it. Carter, you take that smelly old thing away from her."

Suppressing a smile, Carter got up and removed the offending object to the windowsill. "We'll deal with that later. Now," he said, returning to the table, "I think it's time to drop the subject of voodoo and take up the much more appetizing subject of dessert and coffee."

The little group agreed and after consuming Chef Pierre's bread pudding laced with hot whiskey sauce and topping it off with steaming cups of café au lait, they strolled back to the house for after-dinner drinks.

No sooner had the brandies and sherry been poured than two strangers came into the parlor. "Prestwood and

Elaine," Carter said, standing and crossing the Oriental carpet toward them, "I'm delighted you could stop by."

"Oh, my sister here wouldn't miss the chance to meet her favorite cook-show host and cookbook writer," the sandy-haired man with the neat mustache replied favoring Ordell with a smile. The man gestured at the woman who stood next to him.

Ordell beamed. "Your sister is a woman of rare discernment, or as we like to say in the business, ahem, good taste." The others groaned but Ordell ignored them.

Laughing, Carter turned to the group. "Let me introduce my neighbors and good friends, Prestwood and Elaine Matthews—they live in Lilyvale Plantation, which is just a quarter of a mile down the road—and, I might add, well worth a visit if you have the time."

As she heard this, Abby who'd been sipping a small glass of sherry almost choked. Matthews. Immediately her thoughts went back to that afternoon in the Archives when she'd read the handwritten account of Lydia Stewart's trial. Could these be descendants of Jerome Matthews—the man who'd been so virulent in his condemnation of Lydia on that muggy afternoon 130 some-odd years ago?

As Carter made the rest of the introductions, Abby straightened in her chair and tried to mask her sudden emotions with a polite smile. But all the while, she studied the Matthews siblings with a fascinated gaze. Since they were busy exchanging witticisms with Ordell and Carter, she could observe them closely without seeming rude.

Prestwood Matthews was impressive looking, tall and greyhound lean. With his pointed gray gaze, sharp features and self-conscious stance, he reminded Abby of men she'd met who were only happy when wheeling and dealing politics.

His sister, Elaine, on the other hand, struck her differently. Though her fair coloring was similar to her brother's and she, too, was tall, she had the looks of a beauty who had somehow let her potential wither away into nothing but a faded memory. She wore a conservative shirtwaist in a pale beige that made her appear even more reedy and bleached out. And her light brown hair seemed frozen in one of those chin-length flips that had been popular in the early sixties.

As she considered the woman, Abby guessed that though Elaine Matthews might appear older than she really was, she was probably Carter's age—somewhere around thirty-nine. Abby figured her brother, Prestwood, was probably a year or two younger.

"Are y'all staying for the pageant next week?" Prestwood asked coming up to Abby and Joanna and taking a seat between them.

"Oh, yes," the women said in chorus. "We're looking forward to it."

Prestwood eyed Abby appreciatively and went on, "I dare say Carter's told you all about The Prize's history."

"Yes, and it's utterly fascinating, particularly the stories about that swashbuckling pirate—it sounded as if he came right out of an Errol Flynn flick," Joanna said over her shoulder before excusing herself to refill her glass.

"Yes, the pirate's an interesting fellow but I think," Abby said, weighing her words, "that what I've heard about Lydia Stewart and Byron Forbes is even more fascinating."

"Well," Prestwood said, leaning one elbow on his knee and favoring her with a smile, "I'm glad you said that. I'm a history buff myself and I'm just putting the finishing touches on a script about that for the pageant's play."

Abby raised her eyebrows encouragingly and Prestwood went on, "I hope you're going to see it. It's all about how Lydia Stewart betrayed Byron and stole the ruby and cipher disk and how the Forbes family emerged from the ashes of her perfidy to fight a glorious battle for the Confederacy." His voice rose in a dramatic flourish.

"You don't say? I'm looking forward to seeing it," Abby said. "I'm curious," she added, swirling her brandy in the snifter she held, "does the Matthews family trace its history as far back in this area as Carter's?"

"Not quite. The Forbes have been here since the early 1700s. My ancestors, on the other hand, immigrated from Scotland to Virginia around that same time but it wasn't until shortly before the Civil War that my great-great-grandfather Jerome Matthews found his way to Baton Rouge."

"Oh," Abby said, very much interested. "What brought him to these parts?"

"He was a schoolmaster hired to instruct the Forbes's children—they had quite an extended family, you know."

Remembering Byron Forbes's dashing dark good looks, which seemed to be dominant in his family's genes, Abby had no doubt of there being plenty of offspring. "Does Jerome Matthews appear in your play?" she asked, maneuvering the subject back toward Lydia's accuser.

"Indeed he does. Jerome played a significant role in uncovering Lydia's duplicity. He was very loyal to the Forbes family and it was he who first alerted Byron to what was going on."

"He sounds like quite a hero."

"Oh, he was no ordinary schoolteacher, I'm proud to say. Indeed, I suspect if it weren't for Jerome, Lydia Stewart might have caused a lot more damage. As it was, Byron Forbes was able to salvage some of the work he'd done for the Confederacy. All this, naturally, will come out in my play." Prestwood shot her a playful smile.

"You've really whetted my interest," Abby declared. "I'd love to read the script."

"I'd be flattered to have a professional writer's opinion," Prestwood answered. "I'm merely an amateur with a frustrated poet's love of words. We'll be having some rehearsals this week but if you have the time to stop at Lilyvale before then, I'd be obliged if you'd cast a critical eye over my dialogue."

"I'd be pleased to," Abby replied. "In fact, if you don't mind, I may stroll down to Lilyvale tomorrow."

"If you know when you'd like to come, I'll pick you up," Prestwood offered, obviously pleased by her interest.

"Thank you, but I'm not sure. I may walk over, though." Truthfully, if she did go to Lilyvale it would be to snoop for who knows what. Some sixth sense told her not to leave any stone there unturned. But the role of secret agent was not coming naturally to Abby. Because of what she hoped to uncover, she didn't want to be any more obligated to this man than necessary. "I think after all this wonderful food, I'll probably need the exercise," she added to soften her refusal of Prestwood's proposal to drive her.

"Well, walking's great exercise," Prestwood agreed. "But, Ma'am," he went on, eyeing her trim figure, "you look just right to me."

At that moment, a flash went off in their faces and blinking, Abby and Prestwood turned toward its source.

Mary Lou stood holding a camera. "Oh, just go ahead and act natural," she declared. "Carter gave me this instant camera for Christmas and I've been meaning to try it out." She held out the picture and watched it materialize. "I want pictures of our first guests for my storybook."

Late that night, back in her cabin, Abby kicked off her sandals, lifted the gauzy dress over her head and slipped it off. Then padding to the bathroom, she wrapped the white terry robe that The Prize had provided around herself. As she washed up, she smiled, thinking about how the evening had ended. Callie had paraded in her troop of hounds and, borrowing Mary Lou's camera had, like a miniature Cecil B. De Mille, directed each of the guests to pose with the affectionate creatures.

After brushing her teeth, Abby finished undressing and put on a thin cotton nightgown. But before climbing into bed, she went over to the armoire and, balancing on a chair, reached up and took down the old diary. Opening its yellowed pages, she turned to the passage describing Lydia's first meeting with Byron Forbes.

As my friend Annabelle Litton's carriage brought us up the long, shady drive to The Prize of India, I looked around with a feeling of awe. The mansion, with its fields of cotton and its alley of live oaks draped with Spanish moss, seemed so exotic and beautiful.

No sooner had my friend and I stepped out of the carriage and lifted our skirts to climb up to the veranda, than we heard the clip-clop of hooves and saw a horseman riding up at a furious pace toward us.

"Byron, you handsome devil," Annabelle cried out. "You're just in time to greet my friend Lydia from Baltimore."

The rider, a broad-shouldered gentleman in a white linen shirt, gray trousers and frock coat, looked at me. At first his hat brim shadowed his face and I could only see his strong chin and firm, smiling mouth. But then, he swept it off and I saw his whole face—his dark eyes, his aristocratic features, his curly black hair glistening in the sunlight. I will never, ever, forget that moment.

Abby's eyes left the faded writing and her gaze went to the

window. That passage had always moved her but now that she, too, had stood on the veranda at The Prize of India, the description seemed almost unbearably vivid. For a long time, she stared out at the moonlight, lost in a reverie of the past. At last, with a sigh, she replaced the diary in its hiding place and switched off the light. Then, pulling down the counterpane on her bed, she climbed under the covers, closed her eyes and tried to sleep.

But it was impossible. There was just too much going on in her head. Memories of the evening at The Ruby, snatches of conversation, Prestwood and Elaine Matthews with their faded Southern charm, Mary Lou and her camera, Joanna's and Ordell's amusing banter, Callie and her gris-gris—and Carter with those dark eyes—filtered through her thoughts mixing with all the emotions and fears stirred up by her mission.

Suddenly Abby sat up and tossed back the covers. What she wanted and needed was some time by herself to gaze at Lydia's portrait. Switching on the light, she went over to the dresser and picked up her room key and the one for the main house's front door. With everybody asleep, now might be a good time to study the picture.

Pulling on her terry-cloth robe and slipping her feet into a pair of canvas espadrilles, Abby turned on the light and opened the dresser drawer where the flashlight was kept. Armed with it and the keys, she headed out into the warm night and walked up the path to the house. Her passage, though quiet, drew the attention of Goldie who padded over and nuzzled Abby's leg, all the while wagging her plumed tail furiously.

"Good girl," Abby whispered, patting the dog's silky head. "We've got to be very quiet and not wake anybody up."

Goldie seemed to accept that explanation and fell in step next to Abby. Gingerly she unlocked the big front door, opened it and looked inquiringly at Goldie, who, in answer, settled down on the veranda to wait. "I'll be back in a minute," Abby promised as she glided inside.

Only the ticking of clocks and the occasional creaks that all old houses made broke the silence. With her heart fluttering, Abby tiptoed across the polished wood hallway floor through the double doors into the ladies' parlor. Her flashlight sent a bright beam over the antique furnishings and rugs until it came to rest on the large portrait above the mantel.

In the cool white light, the painted figure seemed almost ghostly. Stepping closer, Abby aimed the flashlight directly at the face in the portrait and stared up into her ancestor's features.

The face was so young, so innocent. When it had been painted, Lydia had been looking forward to a life with her beloved as the mistress of The Prize. Knowing how cruelly disappointed Lydia was destined to be made the painting seem all the more poignant to Abby. Her gaze went to the young woman's eyes—as clear and blue and trusting as a child's. Those eyes seemed to speak to her, to implore her to right the wrong that had been done.

Anger welled in Abby and, clenching her free hand, she made a vow. "Lydia," she whispered, "I'm here to set the record straight. I'll clear your name, I swear it."

For a moment more, Abby stood there. Then, suddenly, a creak followed by footsteps in the hallway startled her. Heart thumping, Abby switched off her flashlight and whirled around guiltily. The light in the corridor went on. "Who's there," a deep male voice questioned.

Carter. Abby stood frozen. She knew she should answer, but she didn't want to explain her presence. Maybe he would just go away, she thought irrationally, or maybe she could hide.

However, it was too late. With a click, the crystal chandelier flooded the room with a yellow glow, revealing Abby like a deer caught in a car's headlights.

Carter took a step into the room and, on seeing her, stopped. "What have we here?" he asked, a surprised look on his handsome face.

Flushing to her hairline, Abby stood and faced her obviously amused host. "I know this probably looks really stupid."

Carter nodded but said nothing.

She hurried on, "I couldn't sleep so I thought I'd come up and, well, I was so fascinated by Mary Lou's story about Lydia Stewart that I thought I'd come and take another look at the portrait."

Carter lifted an eyebrow. "In the dark?"

Sheepishly, Abby raised her flashlight. "I didn't want to turn on lights and wake everyone up."

"A little midnight art appreciation, huh?"

"I guess you could call it that. I don't know why I didn't answer you right away." She knew she was rambling. Meanwhile she could feel her face growing redder. Blushing in this man's presence was beginning to feel like a bad habit.

"Maybe a guilty conscience," he joked.

Abby laughed self-consciously. He didn't know how right he was. She'd reacted like a thief because in a sense she felt like one. "I'm sorry. I didn't mean to disturb you."

"It's okay, Abby. Guests are welcome to sit in the parlor as late as they want. It's just unusual for folks to wander around in the dark."

"Well, next time I'll turn on the light," she said, moving out from behind the chair.

Carter stood there, still looking at her with amusement. It was then that she noticed that along with his slippers, he was wearing a robe and, from the looks of his bare legs and what she could see of his chest between the navy-blue lapels, nothing else. Swallowing, Abby drew her gaze away from his collarbone and with a startled realization, she looked down at her own robe and back up at him again. Carter, however, seemed unruffled by their mutual states of dishabille.

"Actually you did me a favor," Carter was saying. "I couldn't sleep, either, and this has been a little adventure of sorts." He put his elbow on the mantel and glanced up at the portrait of Lydia. "I've always thought that Lydia must have been a fascinating woman. You know," he said, backing up and cocking his head to reexamine the picture. He looked from Lydia to Abby then back again. "Maybe it's my imagination, but in this light I swear you look a bit like her. Around the eyes."

Abby laughed nervously and then started to edge away. "It must be lack of sleep. Next thing you know I'll be starting to see a resemblance between you and that figure," she said, pointing to a statue of a robed Buddha.

Carter grunted. "Maybe the full moon is just playing havoc with our imaginations."

Abby smiled and thrust her hands into her pockets. "Well, now that I've played havoc with your good-night's rest, I guess I should let you get some sleep, and get some myself, too, for that matter."

"Yes, before you know it the sun will be creeping up over the fields." He held out an elbow. "Allow me to escort you back to your cabin."

Pointedly Abby looked down at her nightgown peeking from beneath her wrap and then at his bare legs showing from below the hem of his. He followed her gaze and started to chuckle. "Well, if you're willing to risk the scandal, I promise to be a perfect gentleman."

"I have no doubts," Abby said, linking her arm through his, "that you'd be anything but a gentleman—it's the perfect part I wonder about." Despite all her resolve, she shot him a flirtatious look, which he returned with a playful smile.

"Well, I'll just have to prove how exemplary I can be." With that, he turned off the light, closed the door and led her outside.

Chapter Five

On the veranda, Goldie greeted them with tail thumps and a damp nose. "Good girl," Carter said to the dog as he disengaged Abby's arm to stroke the retriever's head affectionately.

Following Carter's lead, Abby, too, gave the dog an affectionate pat. Then straightening, she inhaled deeply. "Ummm, the air smells like magnolia."

"Yes, it's a beautiful, soft, southern night," Carter replied quietly. "One of the best things life has to offer." As they stepped into the moonlight that silvered the gravel path, Carter scanned the sky. "Look at the way the moon gilds the trees. If that novel you're working on has any romance in it, this ought to inspire you."

Abby smiled. "I don't think it's possible to write a novel about the Confederate South without including some romance."

"I think you're right. Brutal as the War Between the States was, it does have an aura of passion and poetry about it." As they walked, he turned toward her and gave her a quizzical look. "How did a nice Baltimore girl like you get interested in writing a novel about the deep South?"

"It runs in the family. My father's a historian who's written a couple of books on the subject, one about the

Battle of Vicksburg, the other, a biography of John Brown. When I was in graduate school, I did my thesis on plantation life. I always thought that someday I'd turn it into a book." She hoped her cut-and-dried explanation masked the emotions that were really driving her research.

Carter nodded. "I guess I can understand that. The Confederacy makes a marvelous tapestry for great dramatic passions to be played against."

Barney had joined their little entourage and Carter ruffled his fur in greeting. "Does your husband teach college as well?"

"I'm not married. Never have been."

"Hmmph," he said, looking at her. "It's hard for me to believe that a woman as attractive as you hasn't been grabbed up by some lucky man. Too busy with your work?"

There was a brief pause and Abby sighed. "Partly that—or at least lately. There was someone once, a long time ago but things didn't work out."

"Believe me, I know how that is."

Abby glanced at his profile, remembering what he'd said about his failed marriage. "It was just one of those things," she volunteered. "Gavin and I had planned to get married, but a month before the wedding we both realized we were really in love with love more than each other."

"A common condition, I'm afraid."

Goldie, who'd been gamboling at their feet, suddenly stopped short and barked. "Oh, she wants to play," Carter exclaimed. "If I don't throw something she'll keep yapping until I do." Pausing to bend over, he picked up a stick and tossed it. Immediately the dog launched herself after the stick. And Barney, who'd been following them at a leisurely pace, suddenly lumbered off in pursuit.

"They're almost like people," Abby said.

"Well, they're spoiled. Callie babies them. She's always sneaking them dinner scraps." The dogs came trotting back and retrieving the stick from Goldie's mouth, Carter flung it once more out into the yard. Goldie beat Barney to it again and the two of them came back, panting slightly, and sat down by Carter's side.

"They make quite a picture," Abby commented, looking at the eager animals.

"That's for sure." Continuing their little ritual, Carter launched the twig again. "In fact, I spend a lot of time photographing them. Back in my studio, I've got some great shots of Callie and her whole brood."

Abby studied him thoughtfully. "I guess that makes sense."

"What makes sense?"

"I knew you made travelogues but I suppose it's only natural that you do still photography, too."

"Oh, yes. I seldom travel without my cameras. I enjoy messing around in the darkroom."

"Then you do your own developing?"

"Absolutely. In fact, my studio's that building over there." He gestured toward a barnlike structure not more than fifty yards away. The moon was so bright that the building took on a pearly-gray glow.

"I'd like to see your photos, sometime."

"Anytime you want." He gave her a questioning look. "As a matter of fact, you might be interested in some of the old, old photographs I have of The Prize of India."

Abby tried to contain the excitement that was rippling inside of her. "What sort of photos?"

"Oh, some of the house and buildings that were taken in the late 1800s, even a couple that were taken during the Civil War. I've made some prints of the old daguerreotypes and negatives for an exhibit on The Prize's history and I'm planning to display them during the festival. Eventually I plan to publish them in a book."

"How interesting!" Abby clasped her hands together. "I'd really love to see them." Already she was hopeful that the collection might include pictures of Byron or Lydia. "When can you show them to me?"

"Well," he said, shrugging, "if you're still not sleepy, I'd be happy to show them to you right now. Or," he added quickly, "if you'd rather wait until we're a little more properly attired, we can do it another time."

Quickly Abby debated the situation in her mind. All during their stroll, she had been conscious that anyone peering out his window and seeing the two of them walking around in nightclothes would draw some wrong, but not illogical, conclusions. On the other hand, she wasn't the least bit tired. The night air and Carter's nearness was working its magic, along with the shot of adrenaline that had fizzed through her at Carter's mention of his antique photos. She'd waited so long to get down here to the Prize and to solve the puzzle that had fired her imagination. Now that she was so close, she wouldn't, no, couldn't go back to bed until she'd examined Carter's photos. They could well hold her first real clue.

"I'm really not sleepy yet," she heard herself replying. "So why not do it tonight? I'm game."

A pleased smile crossed his face. "Well, then, follow me," he said and they veered off the path toward the barn. At the door, he told Barney and Goldie to stay and then opening it, he led Abby into a whitewashed room lined with bookcases and file cabinets. A large desk awash in paper and photographic materials dominated one wall. Behind it sat a large leather chair and to its side a table overflowed with slide mounts, rubber stamps, plastic envelopes and photography books.

"Not as neat as it should be," Carter apologized. "But this is where I spend a lot of my time when I'm not on the road."

Several prints on the wall immediately caught Abby's eye. "Oh, these are wonderful," she said going over to examine a set of white matted photos showing Callie romping with her crew of assorted pets. It was obvious that the pictures had been taken with love, for Callie's exuberant personality shone from each image. Next Abby's eye was drawn toward a photo of Carter dressed in a plaid shirt and old blue jeans. He sat by the riverside with his back against a tree. A half-eaten sandwich lay on a piece of wax paper by his side and he held a fishing pole in his hand. "Who took this?" Abby asked.

Carter's dark eyes glowed as he studied the portrait. "Callie snapped it when I wasn't looking," he said. "She has a pretty good eye for composition, doesn't she?"

"Very good. Takes after her father." Abby was thinking that Callie also had had a good subject. In the photo Carter looked so relaxed and comfortable with himself—like a man who knew exactly who he was and where he belonged. He also looked terribly handsome, Abby thought.

Suddenly she became aware of Carter standing behind her and she realized that she'd been staring at the image for a good long time. Embarrassed she turned away from the wall, only to have her eyes meet and hold Carter's. Quickly she looked away and went back to the prints, but as she tried to focus on the pictures in front of her, her concentration was broken by a stream of emotions that seemed to flow between them.

It was Carter who eased the tension. "Ah, but I'm sure it's not shots of me you came here to see. Let me show you the old Prize photos."

With that he went over to the file cabinet and pulled out a box from the bottom drawer. Bringing it over to the desk, he opened the lid. "I keep the prints in this archival box—it's acid-free and helps preserve them." Carefully he lifted out a stack of photographs with layers of tissue sandwiched between them. Taking the artwork over to the desk, he cleared its surface with a push of one hand and began laying out the prints. "Some of the oldest negatives and prints were very brittle and not easy to work with but I think I did a pretty good job with them."

Abby, at pains to contain her excitement, leaned down to examine the collection. There were sepia-toned shots of the old house that had a painterly quality, looking as if they'd been drawn by hand. Many were of the plantation's outbuildings with people in front of them, whom she assumed were slaves or servants. Nowhere, however, did she see anyone who looked like the principal characters in the drama that she'd come to investigate.

"These are beautiful," Abby said as her gaze moved from shot to shot.

For the next few minutes, Carter told her what he knew about each photo, pointing out the different structures and identifying the people in them. The picture that interested her most was of the old schoolhouse—a one-room clapboard building that, according to Carter, had once stood behind the barn. "Is there nothing left of it at all?" Abby asked.

"Just the old stone foundations. The schoolhouse, I'm sad to say, fell victim to neglect. It had been long abandoned, and back when my father was small, it just toppled over like a house of twigs. I think his parents and the tenant farmers used what was left for firewood."

"That's where Jerome Matthews taught school, isn't it?"

Carter nodded and shot her a sideways grin. "I see Prestwood's indoctrinated you. I was wondering what you two had your heads together about this evening." As he spoke, Carter took another box out of the file drawer and opened it. "Here, now that you've gotten the Forbes family orientation tonight, you may find this set interesting. This print, for instance, is of Prestwood's great-great-grandfather Jerome."

Abby's eyes widened. This was too good to be true, she thought as she gazed at the image. Frozen in time, the tall, lanky schoolteacher stood stiffly posed in front of the schoolhouse. Wearing a black frock coat and dark pants, mutton-chop whiskers and carrying what looked like a Bible, he gazed sternly into the distance.

"Hmmm. I can't tell if he resembles Prestwood or Elaine," Abby said. "But no matter, he looks very forbidding. I can't say I'd want to have him instructing me in the three R's."

"He does look as if he did his share of rapping young knuckles with his ruler." Carter reached inside a drawer and grabbed a loupe, "As for the family resemblance, here take a look. What do you think?."

She held the magnifying glass over Jerome's face and studied the ascetic features. Yes, this looked like a man who could point an accusing finger when it suited him. He probably wore that same grim expression the day of Lydia's trial. She straightened and turned back to Carter. "Yes, I do believe under all those whiskers he looks like Prestwood—something about the eyes."

"A little like Elaine, too, for that matter."

"Yes, I guess so." Though Elaine, Abby thought, was more like a shadow than a carbon copy.

"Now for the piéce de résistance," Carter announced as he raised the veil of tissue paper and placed the next photo down on the desk.

Abby drew in a breath. "That's Lydia Stewart and Byron Forbes together," she exclaimed.

"You've got it. What you see before you, my dear lady, is a very rare engagement photo. As a matter of fact, I didn't even know this picture existed until a few months ago when Mary Lou found it in some trunks in the attic. Isn't it something?"

"I thought people had their portraits painted—not photographs made—back then," Abby said, staring down on the couple gazing into the eye of the camera.

"You're right. Photographers were rare in antebellum times. Byron had to bring this photographer up from New Orleans to take this series of pictures of the plantation. You can imagine what an expensive project the whole thing was. I guess Byron was so in love with Lydia that he wanted to capture the image of them together no matter what the cost." Carter shook his head. "Seems such a shame—given all that happened later."

Abby didn't say anything. The faces in the picture moved her almost beyond words. The betrothed couple seemed so right together. You could see it just by looking at them. In those days before instant cameras, they'd probably had to sit and maintain their pose for a long time. Even so, the hint of warm smiles played around their mouths, lending an intimate quality to the image. It was almost as if at any moment they might turn toward each other and embrace.

"Obviously the photographer was very talented," Carter went on. "He seemed to have kept his subjects at ease, a not-so-easy feat in the days of four-minute-long exposures."

"That's true. They don't look wooden the way so many of the people in old photographs do."

Carter picked up the picture and rewrapped it. "Actually," he commented, "they look like lovers who were meant for each other." Carefully he laid the print back into the box. "I must say that, despite the fact I wouldn't be here if Byron had married Lydia instead of my great-grandmother Emily Woods Forbes, I still feel sad looking at that picture." Closing the box, he placed it back in the cabinet. "I'll never understand why Lydia betrayed Byron. Someday I'd like to solve the mystery of why she did it. I suppose as a Northern spy, she must have seen her actions as justified, but still, to betray the man you love..." He shook his head again.

Well, Abby thought, we may not be seeing eye to eye but we do have the same goal at heart. The thought made her feel less guilty. Possibly, when she uncovered the truth, Carter might be willing to accept it. Of course, she conceded, what if Lydia really had been a spy? She pushed the thought from her mind. No, it didn't make sense based on what Lydia wrote in her diary. Yet how did everything—patriotism and loyalty, love and war—all fit together?

Meanwhile Carter had taken out yet another box, and for the next twenty minutes, they leafed through more photos of Byron, Emily and their family and The Prize. Mentally Abby matched the scenes before her with those Lydia had painted in the diary. She asked Carter questions, sorting through his answers, trying to piece the puzzle together. But the later it got, the harder it was for her to keep all the facts straight.

At last, Carter put the box back, switched off the light and escorted Abby back to her cabin.

As they neared its front porch, Abby became more and more conscious of her growing attraction to the man walking next to her. True to his word, he'd been the perfect gentleman even when they'd been alone together in his studio. But whether it was the moonlight, the lateness of the hour, the scent of magnolias or the fact that they were dressed for bed, she found herself wondering how she would react if he stopped being so gallant and swept her up into his arms. She could almost feel the touch of his lips on hers. The thought was so vivid that she drew a little away from Carter and hoped he couldn't read her mind.

But Carter was too taken up with his own wayward impulses to divine hers. Ever since discovering Abby in her nightdress in the main house, he'd been wondering what it would be like to hold her and kiss her. She looked so delectable in her robe, with the flounce of her white cotton gown peeking out beneath its hem. His fingers itched to undo the tie of her wrap and explore the soft flesh beneath. All during the time in his studio, he had had to keep a strong curb on his impulse to touch her. It was a good thing she'd been sincerely interested in looking at those pictures. If she'd ever really looked at him, instead of them, she would have seen the desire in his eyes.

Since Carter's divorce there had been more than one lady in his life, but no one serious. From the moment he'd met Abby, he'd sensed that she was not the kind of woman he could have a casual relationship with. What's more she was his guest. And now with the premiere of the Louisiana Heritage Festival and Pageant, what he and Mary Lou hoped would be an annual event, this was not the time nor the place to open a potential Pandora's box.

By the time their feet had hit Abby's porch, Carter had decided to suppress his romantic urges. He waited while she unlocked the door. Then she turned to face him.

"Thank you for an interesting evening," she told him.

"Photographers always like an appreciative audience."

"Well, you certainly had one tonight," Abby's lips parted slightly and she held out a hand. With Carter towering over her, his body only inches away, she could feel the heat between them. He took her proffered hand and clasped the fingers and once again their eyes met and held. Suddenly under the pressure of his touch, Abby knew he wanted to kiss her just as much as she wanted to kiss him. So strong was the desire that she had to force herself to keep from stepping toward him.

His willpower had obviously also won, for he released her fingers and took a step back. "Good night, Abby. I hope you sleep well."

"Thank you," she responded, feeling a bit let down but also relieved. "You, too."

"I'll see you at breakfast." Then he turned and, trailed by the two dogs, strode away into the moonlight.

WITH SO MUCH TO THINK ABOUT, it was hours before Abby fell asleep. When she did wake up the sun was filtering through the lace curtains at an angle that told her she'd overslept. A glance at her watch confirmed this. Kicking back the quilt, she slipped her feet over the edge of the bed and stood blinking. It was probably too late to see Carter at breakfast and, after last night's unexpected encounter, maybe that was just as well. She sighed and stretched her arms over her head. The man with his Southern charm and easy smile might soon be able to make her forget her priorities.

After a quick shower, she donned a pair of natural-colored linen Bermuda shorts, a pink camp shirt and white sneakers and started toward the main house in search of coffee.

It was a fine, cloudless day, but it promised to be hot. The sun had already dried the dew from the leaves and she could feel fine beads of perspiration forming at her nape. Even the dogs had already staked out shady spots under the oaks to doze.

Cutting through the gardens, she headed toward the kitchen veranda. As she pulled open the screen door, the fragrance of café au lait and hot cinnamon wafted past her. Good, she wasn't too late after all.

"Come in," Mary Lou called out from her perch on a kitchen stool. Around the trim middle of her pastel flowered dress, she wore a clean white apron and, she held a spatula in her hand. "We were just thinking about sending out a search party."

"It's lucky you came when you did," Joanna said from the end of a long rough-hewn harvest table, "because I suspect Ordell wasn't going to let us send that party out until he'd polished off the entire cinnamon coffee cake."

"My dear lady, my dear lady," the portly food writer intoned pulling out a seat for Abby. "Don't pay any attention to these disparagers of my good intentions. Of course, I would have saved you a generous piece," he said, spreading his fingers apart to indicate a thickness of a half inch. He chuckled. "Anyhow, I'm watching my diet."

"And eating it," Joanna parried with a reproving twinkle as, smiling, Abby accepted a cup of coffee and took the chair Ordell had offered.

"Unfortunately you've missed the big breakfast down at The Ruby," Mary Lou said, "but I can fry you up some eggs if you like."

"Oh, no," Abby replied. "This coffee cake smells wonderful and that will be plenty."

"Well, much as I'd like to join you in another piece," Ordell said, "Joanna and I must be off. Mustn't keep Chef

Louis over at the Commander's Court waiting,'' he added, referring to a distinguished Baton Rouge eatery.

''Yes,'' Joanna said, gathering her purse and notebook. ''Off into battle. Another round of quenelles, baguettes and other heavenly delicacies.''

''Finished by a battery of bombes,'' Ordell chimed in, slapping a broad-brimmed white hat onto his balding head. With a little flourish, he held open the door for Joanna and ushered her out.

After they'd gone, Mary Lou took off her apron and sat down beside Abby. ''Callie, of course, is at school and Carter had to go into town. He's got so much to do with that travelogue deadline next month and with this festival only days away. But I'd be happy to take you around to see anything you want,'' she added dutifully.

''Oh,'' Abby replied, placing the empty coffee cup down. ''I'm not expecting you to drop everything to entertain me. I can imagine that you have an awful lot to do for the festival, too.''

''Well,'' Mary Lou admitted, ''that's true. Today I've got to have a meeting with some of the other ladies who are sewing costumes and there's the carpenters to supervise. They're setting up the stage for our play and heaven knows what disasters-in-the-making await us.''

While Mary Lou described all the problems of putting on such a large festival Abby nibbled her cake between sips of coffee. ''You're so busy. Please don't give me another thought. I'm perfectly happy puttering around here and soaking up atmosphere on my own. As a matter of fact, that's probably the best thing I can do for my article and book.''

''Well, you have the run of The Prize and all its buildings. As a matter of fact, if you'd like to borrow a car,''

Mary Lou went on as she refilled their coffee cups, "we have three—a sedan, a Jeep and a station wagon."

"For today, I'll just walk around the house and grounds and maybe take a look around your library, if you don't mind."

Mary Lou looked pleased to be relieved of the responsibility of playing hostess. The last thing she needed right now, Abby thought, was a difficult and demanding guest.

They chatted for a few minutes more and then Mary Lou excused herself to begin her round of errands.

Even after she was gone, Abby lingered over the milky chicory coffee while reading the local paper. Between news of a proposed shopping center and a story about a foster parent, a piece on Prestwood Matthews caught her eye. He was announcing his bid to run for state senator. Abby smiled. She'd had him pegged right—a politician.

When she was done with the paper, she got up from the table, rinsed off her dishes and placed them in the washer. At that moment Maria the maid bustled in. "Oh, just leave that, honey, I'll take care of cleanup when I've finished vacuuming."

"Oh, thank you," Abby said. "Did you bake the cake? It was scrumptious."

"No, child, that's Miz Mary Lou's specialty. She cooks that up whenever she has houseguests."

"Well, we houseguests are pretty lucky," Abby commented.

"So will the regular paying guests be," Maria added as she gave the counter a final swipe with the dishcloth. "The chef is going to be baking up batches of it for breakfast once we're open for business."

Moments later, Abby wandered out into the back hall and stood looking around, trying to decide on her plan for the day. As she considered her choices, the scent of lemon polish and freshly cut flowers drew her attention to an antique game table. Like everything else in the house it was time-honored and exquisite. Atop its mahogany surface lay twelve photos from the night before. Smiling, Abby picked up the prints and studied them.

Several of the photos were of her with Prestwood. But two others caught her eye—one of her laughing as the dogs licked her face and another of her standing near Lydia's portrait. Later on, she'd find Mary Lou and see if she would give them to her for her father.

Putting the photos aside, Abby picked up a leather-bound gardening book that was sitting alongside them. Idly she lifted the cover. Inside there was a bookplate with a line drawing of The Prize engraved on it. "From the Library of the Forbes Family" the scrolled label read.

Abby's brow lifted. "Hmmm," she murmured. "An omen. I guess I'll start by hitting the books." With the hum of the vacuum cleaner upstairs drowning out her footsteps, Abby followed the connecting hallways to the other side of the house. From the tour she'd taken yesterday, she had a pretty good idea where the library was and she found it fairly quickly. Opening its French doors, she stepped in.

The tall bookcase in the cyprus-paneled room were in shadow and there was a mustiness in the air from hundreds of tightly packed leather-bound volumes that had endured decades of humid Louisiana summers before the advent of air conditioning. Her eye was drawn to the fourteen-foot ceiling with its ornate plasterwork moldings and then to the tall windows framed by fringed blue silk swags and jabots. Presently most of the light from them was cut off by narrow slatted wooden blinds that had been closed against the sun.

Snapping on a lamp, she began to walk along the perimeter of the room to admire the beautiful books. One bookcase had been devoted to contemporary works whose subjects ran the gamut from travel to spy adventures, architecture and history. Her finger ran along the Louisiana travel titles until it came to a stop on the word "Forbes." With a start, she looked closer. There were four books bearing Carter's name. Impressed, she pulled one of them out and flipped through it.

It was a large book full of lush, color photos of Southern plantations. The text accompanying them was lyrically written. The other volumes, on Southwest Indian pueblos, Spanish castles and Caribbean houses all looked equally fascinating. What varied interests Carter had, she thought. And how well he serves them. Abby eyed a shot of a beautiful native child barefoot on the wooden porch of her bright pink chattel house in Barbados. Another showed a man carving bamboo vases in Tobago.

She sighed. Carter Forbes was seductive. The more she found out about him, the more she wanted to know. For the next thirty minutes she was lost in his books, unable to tear herself away from his colorful images and poetic prose.

When Abby heard the grandfather clock in the hallway strike the half hour, she reluctantly put the last book back. She needed this time to delve into her project, she reminded herself sternly as she crossed the Oriental rug to the bookcases containing the antique volumes. Scanning the titles, she found old books on landscaping, agriculture, animal husbandry, art. Among the classics—some in the original Greek, she discovered the complete plays of Shakespeare, gilt-edged volumes of poetry and Victorian novels. So tall were the bookcases, however, that she couldn't see the top shelves. She was just moving the library ladder over to investigate when Mary Lou opened the door and poked her head in.

"There you are, dear." The silvery-haired spinster glanced around. "My goodness, it's so dark in here." She hurried in and pulled open the blinds on the windows so that the room was suddenly flooded with sunlight. "That's better." She turned back to her guest.

"Thank you," Abby replied, taking her foot off the ladder. "I thought you might want to keep them closed so the books didn't fade."

"Well, we do like to keep them shut when no one is using the library, but we always open them when we're in here. Otherwise it's hard to see your hand in front of your face." She squinted dramatically at her hand and laughed.

"It's nice to have someone interested in the library," Mary Lou went on. "And lucky you, you have it to yourself today—there are no tours scheduled." She took a step closer to the ladder and peered up. "We have some wonderful old tomes that never get looked at. Why, up there somewhere we even have some old account books from the days of Byron Forbes and a log book from that old rascal Warwick Forbes—you know, the pirate who snatched our ruby from that Indian mogul's treasure ship."

"Oh, yes, Carter told us that story," Abby replied. "You mean you really have his log?"

"Oh, yes indeed, though its practically illegible—and his idea of spelling is quite imaginative." Mary Lou gestured at the upper shelves. "And we have several family bibles and heaven knows what else moldering away up there. You're welcome to look through whatever you like. It's time someone knocked the dust off of them. All I ask is that you don't take them out of the library. They're quite fragile. The only other person besides Carter who spends any time up on the ladder with those books is Prestwood. He wanders over to poke around now and then. I understand he's putting together some sort of genealogy. The history of the Forbes and Matthews families have been quite intertwined, you know."

"Oh, really," Abby said. Mary Lou's information interested her so much that her fingers itched to grab the ladder so she could scale it and start her own research immediately. Containing herself, she chatted with her hostess for several minutes more, but as soon as Mary Lou left, Abby climbed up to examine the old tomes on the top shelf. She pulled out several volumes and glanced at them—several ledgers detailing crops for the years 1832-1858, a bible with the Forbes family tree written inside its front covers, and a detailed notebook on the plantation's ornamental gardens.

All of those looked like good sources for her research but for right now she put them aside hoping for something even more promising. Her next find was a stack of small, leather-bound volumes. As she opened the first her eyes fell on a title that made her inhale sharply. A faded gold script on marbleized paper read, *The Journal of Byron Forbes*. She sifted through the volumes quickly until she found the one that covered the time Lydia had been in the South.

Chapter Six

It was only when her stomach rumbled that Abby thought to pull her gaze away from Byron Forbes's journal and look at her watch. The thin gold hands on the heirloom timepiece read 2:30. "Phew," she said, rubbing her neck and stretching. Nearly three hours had passed since she'd first laid her eyes on the bold slanting handwriting that covered those parchment pages. Even so, she was reluctant to put down her fascinating find.

Though it had been slow going deciphering his antique script, in the pages she'd covered so far, Abby had learned that the former master of The Prize of India had been an interesting, intelligent and complex man. Much to her surprise, Byron's accounts of his daily life had included many passages where he'd wrestled with the issue of slavery and the morality of being a slaveholder.

At one point, he'd even tried to work out a plan to free his slaves, yet still keep his cotton plantation going. But as the tensions between the North and South had escalated, Byron's anguish had grown. And in the end, with his beloved land and heritage threatened, Byron had donned the Confederate gray.

Nevertheless, even in the depths of his turmoil, one subject sent Byron's spirits soaring—Lydia. Whenever he wrote about her, his words took on a lighter, more carefree tone, especially in the early entries when his accounts of their meetings and visits were filled with the exuberance of youthful dreams and love. Reading those passages now and knowing the unhappiness that would come later brought tears to Abby's eyes. Once again, she turned to Byron's description of his first meeting with Lydia.

> Today as I rode in from Baton Rouge, I came upon the loveliest of young women. Her hair was like gold spun from sunshine and her eyes were the color of the sea. The fair young woman's name is Lydia Stewart and she has traveled by coach from Baltimore to visit Annabelle Litton at Lilyvale.
>
> We stood on the veranda of The Prize and spoke no more than a few brief words, but that was enough for me. Having seen this lovely vision, I can think of no other woman. I count the hours until Annabelle's party where I pray I shall see the fair Lydia once again.

Abby closed the book and put her head in her hands. How sad that all those eager hopes would soon crumble under the grim realities of war and the weight of so many lies. As much as she wanted to continue reading, squinting over the faded handwriting had given her the beginnings of a headache. Regretfully putting the book back with the others on the shelf, she vowed to return and finish it over the next few days. Right now, she needed lunch and fresh air.

A few minutes later, downstairs in the kitchen, Abby found Maria in the midst of mixing bowls, flour and sugar canisters and an assortment of spices and spoons. "Have you eaten, Miss Heatherington?" the young redheaded maid asked when Abby walked in. Without waiting for an answer, Maria wiped her hands on the towel and opened the refrigerator. "Here, let me fix you something."

In no time, she'd made a chicken salad sandwich on homemade oatmeal bread and placed it on a blue willow-patterned plate. Then pouring Abby a glass of herbal iced tea, she snipped a sprig of mint from a clay pot on the windowsill and stuck it on top of the cool liquid.

"Oh, that looks wonderful," Abby said. "Thank you."

But when Maria went to clear a place at the table for her guest to sit down, Abby shook her head and said, "I think I'd like to sit outside for a while."

"It's pretty warm out," Maria warned. "But there's a table in the back beneath that old live oak. Maybe you can find a cool spot to eat there."

Nodding and smiling, Abby carried her food outside and headed toward the wrought-iron table. Maria followed with a large white cloth napkin and a pitcher for refills of the tea, then she excused herself and went back into the house.

Abby kicked off her shoes, wiggled her toes in the grass and took in the manicured plantation grounds. Despite the high temperatures, it was a beautiful, sunny, cloudless afternoon. A hummingbird twittered around the gardens, its wings fluttering so fast they were barely visible. Beneath the bird's flight path, azaleas and camellias provided cheery splashes of pink and white around The Prize's stone foundation and along the brick pathways.

Settling into the metal chair, Abby spread the napkin on her lap and picked up her sandwich. However, no sooner had she taken a bite into the bread when Goldie and Barney ambled over to investigate.

"Oh, all right," Abby said with a laugh. She took two small pieces of meat and fed them each a taste. Her generosity was a mistake for the dogs then settled themselves in front of her and watched every movement of her hand.

Goldie, the more persistent of the two, began whimpering as if she hadn't been fed in days. Finally Abby told the begging duo to lie down, and with a groan, the pair threw themselves beneath the table at her feet. Abby ate the rest of her lunch guiltily saving only a corner of sandwich for each of her canine companions. Then she sat sipping her tea and enjoying the warmth of the southern afternoon on her skin.

She was half-asleep when the dozing dogs suddenly sprang to life. With barks of joy, they jumped up and tore down the path where Callie, laden with books, a light sweater and her lunch box, was hurrying along toward the house followed by three other yapping mongrels. A ginger-colored cat with its tail up in the air to express its joy had joined the entourage.

Dropping her burdens on the ground, Callie stooped to hug her frisky menagerie. "You silly animals, did you miss me," she cried as Goldie reached out a long pink tongue to swipe her nose, followed by Barney thrusting his damp muzzle into her ear. Giggling, Callie looked up and spotted Abby who waved at her.

"Hello, Miz Heatherington," Callie said, scooping up her books and heading over to set the ragged pile on a bench near Abby. "You're all alone! Where is everybody?"

"I've been abandoned," Abby joked. "Your dad's doing errands. Mr. Bradley and Mrs. Hudson are in town at a restaurant and your Aunt Mary Lou is out at a meeting of the costume committee."

At the mention of the committee, Callie made a sour face. "They're probably sitting around sewing fifty more flounces on my dress." She pretended to mince through the grass like a mock Scarlett O'Hara. "I thought this pageant was gonna be fun until those ladies on the costume committee started using me for a pincushion."

Abby laughed. "It couldn't be all that bad, could it?"

"Worse," Callie declared. "You should see the getup I've gotta wear—all this silly lace and a crinoline with a skirt that goes out to here," she insisted, holding her arms out as far as they could go. "Can't sit in those things or even walk through a doorway. No matter how hard I try to be graceful, I bump into things and trip on the hoop. And every time I've got it on, it somehow tears or gets a smudge and then they're all mad at me." Callie grimaced and shook her ponytail.

"But just think if you'd been born more than a hundred years ago, you'd have to wear those kinds of dresses all the time," Abby consoled.

"No wonder everybody back then treated girls like they were helpless. There's no way you could be anything but a ninny in those kinds of outfits. All girls did was stay home and sew samplers." She put her hands on her blue-jeaned hips and looked disgusted. "No way you can climb a tree, row a boat or even gallop on a horse in those stupid dresses."

Abby couldn't dispute logic like that. "Girls had it hard in those days," she agreed. "Anyhow, I'm with you. I wouldn't want to wear big skirts all the time, either. I enjoy my freedom too much."

Callie cocked her head. "I wish Aunt Mary Lou would let me dress like a boy for the pageant. I wouldn't really want to be a boy," she added quickly. "I think girls can do anything boys can do and sometimes even better. But I'd sure rather dress like one for the festival."

"Well, if I were in charge of costumes, I'd let you. But I have a feeling your Aunt Mary Lou has her heart set on your wearing that gown. After all, Callie, it's only for a day."

Callie sighed and kicked at a stone. "I guess you're right but I'm not going to like it one bit."

The two went into the house where Maria took Abby's lunch dishes and gave Callie some lemonade and a plate full of freshly baked cookies. While Callie wolfed down her snack, Abby nibbled on a couple of the warm gingersnaps. "They're wonderful, Maria."

"Yeah, they're great," Callie said. "Can I take some more with me?"

Maria lifted an eyebrow. "Where are you heading for, child?"

"Oh, Jimmy and I are going to put a coat of paint on *The Pirate's Pursuit*."

"*The Pirate's Pursuit*?" Abby said.

"Yeah, my boat."

"You don't take it out on the river, do you?" Abby asked, thinking of the big barges and towboats on the Mississippi.

"Oh, no—that's too dangerous." Callie drained her glass of lemonade and put it in the sink. "But I do take it out into the swamp sometimes, though my father doesn't like me to go by myself. Would you like to see *The Pursuit*?"

"Sure."

"I'll go get changed and come right back down."

Ten minutes later, Callie reappeared in ragged jeans and a worn T-shirt that said LSU on it.

"I'll bet your dad went to school there," Abby said, eyeing the emblem.

"Yep." Callie grabbed a fistful of cookies, opened the screen door and looked at Abby. "Are you ready?"

"Absolutely."

Outside, the twelve-year-old bounded down the dusty path, forcing Abby to jog to keep up with her. The dogs, yapping and clambering along as usual, completed the party. A twenty-minute excursion through the fields brought them to the bayou and to the boat that was pulled up on a muddy embankment.

Abby noticed several wooden shacks dotting the ragged shore. When Abby asked about them Abby explained they belonged to transient families who squatted on the public land and worked at odd jobs in the area. "When he hired him as our handyman, my father tried to give Jimmy a nice house close to ours," Callie explained, "but Jimmy is an old-time Cajun who likes to live on the water where he can fish."

At that moment, a grizzled gap-toothed middle-aged man in a red baseball cap came out carrying a large can. "Hi y'all," he shouted and then rattled off a line of garbled-sounding syllables in a Gallic accent. Callie introduced Jimmy and Abby. Abby smiled and did her best to make out what he'd been saying but the Cajun seemed to be speaking a language all his own.

"Jimmy and I are going to paint the whole boat this afternoon," Callie said as the man handed her a brush. "But it ought to be okay to use tomorrow." She worked the bristles in her hand to take the stiffness out of them. "Would you like to go into the swamp with me? We could visit Aunt Hat."

"That sounds like fun," Abby agreed, inhaling the gamey fragrance of the damp earth and weedy water.

Jimmy, who was wiping his hands on a spattered rag, said something that sounded like, "Very nice, the swamp."

"Sounds great," Abby replied, hoping that she'd understood his remark correctly.

"Okay. You and me will go when I get home from school tomorrow," Callie said, settling down on the ground and dabbing paint on the boat's stern.

Abby watched for a while as the girl and the Cajun worked. Then she looked out past the houses to a dusty ribbon of road in the distance. "Where does that go?" she asked, gesturing toward it with her head.

Jimmy rattled off something inscrutable and Callie interpreted. "If you turn right, you can get back to The Prize that way. It would take you a few minutes longer than cutting through the fields, though."

"And what happens if I turn left?" Abby asked.

"Baton Rouge," Jimmy answered.

"But before that—Lilyvale—that's where my dad's friend Prestwood lives," Callie chimed in.

Abby put her hand up to her forehead and gazed out at the road. She was remembering Prestwood's invitation and Byron's diary where he talked about Lydia staying with her friend Annabelle at the neighboring plantation. Suddenly Abby knew exactly how she'd spend the remainder of the afternoon. "How long a walk is Lilyvale?" she finally asked.

Callie shrugged. "Not too far." She conferred with her Cajun compatriot and then turned back to Abby. "Probably twenty-five minutes or so." Jimmy nodded as if his head were on a spring. "You just have to follow that road until you reach a big paved one, then you cut over to the right and walk about half a mile. There's a big white sign with a water lily painted on it."

Perfect, Abby thought. That ought to give her plenty of time to look around over there and still get back before dinner at seven. "Well," she said finally, "if you all will excuse me, I think I'll meander over there and say hello."

THE LANE LEADING FROM THE BAYOU was so dusty that Abby had to stop several times and empty her shoes. Once she found the paved road, she took a moment to wipe her bare feet free of grit in the grass and push her damp hair off her neck. Her throat had grown dry from the dust and she was beginning to fantasize about large glasses of cool water. Meanwhile, she tried walking beneath the shade of the scrubby trees that lined the road.

At last she spied a white gatepost with a large white octagonal sign announcing Lilyvale. The French planter-style house that stood behind it was less imposing than The Prize but still very pretty. Nestled behind draping Spanish moss that hung from an alley of live oaks, the white wooden house had a classical look with columns of triangular brick and a sloping roof broken by dormers and topped by two high brick chimneys. An outside stairway led to a wide upper gallery. Through the wispy screen of Spanish moss Abby could imagine the ghosts of Lydia and her friend Annabelle leaning over the balcony. Maybe Lydia had watched for Byron from this second-story perch, Abby speculated.

As she walked up to the house, more scenes from the diary played in her mind. So vivid were her imaginings that it was a shock to come upon a shiny blue Buick parked off to the side in the circular drive. Assuming from the presence of the car that someone was home, Abby walked up to the front door and lifted the brass knocker. She waited, but no one answered. After several more fruitless tries, she decided to go around back. Maybe Prestwood or Elaine were out in the yard.

The back was as deserted as the front and when she peered into the kitchen from the screen door, no one was in sight. "Hello," she yelled out, looking longingly toward the kitchen sink with its promise of water. If nobody was home, she could always come back but she really didn't think she could walk all the way home to The Prize without getting a drink.

Finally her thirst won out over her good manners and feeling guilty, she tried the handle of the screen door. When it yielded, she stepped inside and headed for the faucet. While her eyes adjusted to the gloom, she looked for a glass. There were several that appeared clean in the drainer and she quickly filled one and took several gulps. As she was finishing the glass she looked around the kitchen.

It was a simple square room that in a former age was probably an office or bedroom. From the looks of the painted cabinets that lined its yellow walls, someone—perhaps Prestwood's family—had converted it into a kitchen back in the 1920s. A table, covered with papers, books and material, sat in the center of the brick floor, surrounded by four Hitchcock-style chairs. As Abby gazed at its cluttered surface, her eyes widened.

On a small velvet cushion, almost hidden behind a stack of magazines, sat an enormous red gemstone. Placing the glass on the counter, Abby crossed over to the table and stared down at her find. Round and cut like an old-fashioned diamond with many facets, it looked like a mogul's gem. Abby's heart skipped a beat as her fingers reached out to touch it. Picking the jewel up out of its nest, she took it to the window and held it to the light where it sparkled with a dark red fire.

"Ahem," a voice said at her back, startling her. She whirled around to stand face-to-face with Prestwood. "Careful," he said as he came forward with his hands held out. "Don't drop that. It's breakable and we need that prop for the pageant."

Of course, Abby thought, it's only glass. Handing over the bogus gem, Abby flushed with embarrassment and stammered an apology for coming into the house without permission.

"Well, I certainly wouldn't deny a glass of water to a thirsty guest," the tall man replied as he replaced the ruby on its cushion. "I'm sorry, I didn't hear you call out. I was upstairs on the phone with a client."

"Well, I hope I haven't come at a bad time," Abby said. "I could always return tomorrow or the day after if you're busy."

Prestwood held up a hand. "No, no, no. No problem. Just let me tell Elaine that you're here. She's in the basement, cataloging her homemade jams and jellies. Home canning is her passion, you know. And she's quite famous for her peach chutney. She's going to be selling some at the pageant."

"I'll have to pick up a jar," Abby said politely.

"Better yet, I'll bring one up for you." Excusing himself, Prestwood disappeared into the hall and through a small door. A minute later, Abby heard the sound of footsteps coming up and Prestwood reemerged with a slightly ruffled-looking Elaine in tow. She clutched a jar against a dusty apron that covered her pale blue shirtwaist dress and her blond hair was tied back with a paisley bandanna.

The two women exchanged pleasantries and Elaine presented Abby with the jar of chutney. After thanking her, Abby protested once again, "If you're busy, I really don't want to disturb you. Why don't I come back tomorrow?"

For a moment, Elaine looked distracted, as if she'd like to take Abby up on the offer, but didn't have the nerve. However, Prestwood immediately intervened. "Heavens no. Our small house doesn't compare with the grandeur of The Prize but my sister and I are very proud of Lilyvale and are always glad for the opportunity to show it off." He gestured expansively. "Would you like to take a little tour now?"

"Oh, I'd love that. Perhaps you could tell me some of the history of the house," Abby added as they left the kitchen and went out to a dark parlor stuffed with eighteenth-century antiques.

Elaine walked over to the marble mantel filled with framed needlepoint and export porcelain plates and struck a tour guide's pose. "Lilyvale was originally owned by the Litton family, who came to this area to grow indigo in the early 1700s," Elaine said, going into what sounded like a prepared speech. "They were very prosperous and at one time owned five hundred acres. But the Littons, like many in these parts, were ruined by the War Between the States."

"During reconstruction, carpetbaggers took over the property for a while," Prestwood added. "And everything fell into disrepair. Fortunately my granddaddy bought this house for a song around the turn of the century."

"Are you talking about Jerome Matthews, the man who was involved in the Lydia Stewart trial?" Abby asked, hoping to swing the conversation around to the subject that interested her most.

"No, my granddaddy was his son. Jerome was killed during the war, in the Battle of Vicksburg."

"He was quite a hero in these parts, you know," Elaine interjected. She brushed some dust off her apron. "It's because of him and what he did that the Matthews have prospered in this area." She shot her brother a proud look. "Prestwood is running for state senator. Even after all these many years, a lot of people will vote for him because they know Jerome's story and remember what a hero of the South he was."

"Senator." Abby could tell Elaine expected some enthusiastic reply. "Goodness, that's quite impressive."

"Oh, not really," Prestwood said. His gray eyes regarded her steadily. "Carter could have had the nomination if he'd wanted it. The Forbes family are the real aristocrats of this area and they're very well liked by everyone."

"But Carter is such a free spirit," Elaine said with a wry little shake of her head as though she knew the man and all his secrets through and through. Which she might, Abby reflected, feeling very much the outsider. After all, these people had grown up together.

"Carter just thinks politics is too confining, so it's up to me to carry the standard. I only hope I can do the job Carter would do." Prestwood's modest statement was belied by the confidence in his voice.

"I'm sure you'll be great," Abby murmured.

"Well," said Elaine, clasping her hands together. "Why don't we get on with the house tour?"

The trio continued on, going from room to room where Abby admired such things as Spanish-moss-stuffed chairs, antebellum paintings and fine brocade hangings. When they poked their heads in the doorway of Prestwood's study, he joked, "And there's my antique computer. It's all of four years."

"Prestwood is a very successful real-estate broker," Elaine told Abby. "He's the best in all of Baton Rouge. Why, last year his sales topped—"

Prestwood broke in, "Elaine, let's not bore our guest with numbers."

"Well, it's just that I'm proud of you," his sister answered. "I declare Prestwood could sell heat lamps to a Hottentot."

Prestwood turned to Abby. "Hmmmph. Well, here's a test," he said, nudging Abby. "Wanna buy five hundred acres of genuine Louisiana swamp?"

Abby smiled and shook her head.

"Well, then, how about a nice little plantation house complete with barn, stables and outbuildings?"

She shook her head again.

He turned to Elaine. "If we can't tempt Miss Heatherington with that, why don't we get out this month's listings?" He shot Abby a sly, playful grin.

Misinterpreting the gleam in his eye, Elaine looked alarmed. "Oh, I'm certain Miz Heatherington wouldn't want to settle here. Baltimore is a wonderful city—I'm sure," she insisted. She looked nervously at Abby. "You would be bored down here in our little corner of the world."

"Elaine," Prestwood said. "Where's your sense of humor and your Southern hospitality? You don't want Abby to think you're anxious for her to leave, do you?"

Everyone laughed but Abby sensed that Elaine was joining in only halfheartedly.

"By the way," Prestwood said, pointing to the computer screen. "This is where my great literary masterpiece, *The Jewel and the Spy* was composed."

"Your play for the pageant?" Abby asked.

"Yes, here's a copy of the script." Prestwood held up a sheaf of papers bound in a clear plastic cover.

Elaine put a hand on her brother's arm. "Now, Prestwood, you're not going to make Abby read your whole play now, are you? It's almost dinnertime and I want to show her the rest of the house before she leaves."

"Well," Prestwood said, weighing the manuscript in his hand, "I guess Abby's critique will have to wait for another time."

"Oh, well. I guess it *is* too late to look at it now, but maybe later this week...." Abby replied.

The last stop on the tour was Elaine's flowery bedroom. Pink-and-green chintz draperies swathed the large windows and matching upholstered chairs flanked a massive armoire. Dominating the room was a carved mahogany four-poster and on it lay a sumptuous green ballgown.

"How gorgeous," Abby exclaimed when she glimpsed it. Making her way over to have a better look, she realized she'd seen the garment before. It was a copy of the dress Lydia Stewart wore in the portrait that hung over the mantel at The Prize.

"I'm to be Lydia Stewart at the pageant," Elaine declared. She took off her bandanna and apron and lay them over a chair. Going over to the dress, she lovingly picked it up and held it against herself. Then with a dreamy expression on her face, she turned to the standing full-length mirror.

Behind her, Abby gazed at the image reflected back. To her mind, the only thing Elaine had in common with Lydia Stewart was her blond hair—and Elaine's was but a dull version of the original. Yet Elaine appeared to be entranced with what she saw before her.

"How did you get the part of Lydia?" Abby asked, unable to restrain her curiosity.

Prestwood chuckled. "When my sister heard that Carter would be playing Byron, she worked on her big brother the playwright to put in a good word for her."

Elaine, who seemed suddenly animated by the dress she clutched to her bosom, took a playful swipe at Prestwood with her free hand. "My dear brother is just the biggest tease." Spots of color had come into her cheeks and her pale gray eyes glistened. "Prestwood, you make me sound like a lovesick fool," she scolded. "The real story," she said, directing her comments to Abby, "is that acting is my hobby. I've done a lot of local theater and," she said with unusual directness and with what seemed like a touch of defiance, "I wanted this part. And I'll be damned good in it."

BACK AT THE PRIZE, Abby discovered that Elaine's statement was no exaggeration. Abby had returned to her cabin, courtesy of a lift from Prestwood, in time to shower and change into a light cotton dress for dinner. As a matter of fact, she was a bit early and when she strolled over to The Ruby, she found Mary Lou alone with the chef and his assistant, bustling around with preparations for the evening's meal.

As Abby helped her hostess bring out a tray of cheeses and arrange vases of freshly cut flowers for the small group of writers, she described her visit to Lilyvale. "And the gown Elaine will be wearing to play Lydia is just beautiful," Abby finished.

"My land," Mary Lou exclaimed as she rested a silver tray of French bread on the white tablecloth. "The trouble we've had getting that dress right for Elaine." She threw up her hands. "Politics, my dear, everything is politics." She patted her carefully waved silver coif. "Frankly, between you and me," she said, leaning toward Abby conspiratorially, "I would have liked to have seen the Smith girl from down the road take the part. She's a lovely little thing and is just about the age Lydia was when the story took place. But when Elaine found out she wasn't the only one in the running, she was madder than a wet hen caught in a car wash. She insisted that the part should go to her. Threatened to wreak more havoc than a tornado if it didn't." Mary Lou stood back to admire her table arrangement and went on, "To make a long story short, with everything else that was happening—you know, all the work that needed to get done for the festival—it just wasn't worth the aggravation." She sighed. "Elaine may come across as quiet but when she gets a bee in her bonnet—look out. She just plumb wore us down."

"Why do you think the part is so important to her?"

"I suspect, that that's the reason," Mary Lou said, pointing through the window.

Following the older woman's finger, Abby peered through the pane. Carter, handsome in a dark suit, had pulled into the side lot and was just getting out of the car and heading toward the house. At the sight of him, Abby felt her heart lurch. Though she hadn't admitted it, she had missed him today and had been looking forward to being with him this evening, even if it was just across a crowded dinner table.

"Elaine has always fancied herself the Juliet to Carter's Romeo, poor girl," Mary Lou explained. She picked up one of the vases Abby had just filled and began arranging the flowers in it. Abby turned her attention back to her loquacious hostess.

"It's been like that ever since they were young'uns. Why when Carter brought Diana home to The Prize and announced their engagement, Elaine threw a temper tantrum that they could hear clear into Mississippi." Mary Lou stuck a fern into the arrangement of hibiscus and took a step back to admire the effect.

Abby smiled at the picture that sprang to mind, then she asked, "Had Elaine and Carter been dating?"

"Carter didn't consider an occasional dinner invitation at The Prize for her and Prestwood dating, but apparently Elaine did. Oh, but I'm rambling," Mary Lou declared, placing the glass salt-and-pepper shakers next to the arrangement. "I didn't mean to dump all this on you. Forgive me, Abby. It's just nerves from trying to get everything done for the next week, that's making my mouth run off like an old gossip."

"And just who have you been gossiping about?" a deep voice inquired.

Both women turned toward the door a shade guiltily. Carter stood there, tall and tanned, and though he'd addressed his remark to both women, his dark, admiring gaze was fixed on Abby alone.

Chapter Seven

Ordell wiped his mouth with a starched white linen napkin. "Superb, my compliments to Chef Pierre," he said as the waiter cleared away the last of the bread pudding dishes and offered refills on the coffee.

"No more for me, thanks," Abby said, holding a hand over her cup.

"Nor for me," Carter added. He smiled at Abby and she smiled back. All through dinner she'd been powerfully conscious of him. Her gaze had lifted to meet his across the table so many times that it was becoming embarrassing. She'd hardly tasted her trout almondine at all. This is ridiculous, she told herself sternly. You're reacting to Carter Forbes as if you were lovesick.

"Callie," Mary Lou said as everyone was finishing up their coffee. "Have you done your homework?"

"I don't have any tonight."

Mary Lou clasped her hands on the table in front of her and leaned toward her niece. "Well, then I need a favor from you."

"What's that, Ma'am?" Callie peered over her glass of milk suspiciously.

"I need to rehearse my lines for the pageant," Mary Lou declared, "and I think you might need to rehearse yours. How about we spend an hour or so practicing?"

Callie opened her mouth to protest but Mary Lou rushed on. "Callie, it will be loads of fun. And we really need to do this. After all, we don't want to flub our lines onstage." She waved her hand as if swatting away the unhappy scenario. "This way I can prompt you and you can prompt me."

"Oh, are you going over the script for the pageant's play?" Joanna asked, putting down her coffee cup. "If you need any extra coaches, I'd be delighted to read any of the other parts."

"And I, too, have a thespian flair, or so I've been told," Ordell announced. "If you have a role for a handsome rogue or perhaps a learned, sophisticated worldly gourmet—"

"Absolutely," Mary Lou broke in.

Carter laughed. "Actually I could use a little rehearsal time myself. Can I join you?"

Mary Lou clapped her beringed hands. "Delightful. What a wonderful cast we'll be!" Then she turned to Abby. "How about you, dear? Are you interested?"

"Sure," Abby replied cautiously. She was certainly curious to see how Lydia was portrayed in Prestwood's script. However, the whole subject of her ancestor was so sensitive to her that she knew she'd have to be careful to keep her emotions under control.

"Splendid," Mary Lou said as they all rose from the table. "Let's go back to the house and make ourselves comfortable in the parlor."

Sunset had brought a drop in the temperature and the night air felt pleasantly cool against Abby's skin. As the little group strolled back to the house, Carter fell into step next to her. Even though it was dark, Abby was very much aware of the good-looking man walking beside her.

"Callie tells me you're going to venture out with her into the bayou tomorrow," Carter said, turning toward Abby. "I hope she didn't badger you into doing this. Callie loves to boat around the swamp but I don't let her go out alone. I believe in the buddy system. If something happens, two heads are better than one."

"I quite agree with you," Abby replied, smiling up at him. "But as for the invite, Callie didn't have to twist my arm. She's charming, Carter. And I was thrilled to be asked. This excursion fits right in with the research I'm doing on the area."

"Great," Carter said, then his voice grew serious. "Abby, sometimes I worry about Callie growing up wild. Her antics drive my aunt crazy." He shook his head. "But I think Callie's just high-spirited. She's her father's daughter, I guess—born with a taste for adventure. It comes with the genes."

Abby smiled. "Well, there are no pirates in my family, but I can identify with Callie's attitude. I was a bit of a tomboy myself."

His gaze skimmed over her, taking in the trim figure and her shoulders, which were smooth and bare above the bodice of her tropical print sundress. "That's hard to believe, Abby. But," he amended, "I'm beginning to realize that underneath that soft exterior is a woman of real spirit."

Abby blushed. "Well, I hope that's true. When I was a kid, I was always the one who climbed the willow tree to rescue the neighbor's cats. And I was forever coming home with scraped knees and torn jeans."

"Your mother didn't fuss?"

Abby shook her head. "I don't remember my mother. She died when I was a baby. My father raised me and, I must admit, spoiled me."

"Then you and Callie really do have a lot in common," Carter said, cocking his head. "I'd like to talk to your father sometime. I find it pretty tough playing the role of both parents—particularly when I'm on the road so much of the time. Maybe with this new venture—the guest cottages and restaurant—I'll be able to stay home more."

For a moment they were silent. The sound of their footsteps crunching on the gravel played counterpoint to their private thoughts. "Well," Abby finally said, "fortunately, with my dad teaching college, his hours were flexible. That made it a little easier for him to be around when I needed him."

Carter looked at her. "I remember you telling me that you got your love of history from your father."

"Definitely. Dad and I are both passionate about anything old—books, furniture, buildings—and we love wandering around historic places." Abby smiled. "You'd laugh if you saw us at old battlefields, the two of us with maps in our hands, trying to figure out who shot whom, when."

Carter looked into her face and grinned. "Abby, you encourage me. I hope when Callie's grown-up she'll talk about me as fondly as you do about your dad."

"I'm sure she will."

"I hope so. My divorce was a little hard on Callie and since then we've steered through some rough times. But things have gotten better. Like you and your father, we have a lot we like to do together—fish, take hikes, fool around with cameras. And Callie's been a great help with getting The Prize ready for guests. She helped paint some of the cabins and spruce up the flower beds." He looked at the moonlit fields. "I think Callie loves this place as much as I do."

The love of the land, along with their obvious devotion to each other, seemed to bind all of the members of this family tightly, Abby mused. "From what I've seen," she finally said aloud, "Callie adores you. I don't think you have anything to worry about."

They smiled at each other and, with Carter holding open the screen door, Abby went into the big house.

A few minutes later when everyone had settled into their chairs in the parlor, Mary Lou passed out the photocopies she'd made of Prestwood Matthew's script, *The Jewel and the Spy.* "Now let me see," she said, putting a finger to her mouth. "Who shall play what? Carter, you of course, will be Byron—just as you will in the pageant. Naturally Callie and I will play our roles. That leaves the parts of Lydia, Jerome, Maggie the maid, the judge, the lawyers and a bunch of minor characters. Some of us will just have to double up on roles."

Her assessing gaze swept over the little group and lit on Abby who suddenly knew what was coming next. "Abby, dear, you'll play Lydia, won't you?"

Unaccountably alarmed, Abby looked down at her lap. "Oh, I'm not a very good actress. Maybe I should take a smaller role."

"This is the woman with the sense of adventure? Come on, Abby," Carter teased. "You'll be perfect. You're a natural to play Lydia."

"Yes," the others encouraged. And Ordell looked up at the portrait over the mantel and exclaimed, "Girl, with your delicate features and heart-shaped face you even resemble the turncoat temptress! All you need is a blond wig and blue contact lenses."

Abby felt her neck go warm and made a quick decision not to draw any more attention to the resemblance between her and her secret ancestor. "All right," she said, holding up her hands and opening the script. "Lydia it is."

After assigning the rest of the parts, Mary Lou cried "Action" and the reading began.

The first scenes of the opening act took place at The Prize with Byron proposing to the lovely Baltimore debutante. Though this tender love scene had been stiltedly written, Abby couldn't help but be moved by it. It was so easy for her to imagine the real emotions that Lydia must have experienced, especially with Carter speaking Byron's words. Though they were sitting on opposite sides of the room, the electricity of that long-ago declaration of love seemed to charge the air between the two actors.

"From the moment I first saw you, Lydia, you captured my heart," Carter was saying.

"Oh, Carter," Mary Lou broke in. "How can you sit there like a stick? You're proposing to the girl. Go over to Abby and get down on your knees."

Carter shot his aunt an amused look. "And they said Otto Preminger was a tyrant."

"Be nice now, boy. Pretend you're Clark Gable in *Gone With the Wind*."

With a faintly sheepish grin on his handsome face, Carter crossed the room toward Abby and, with an exaggerated flourish, dropped to one knee and took her hand.

Ignoring his audience, Carter began his speech. "From the moment I first saw you, Lydia, you captured my heart. Now, beautiful lady, I offer it to you along with my pledge to love and cherish you. Will you do me the honor of being my wife?" As Carter finsihed speaking, he lifted Abby's hand and dropped a kiss on the sensitive flesh of the palm.

"That's not in the stage direction," Ordell whispered to Joanna as he peered into his script.

The remark sailed past Abby who was recovering from the sensations that Carter's lips on her flesh had evoked. All that she could think about as he looked into her eyes was how appealing she found him and how it would be almost as easy for this man to win her heart as it had been for Byron to win Lydia's.

Abby didn't have to look down at her page to know the response. It was as if Lydia was speaking through her. Placing her free hand over her heart, Abby replied, "I would be more than honored to be your wife. Oh, Byron, my dearest, my answer is yes."

Though there were no more lines in the scene, for a long moment the two continued holding hands and gazing at each other. Again, Abby felt the mesmerizing power of Carter's eyes, which drew and held her more than those in the photograph of Byron Forbes had.

"Cut," Mary Lou shouted and, with sudden realization, the pretend lovers broke contact and Carter got to his feet.

A loud "bravo" came from the doorway and everyone's attention turned to the tall, thin figure who'd obviously come into the room sometime during the scene. "Land's sakes, I had no idea that I'd written such a moving drama," Prestwood said jovially. "Maybe after the pageant we should consider conquering Broadway with it."

"Why not think big?" Mary Lou tossed out airily.

Prestwood walked over to Carter who'd returned to his seat and placed a hand on his friend's shoulder. "Carter, you surprised me, you're quite an actor. I could really hear the feeling in your voice."

"Yes," Ordell seconded. "I was practically ready to follow your example myself."

"I, of course, would have thrown myself at your feet if I weren't already married," Joanna announced, holding her hands out.

Smiling, Prestwood interrupted, holding up a fat jar wrapped in calico and tied up with a pink ribbon. "I just stopped by to bring Abby the chutney she left behind when she came to visit." He walked over to Abby and placed his gift on the tea table at her side. After she'd thanked him, he continued, "I wasn't planning to stay but the performance of this cast is so inspiring, I'd like to stay for the rest of it, if none of you mind."

"Of course we don't mind," Mary Lou declared. "As a matter of fact," she said, pulling out an extra chair, "you can take on your part as Jerome, if Ordell doesn't object." Ordell waved a lazy hand in answer. "That way we'll have to do less doubling up."

The next scene showed Byron working as a spymaster for the Confederacy. Abby paged through the script and saw that there were no lines for Lydia here so she could just sit back and listen. But as Carter spoke his character's words about loyalties and conflicts, she found her attention moving from Byron's speech to Carter's reality.

There was no denying the sensual current that his touch had generated during their scene together. Maybe it was their late-hour rendezvous the evening before or their intimate talk on the way over before the reading, but the electricity that had first crackled between them during their moonlit stroll on the *Mississippi Queen*, took on higher voltage tonight. For that brief moment they'd held hands, it had been as if all the other people in the room had vanished. Had Carter felt it, too? Yes, she decided. The desire had been in his eyes, his voice and in his touch.

When the final scene of the first act came to an end, Mary Lou broke out the brandy and passed around a plate of pralines. Then they took up the second act where the ruby and the cipher were found missing and Lydia was accused of stealing them. Although Abby had known this was coming, with each page she turned, she began to realize just how difficult it would be for her to act the part of the treacherous and coldhearted Lydia who appeared in these scenes. But she couldn't back out in the middle of the reading without creating a scene of her own. Her only option was to get through it as best she could.

Meanwhile Prestwood was throwing himself into the part of his ancestor with heavy-handed enthusiasm. He played Jerome as a passionate man consumed by patriotism and merciless self-righteousness. Pointing at Abby, who was once again Lydia, he thundered, "This woman is a Yankee traitor. She's lied to you and betrayed you, Mr. Forbes. It is she who stole your cipher disk and for that she deserves to hang."

As if they were observing a real life event, the room was quiet. Not even Ordell broke the taut spell. However, despite her resolve not to betray her feelings, Abby couldn't read her lines without her voice breaking. Suddenly it was as if she were Lydia herself, trapped in a fate not of her own making and, hopelessly doomed to a life of infamy, suspicion and loneliness. Before Abby could recite her reply, she felt tears in her eyes and her throat choked up with emotion.

"Excuse me," she said, putting down the script and wiping her eyes. "I can't read anymore."

Catching glimpses of the others' disturbed faces, especially Carter's, she hurried from the room and blindly down the hall in the direction of the kitchen. For a moment, she stood by the sink, breathing deeply and trying to calm herself. Anger at herself and at the script warred inside her. Could she go back and finish? No, she told herself, there was no way she could reenact the trial or the scenes portraying Lydia's duplicity. It was all too far from the loving passages she'd read in both Lydia's and Byron's journals. Shaking her head, she pulled a paper towel from the holder and held it under the tap. She was just bathing her eyes with water when the kitchen door swung open.

"Oh, here you are," Prestwood said. "Carter went outside to look for you and I said I'd check the house."

Carter. What would he think of her, now? "Well," Abby finally managed. "Here I am."

"Did my play upset you?" When she didn't answer, Prestwood rushed on, "You were really into Lydia's character." He regarded her with curious eyes. "Is that why you ran out of the room?"

Abby couldn't meet his gaze. "I guess it was a combination of things. The hour's late. I'm tired and I think I've had a bit too much brandy," she lied.

"Well, I hope my lines about Yankee traitors didn't upset you."

Abby shook her head. She was anxious to escape from him and the house and retreat to the sanctuary of her cabin. She'd appease the man and get out as quickly as she could. "No, not at all," she heard herself saying. "For us in the North the Civil War is just history."

He looked at her thoughtfully. "That's true, I suppose. But we Southerners are a proud people and still feel the sting of the defeat. Many people here lost everything and, even after all these decades, have yet to recover from the War's brutal effects. The Matthews family," he went on, pointing at his chest, "on the other hand, was very lucky. Our family fortunes rose after the War. But that was an unusual case.

"Take the Forbes family, for instance. They do all right nowadays but they were much wealthier before the War.

They had thousands of acres of cotton fields, hundreds of slaves, and a pile of money."

"And the ruby," Abby couldn't resist adding.

"Yes, the ruby." Prestwood walked over to the window and looked out as if contemplating the Forbes's former glory. Then he turned to face Abby. "I thought about that a lot as I was writing *The Jewel and the Spy*. In a way, when Lydia Stewart made off with the ruby, she also stole the visible symbol of the family's success. So, the way I figure it, Lydia's seduction and betrayal of Byron Forbes represents the downfall of the great Southern families and the Confederacy itself."

As Abby took in his words, she could see his point of view and understand what this play meant to him. But from her perspective, the play was rooted in falsehood. Nevertheless, she couldn't stand there and argue with him about it without giving herself away.

"It's really interesting how you pulled these ideas together and I'd like to discuss them with you some more," she said at last, "but right now my head is splitting. Would you please make my excuses to the others?"

"Certainly," he replied, still looking at her speculatively. "Can I get you anything?"

"No, nothing, really." Abby edged toward the door and opened it. "I just need to lie down. See you tomorrow."

Outside Abby hurried through the garden, toward the path to her cabin. As her feet moved along the gravel path, she inhaled the clean scent of the night air. But when her thoughts drifted to the way she'd handled the play reading, her head began throbbing again. In truth, she hadn't been prepared for the strength of her reaction to Prestwood's work. With a little groan, she remembered the surprise and shock on everyone's face—especially Carter's—as she'd fled the room. He probably thought she was crazy. Tomorrow she'd have to figure out how to apologize gracefully.

Suddenly she remembered that Prestwood had mentioned that Carter was out here looking for her. Glancing around, she quickened her step, hoping she wouldn't run into him now. As she reached the safety of her cabin, she turned the key in the lock and breathed a sigh of relief.

Once inside, she swallowed a couple of aspirin tablets then, feeling the need for a relaxing shower, she stripped off her sundress and panties, kicked off her sandals and headed for the cabin's neat little bathroom. As the warm spray slipped over her naked body, she rolled her shoulders and reached for some peach-scented shampoo to massage into her scalp. Vigorously she rubbed it in as if to work out all the embarrassment and anger she'd carried bottled up inside.

Then, feeling a little better, she stepped out of the shower and toweled herself dry. She plucked the white terry-cloth robe off the hook on the bathroom door, donned it, and walked into the bedroom where she sat down on the mattress to towel dry her hair. Afterward, she reached for a comb and ran it through her rich brown tresses. Her hair was fine and had a tendency to tangle so she had to be careful but, as she sat there working on it, disturbing images of what had happened up at the big house began to play through her mind once more.

"Damn," she cried out suddenly as her comb hit a snag and tore some strands from her scalp. Yanking the comb away she studied the knot that was caught in the teeth. Great, if she wasn't careful, she'd not only be a fool but a baldheaded one. She reached out to remove the knot, but before she could do it, a soft rapping startled her.

"Who's there?" Abby called out, placing the comb on the old commode table next to the bed. She glanced at her watch and then down at her bare feet. She wasn't dressed and it was almost eleven.

"It's me. Carter," the voice said.

"Carter?" Her heart skipped a beat. Getting to her feet, she crossed to the entry where she hesitated, wondering what to do. Opening the door a crack, she peered out. "Carter? What is it?" she asked with feigned nonchalance as her green gaze met his dark one. He'd taken off his suit jacket and the white shirt covering his broad shoulders glimmered in the moonlight. He looked at her searchingly, his expression filled with concern. At the sight of him, she felt her pulse quicken.

"I was worried about you," he said. "Prestwood told me you had a headache so I came down to offer you aspirin." He took a plastic bottle from his pocket and held it up. "If you're really feeling bad, I could call a doctor."

"That's very thoughtful, but it's only a headache and I've already taken some aspirin." She opened the door another few inches so as not to seem unfriendly.

Sliding the bottle back into his pocket, he took a step toward her. "Are you sure you're all right?"

Abby clutched the lapels of her robe together. "Oh, yes. I don't know what came over me at the house," she lied. "Maybe it was the brandy."

He cocked his head. "I didn't think you'd had that much. As a matter of fact, I don't recall that you had more than a sip or two."

Abby feigned a laugh. "I must be a cheap drunk." For a moment, they stood looking at each other, the silence between them stretching awkwardly. Abby became more intensely aware that meeting this man in her nightclothes was getting to be a habit.

"I don't mean to be rude, Abby, but are you sure it wasn't something else that upset you?"

She gave a little shrug. "Like what?"

"The play, for instance. Before now I hadn't really thought about how the play might strike a northerner. All this North-South business—it does get to be pretty strong stuff."

She stepped out on the porch and closed the door behind her. "Did Prestwood suggest that?"

"Yes, though it had already occurred to me as well." He raked a hand through his hair. "It makes me worry. If you were affected so negatively, what will visitors, particularly those from the North, think when they see our pageant?"

Abby could no longer contain the emotions still churning inside her from the evening's ordeal. "They'll think what I did," she blurted out, her voice rising, "that you're never going to get beyond what happened during the War. They'll think you're always going to be prejudiced against anyone or anything that you consider Yankee."

He frowned and a defensive note crept into his voice. "But you know that's not true, Abby. We're just reenacting a historical event."

She put her hands on her hips. "As a historian and a writer, I know that there are hundreds of ways to present the same events. It all depends on the interpreter—his point of view and what facts he has." Lifting her chin, she plunged in where she'd promised herself she wouldn't. "In my opinion, you've all twisted the Stewart-Forbes story to suit your own purposes."

Dumbfounded, he stared at her. "I have to admit that I'm not completely crazy about Prestwood's script but it is accurate. Our story's based on the facts," he reiterated.

As soon as her words had left her mouth, she'd regretted her hasty temper. Once again she'd offended her host. Some Mata Hari she was—not to mention how rude her behavior as a houseguest had been. She'd better cover up quickly and make amends or she and her suitcase might be sitting out by the road tomorrow morning. "Oh, I guess North and South will just never see eye to eye," she finally said, trying to make light of their argument.

But Carter didn't look either mollified or amused. His dark brows were drawn together in a scowl and his hands were clenched on his lean hips. "Now you're beginning to sound like my ex-wife." He began to pace back and forth on the boards of the porch and then with a grunt of exasperation, he faced her, his dark eyes blazing. "What is it with me and women anyway? I must have a self-destructive streak."

She stared at him. "What's that supposed to mean?"

"It means that I, like my poor fool of an ancestor, seem to be drawn to Northern women with chips on their shoulders."

Abby threw up her hands. "What are you talking about?"

His gaze locked with hers. "Oh, Abby," he said softly, "back in the parlor when I was holding your hand, all I could think about was how much I wanted to take you in my arms and kiss you. I swear it was almost as if I were Byron and you were Lydia, the Lydia who'd entranced him." He paused and scanned her face searchingly. "And I knew from the way you were looking at me that your feelings weren't entirely different. Admit it, Abby. They weren't, were they?"

Abby dropped her hands to her side. She wanted desperately to be able to tell him that he was wrong, but she couldn't summon the deceiving words. Instead she could only stand there gazing at him mutely.

"Abby," Carter said with a groan as he reached for her. His arms went around her waist and drew her close. "Oh, Abby. You're so damned beautiful." As his lips came down on hers, he pulled her against his broad chest so that she could feel the heavy beat of his heart.

Hungrily his mouth devoured hers and Abby felt her knees weaken. Her hands crept up to encircle his neck and, giving in to his fervor, she returned his kisses. As his lips dropped to her throat, her fingers ruffled the crisp, dark curls that clustered at the base of his neck.

He lifted his head and looked into her eyes. "I've been thinking about being with you this way ever since we stood on the deck of the *Mississippi Queen* in the moonlight."

Abby wanted to admit that she'd been thinking of him constantly, too—even dreaming about him. But where was all this leading, and did it make sense to give in to her feelings for this attractive man this way? Before she could sort out her thoughts, his mouth was on hers again and logic was lost in a whirlpool of feelings and sensation.

As they embraced hungrily, all her senses were alive to him. Carter wore no cologne. His scent was clean and masculine, compounded of soap, brandy and the faint sweetness of the grass he'd just strolled through. To Abby the fragrance was so intoxicating that she seemed to grow drunk as they kissed.

It was only when Carter's hand slid inside the nubby fabric of her robe and caressed her breast that she surfaced long enough from their tumultuous embrace to realize that she shouldn't let this go any farther. She was not going to fall into the same trap as Lydia. No, she would not put herself in a position where she could be accused of using sex to carry out her mission. And as much as her body and emotions longed to make love with this man, her honor said no.

"Carter, Carter," she whispered, gently pushing him away with her hands, "please. Please stop."

For a moment, he looked uncomprehending, then slowly he released her. "What's wrong, Abby? I thought..." She could feel his dark eyes questioning her. Avoiding his gaze, she busied herself retying her robe.

"Carter, you said it yourself. You don't want to get involved with someone like me." The words sounded harsh as she uttered them but she continued. "I'm leaving in a few days, Carter, and I'm afraid I'm not the casual-affair type."

Carter's face went stony and he drew back another step. For a long moment, he stood there looking at her, and when he spoke, Abby could hear the pain in his voice. "I'm sorry," Carter said. "I didn't—"

She held up a hand. "I think we were both just too caught up in the characters we were portraying this evening. You're not Byron and I'm not Lydia."

"No, of course not," he said stiffly. "You're probably right. I guess it was just too much moonlight, brandy and an overdose of legend. Let's forget this happened."

"All right," she agreed, although she knew that neither of them would or could.

Pulling open the door, she took a step inside and then looked back. "Good night, Carter."

"Good night, Abby," he said solemnly and then he walked quickly into the darkness.

When he was gone, Abby shut the door and stood in front of it, collecting her scattered thoughts. She lifted a finger to her lips, remembering with regret the fiery pressure of Carter's kisses. Then she grabbed a crocheted pillow off the rocker and threw it across the floor. "Damn it," she cried. "That was really stupid, Abby. You weren't going to let anything like that happen."

For a good ten minutes she paced back and forth on the rag rug. She couldn't believe all the dumb things she'd done tonight. What would she do for an encore tomorrow, she wondered. Use Byron's portrait for a dart board?

Abby tried to go to bed but as she lay awake in the darkness, all she could think about was Carter—Carter on one knee in front of her, Carter standing in the moonlight, Carter kissing her. In a desperate effort to get her mind off him, she turned her thoughts to Callie and tomorrow's planned expedition through the swamp. A part of Lydia's escape had been through the bayou and Abby hoped to trace her route. At the very least, she would get an idea of what Lydia had experienced.

Unable to concentrate, Abby tossed and turned restlessly. Finally, kicking off the covers in frustration, she switched on the light, climbed out of bed and reached up to the top of the armoire where she'd hidden Lydia's diary. Sitting down on the edge of the bed, she opened it and paged to the passage she'd remembered. It was a description of how Lydia had fled through the swamp in a boat, guided by a slave named William.

> The swamp was green and choked with water lilies and William had to cut through the screen of them. Strange, silent creatures peered malevolently at us from the growth on the banks. Everything about this place seems alien, and alone I would have never been able to find my way safely through this oppressive tangle of green. But William obviously carried a map in his head. Truly V, who's risked everything to provide William, the boat and our food and water, is my savior. Alas, no one will ever know the true nature of his heroics.

Abby touched a fingernail to the single initial. The passage had troubled her every time she read it. "V" whoever he might have been, was mentioned only this once in her aunt's diary. Yet obviously V had played a crucial role in her aunt's escape from the hangman's noose.

Just who had this person been? And why had he gone to such lengths? Byron Forbes had been a powerful man and defying him would have been a dangerous thing to do. Why had V taken the risk and what had he gained from it? Perhaps it was too much to hope that tomorrow's venture would throw any light on that question. But maybe, just maybe, the answer to that secret was hidden somewhere deep in the swamp.

Chapter Eight

By three o'clock the next afternoon, Callie and Abby were cutting through the opaque waters of the bayou in *The Pirate's Pursuit*. As the flat-bottomed craft motored through the lily-clogged expanse, past tall oak and pine trees and drifts of lush greenery and giant cyprus with their beards of moss, Abby craned her neck to see the people fishing from small dinghies hidden in the dense foliage of the bayou. Many waved to Callie who was obviously well-known to them.

The afternoon was warm and damp. The sun filtering through the canopy of leaves seemed, like the rest of this wet world, to be tinted with emerald. Abby reached up to wipe beads of sweat from her brow. Even though they were moving, there was little wind. What must it have been like to row through this soupy world in the August heat, swathed in long, heavy skirts and terrified for your life?

From the moist banks, lazy alligators silently watched them pass by. Nearby wood ducks whistled as they lit on crawfish. And the fussing chatter of swamp foxes and egrets flitted through the thickets of cyprus. Now, as they putputted deeper into the marsh, Abby could understand why Lydia had called this an alien place.

Lydia had heard those sounds and felt those eyes. Had she worried that there might be a hostile human pair among them? How easy it was for Abby to imagine what her great-great-great-aunt's emotions must have been. The gobble of a wild turkey, a comic sound made eerie in the bayou's strange mix of noises and sights, made Abby clutch the open collar of her shirt.

Callie gave her passenger an amused look. "Swamp music." She giggled and rubbed a sweaty palm on her khaki shorts before returning it to the tiller. "It gets even better a little farther in," she added. "Spookier. When Jimmy and I go fishing, he tells me all kinds of stories about the swamp. His grandaddy used to live here and according to Jimmy these bayous are filled with ghosts."

"Ghosts?" Abby fingered her collar some more and looked around at the desolate landscape. "I can believe it. Any in particular?"

"Yes." Callie's grin widened. "Some dead people who didn't go to heaven and even some undead."

Abby lifted her eyebrows. As she looked through a tangle of cyprus roots she could see why people might believe such things. It really was as if they'd floated onto another planet. A primitive universe that sounded, smelled and looked very different from anything she'd seen anywhere else.

As they rounded a bend and passed a wide inlet Abby noticed a trail of oil rigs dotting the shoreline. "See that old well over there," Callie said, pointing at one of the derelict wooden platforms. "Before I was born a man named Tommy La Croix fell off that platform and broke his neck. People see his ghost here all the time. Once I even thought I saw it, only my dad said it was just swamp gas."

The mention of Carter distracted Abby's attention from the scenery. Quickly she blocked from her mind the nearly overpowering memory of Carter's lips descending upon hers. "Does your father come into the swamp often?"

"Sometimes we go fishing." Callie waggled her ponytail thoughtfully. "But not so much anymore. Anyhow, Daddy knows the bayou like the back of his hand because, when he was a kid, he used to play here all the time—just like me."

Abby nodded. She could picture Carter as a boy, poling a boat through these waters. The Huck Finn image made her smile and shake her head. This was a wonderful place for a child to play out his adventures. No wonder Carter was so fond of Louisiana. In fact, she could imagine that it wouldn't be so hard to fall in love with it herself. As strange as the swamp was, it did have a gripping kind of beauty.

"Do many people live out here?" Abby asked. "And, more importantly, how do they survive?"

Callie maneuvered *The Pursuit* around a floating log. "Not too many people actually live in the swamp anymore. Aunt Hat says folks are too fond of conveniences like running water, and grocery stores, and VCRs."

Abby laughed. "But seriously, how do they get food to eat or water to drink?"

"Well," Callie said, throttling down so as not to leave a wake as they passed an elderly couple dangling fishing rods into the water, "Aunt Hat eats a lot of fish and Jimmy drives her into town whenever she needs other stuff. Then, people who come out bring her a lot of things."

"Come out and bring her things?"

"Yeah, in payment for her voodoo work. Yeah, even Miz Matthews, you know, Elaine. She brought Aunt Hat a whole case of homemade jelly."

Abby's eyes widened. "You mean Elaine Matthews actually wanted some voodoo done?"

"Yeah, she paid Jimmy to bring her all the way out in his motorboat so she could get a charm, but Aunt Hat said 'No way, José' and Miz Matthews had to take that stuff all the way back home."

Abby couldn't suppress a smile. The picture of decorous Elaine, bearing preserves, actually venturing into the swamp, was amusing. Despite herself, Abby queried, "Do you know what kind of charm she wanted?"

Callie made a face. "Yeah. A love charm to use on my dad. But Aunt Hat's a friend. She knows how I'd feel about having Elaine for my stepmother, so she turned her down. Boy, you should have seen how mad Elaine was."

For a moment Abby stared in astonishment at her young guide. Elaine looking for a love potion. She would have never guessed it. "How do you know all this?"

"Aunt Hat told me and I saw Elaine after she got back. She was fit to be tied." Callie drew out the last word and then giggled.

Abby mulled this information over. "Hmmm. Is Aunt Hat the only voodoo woman around?"

"Naw. There's lots of others. But it doesn't matter if Elaine goes to anyone else." With a mischievous look, Callie pulled out the forbidden little gris-gris bag, which was hidden in her blouse. "This will counter anything Elaine tries to do to make Daddy fall in love with her. Aunt Hat made it up for me special."

"But Callie, your father may want to remarry someday."

"Yeah, I know," Callie admitted. "That's okay, but it's got to be somebody I like." She thumped her chest with an index finger. "Someone like you who doesn't just sit around all day and fuss at me. I don't want anyone like Elaine who's always so prim and proper. She'd have me wearing dresses all the time and staying in the house. I'd never have any fun—and neither would my dad, I bet."

Abby nodded. Callie might be young but she had a sharp eye. There were no doubts in Abby's mind that Carter and Elaine were all wrong as a couple. Carter was sophisticated, vital, interested in myriad subjects. Elaine, on the other hand, seemed cut off from life, limited in curiosity and, except for her pursuit of Carter, limited in her ambitions.

Just then Callie turned off the motor and yelled "Halloo."

A reedy voice returned the salutation and Callie began to pole toward a tiny broken-down dock that poked out from a thicket of cyprus on the shore. Squinting, Abby caught sight of a wizened figure in a flowered housedress making her way to the water's edge. The woman lifted a pair of black binoculars to look at them and then, dropping them back to her chest, waved.

Now as they drew closer, Abby could see that Aunt Hat *was* an old woman. It was impossible to guess how old. Her dark face was deeply wrinkled and her iron-gray hair was caught back in a bun, but Aunt Hat might well be anywhere from sixty to a remarkably spry ninety.

Callie eased the boat closer and threw out a line. The old woman caught it nimbly. She might be getting on in years but she obviously wasn't weak, Abby thought as Aunt Hat pulled the little craft in and tied it to the dock. A moment later Callie jumped off the boat and Abby followed.

Sweeping Callie into her arms and hugging her, the old conjure woman exclaimed, "Girl, you're a sight for sore eyes." She gave Callie's ponytail an affectionate tug then looked over her shoulder at Abby. "Now, who's your friend here?"

Callie went over to Abby and drew her forward. "Aunt Hat, this is my friend Abby Heatherington. She's a writer and she's a guest at The Prize. She's gonna stay for the pageant."

The elderly lady regarded Abby with friendly shoe-button eyes and gave her a pat on the shoulder. "Welcome, welcome. This is a special occasion. I don't often get writer guests. I'll have to fix us something good to eat."

"Oh, wait," Callie exclaimed and ran back to the boat where she hauled up a cooler. "I brought you some gingerbread that Maria baked and some lemonade."

Aunt Hat clasped her hands. "Wonderful, child." She accepted the cooler from Callie and took a peek under its cover. "I sure do love lemonade and gingerbread. That's a real treat."

"I'll carry it for you," Callie said, taking the white foam container from her and scurrying ahead.

The two women followed. As they climbed the slope, Abby saw a faint dirt path that led through the jungle growth. A humming sound from some sort of machine was the first indication that a dwelling existed on the other side of the clump of scrub pines.

Aunt Hat's house turned out to be a ramshackle wooden structure that looked as if it had stood weathering in this desolate spot for at least a century. "My mammy and hers before her lived here," Aunt Hat said. Stopping to rest, the old woman placed a hand on her chest and beckoned Abby inside.

Callie was already setting out the gingerbread on the ancient kitchen table. For a moment, Abby remained still, trying to adjust to the cool darkness and unfamiliar sweet musty smells. When her eyes had focused, she could see that the house consisted of one room with a fireplace at one end, a cot near it, and what served for a kitchen on the opposite side. All sorts of dried herbs hung upside down from the rafters, and shelves brimmed with jars containing powders, colored liquids and other mysterious objects. One shelf of doll-like figures with bowls of grain set before them drew Abby's attention. It appeared to be some sort of altar.

The buzzing of a lone fly competed with the sound of the generator out back that powered the ancient refrigerator standing catercorner to the shelf wall. And next to the refrigerator was an old metal coatrack that apparently held Aunt Hat's meager wardrobe. Above it a calendar showing a European castle added an incongruous note.

"Well, let's have our treat," Aunt Hat invited pulling over two spindly chairs to join the one already at the rough-hewn table. Callie had spread out paper napkins and placed pieces of cake atop them. Before sitting down, the old voodoo woman took the binoculars, which she had called "her special spyglass" and placed them on one of the shelves. Then she settled on a seat across from Abby.

Callie poured the lemonade into the jelly jars Aunt Hat used for drinking glasses and then handed them out. While they sat sipping the tart drink and nibbling on the spicy confection, the young girl chattered on about the week's events, including the writers' visit.

Meanwhile Abby's gaze went back to the wall of shelves and the charms. She would have liked to get up and read the labels. On the other hand, she thought, catching sight of what looked like a dried bat dangling from a string at the corner of a shelf, maybe it was better not to look too closely.

As Aunt Hat asked questions, Abby was surprised by how much she seemed to know about what was going on at The Prize. "Has Prestwood Matthews finished that play of his?" the old woman queried.

Callie took a swallow of lemonade and answered, "Yeah, we had a reading last night. Abby played Lydia."

Abby's face reddened. This was definitely a topic she didn't want to pursue. But maybe she could steer the conversation away from last night's embarrassment, and toward the information she needed about Lydia's escape route. It was one bit of information she doubted she could get from the records at The Prize.

A moment later Callie did it for her. "Abby's not only writing an article for a magazine. She's also writing a historical book about these parts," Callie told their hostess.

Aunt Hat turned to Abby and poured her some more lemonade. "A book. My, my, my, now isn't that somethin'. What's it about, honey?"

Abby hesitated. "Actually, it's about a plantation—very much like The Prize."

Aunt Hat nodded. "Lord knows there's certainly a bushel basketful of stories about the historical goings-on there," she declared.

"Yes, and one story I've been hearing—the one about Byron Forbes and Lydia Stewart is very romantic."

Aunt Hat squinted off into the distance. "Oh, yessum. My granny was the cook at The Prize when all that to do happened so I heared lots of stories about that pair." She scratched her head. "Seems like everybody's got a different version of what happened."

"Oh," Abby said, "all I've heard is the official version—the one in Prestwood's play."

Aunt Hat put her hands together on the table and leaned in toward Abby. "Well, I don't know nuthin' about Mr. Matthews's play but according to my granny, Byron wasn't the only one in love with that Lydia."

"Oh?"

"Jerome Matthews, he was in love with her, too. But she wouldn't have no truck with him, no sirree. He was beneath her. Only a schoolmaster."

"Whoeee," Callie exclaimed. "I never heard this stuff, either. If Jerome was so crazy about Lydia, then why was he so all-fired eager to get her hanged?"

Aunt Hat lifted her thin shoulders. "She done turned him down and if he couldn't marry her, he sure didn't want no one else to." Aunt Hat thumped the table and sat back like a judge who'd just passed sentence.

"What about all the spy accusations?"

"I don't know about all that stuff, honey," Aunt Hat answered. She looked from side to side. "Some in these parts still think that it was a put-up job, but there's no way of telling after all these years."

"Wow," Callie said.

Abby took a thoughtful sip of her lemonade. "I've heard Lydia Stewart escaped through the swamp. Would you know anything about that?"

Aunt Hat put her hand to her brow and closed her eyes. "Seems to me I used to know sumpthin' about that. Let me think now."

"I heard something about a shack by three twisted trees," Abby prompted, reciting a detail she'd found in Lydia's diary. "Supposedly Lydia stayed there one night while she was on the run."

Callie gave Abby a surprised look and put her hands on her hips. "Gee, it's my house and my family but you folks seem to know more than I do! How do you know so much about Lydia and the swamp?" she asked Abby.

"Oh, from a book," Abby answered truthfully and turned back to Aunt Hat.

"Twisted trees. Three of 'em. It's coming back." The old woman rubbed her forehead as if she were massaging an old memory back to life. "Now there's lots of twisted trees in this swamp but there's the footings of an old shack down around Devil's Fork. Seems to me there's three old cyprus trees smack dab in front of them."

"Oh, Devil's Fork—I know where that is," Callie exclaimed. "Daddy says not to go down there 'cause there's quicksand."

ON THE WAY BACK from Aunt Hat's later that afternoon, Callie pointed out Devil's Fork. Even from the middle of the waterway Abby could see the trio of ancient cyprus trees looming out of the water like hoary witches. As they drifted past the point, Abby strained her eyes. There was no sign of any structure on the shore, however. When she mentioned the fact to Callie, the girl said casually, "Oh, it's probably there under all those swamp weeds."

"My binoculars are in the box over there," Callie added gesturing toward a small wooden container that she'd stowed under the seat.

Gratefully, Abby took out the glasses and adjusted their focus but, even with the magnified view, all she could make out was the tantalizing outline of an old brick chimney covered with vines. "Did they search there for the ruby or the cipher disk?" she asked, turning to Callie.

The girl shrugged. "I suppose so." But she obviously had no idea. Abby decided to check the records in the library for any mention of Devil's Fork. She wouldn't have much time before dinner, but it would be enough to make a start.

Once again Abby raised the binoculars to her eyes. What might she find, she wondered, if she could investigate the remains of the old shack here on her own? Might there still be some evidence of Lydia's flight buried in the sand there, or had it happened too long ago for anything to remain?

THAT EVENING Abby, Carter, Mary Lou, Joanna and Ordell were hosted by Chef John. His restaurant was a two-story gray building on the river. They dined upstairs in a small room filled with art. Ordell and Joanna were in high spirits, trading quips and war stories with the chef who plied his guests with magnificent plates of sautéed fillets of catfish in *sauce meunier*. As they ate, Mary Lou entertained everyone with accounts of her most recent last-minute pageant disasters.

"You all should have seen the expression on Lucy Deveraux's face when she opened her costume box and found she was going to be the first topless woman in Civil War history. It appears that the seamstress forgot to attach the bodice. And," Mary Lou went on, flipping her hand dramatically, "where was the missing bodice? In Jack Worthington's Confederate frock-coat pocket, of all things! Lordy, I can't believe we're all still in such chaos and the pageant is only days away."

It should have been a highly enjoyable evening, and indeed for the rest of the group, it seemed to be. Abby had dressed in an off-white suit trimmed in pale pink that normally made her feel as though she could go out and conquer the world. Nevertheless, the evening soon became an ordeal for her.

Carter had obviously decided to go for the nonchalant pose. He acted as if she meant no more to him than any of the other guests. But she knew it was a charade. Whenever their eyes met, she saw him look away as quickly as she did, obviously afraid that the strong emotions they were struggling with would show. Keeping up the act was exhausting.

Later when they adjourned to The Prize's parlor for after-dinner talk, Abby stayed only briefly and then excused herself. To her surprise, Joanna, too, made her good-nights early and accompanied her out into the garden. Barney and Goldie, ever vigilant, thumped their tails and trooped after the two women.

"I was worried about you last night," Joanna confided, petting Barney's soft fur and then brushing his hairs from her paisley skirt. "Are you feeling all right?"

"Oh, fine," Abby said airily. "I had a headache last night but it went away after I took a couple of aspirin."

"Well, you certainly don't look any the worse for wear this evening," Joanna said, casting an admiring glance over Abby's trim figure. "And I'm not the only one who thinks so. I swear, when you're not around, Carter always finds a reason to talk about you. And when you *are* around, he can't keep his eyes off you."

Abby stopped and looked at Joanna. "He talks about me?" She narrowed her eyes. "What does he say?"

"Believe me, everything good. He's very interested in what you're doing. And he admires you for tackling a big project like this book you've told us about. Carter may be a southern gentleman of the old school but he's no male chauvinist. He really admires a woman with gumption." Joanna shot Abby a mischievous smile. "Oh, of course, it doesn't hurt if she's also pretty and single."

"Well, I'm flattered," Abby stammered. "But I'm sure he admires you and Ordell as much as he does me."

Joanna laughed. "I may be vain, but I'm not an idiot. I've noticed from the beginning that Carter Forbes has a thing for you, Abby. As a matter of fact, I'll bet he wouldn't mind extending your invitation to The Prize indefinitely."

Abby shook her head, wishing she would have the opportunity to stay, but knowing it was unlikely. "Oh, I don't think so."

Joanna patted Abby on the shoulder. "Well, maybe I'm wrong, dear, but when you and Carter are near each other, there's more than magnolia in the air."

THAT NIGHT Abby lay awake thinking about Joanna's words. Though she tried to laugh the comments off, she knew that her friend was right, the attraction between her and Carter *was* growing more intense. With a little shiver, Abby remembered last night's kisses. Under other circumstances, she wouldn't have sent Carter away.

It wasn't just that she didn't want to repeat Lydia's mistakes. And there were other impediments. What would happen when Carter discovered that she had deceived him in coming here—that she was actually a spy herself determined to rewrite his family history. And not only that, she meant to publish her revision of the Stewart-Forbes affair in a book? Doubtless, he would be furious and feel betrayed, used. And what about Callie and Mary Lou? Abby winced and twisted her bedsheet around her fingers. She particularly didn't want to hurt Callie. Callie had been so open about sharing her friendship with Aunt Hat and her love for the wild bayou.

But, on the other hand, Abby knew that she owed it to her father, herself and even Lydia to set the record straight. That being the case, there was simply no hope for her and Carter. No, the best thing for all of them was to complete her mission as soon as possible, then leave and write the Forbes family an apology just before her book was published.

Even with her decision made, the issue nagged at Abby all through the next morning as she accompanied Ordell and Joanna, along with a local public relations man, to a sugar cane processing plant and then later to the Evangeline Oak where the famed heroine of Longfellow's poem had waited for her lover on the banks of the Bayou Teche so long ago. Along with the other writers, Abby copied down the inscription on the plaque and then snapped a photo for her article. Afterward, as she stared at the statue of the tragic heroine who'd loved and lost, Abby couldn't help but feel that she and the lovelorn Evangeline had something in common.

"Ooof, it's a scorcher today, isn't it," Ordell said as they returned to The Prize. He fanned himself with his broad-brimmed white hat as they got out of the car and walked up the gravel pathway. His eye lit on Barney who, as usual, was sacked out in the shade of a large live oak. "I think I'll follow that intelligent creature's example and find a shady spot for a midafternoon siesta."

Joanna wiped her neck with a handkerchief. "Me, too. My feet are tired from all that walking."

"Sounds like a good idea to me," Abby agreed.

But once Abby was back in her room, she grew fidgety. Her mind was filled with disturbing questions. Finally, giving in to her restless nerves, she got down Lydia's diary. Turning to the passage about the swamp, Abby noticed how tight and blotchy Lydia's handwriting was. She'd obviously been agitated when she wrote the passage.

> I am truly in fear tonight, so frightened that even if I were on a feathered bed rather than on the rough floor of this dank wooden shack, I wouldn't be able to sleep. I'm so grateful to have William, that kind and faithful soul, sitting guard outside with a shotgun across his knees. Even so, the knock on the door was enough to make my heart stop—

The entry ended there, leaving Abby curious about what had happened next. Oddly Lydia's next entry made no further mention of the incident. And there was no mention of the ruby or the cipher disk, either.

Abby put a finger to her chin and thought. What if Lydia *had* stolen the disk and the jewel? Had the person who'd knocked been a coconspirator? The unidentified V? And might Lydia have hidden her booty in the foundation of the old cabin where she'd spent the night? The latter question had been in her mind since yesterday. Even though Abby was sure of Lydia's innocence, she had to satisfy herself by searching through that site. Could she get Callie to take her out there? Callie, of course, would have to stay on the boat since Devil's Fork was off limits to her. The Cajun Jimmy was probably a better bet.

Decisively Abby changed into shorts, tennis shoes, T-shirt and visor. After dropping her key into a small purse attached to her belt, she hurried out the door and walked toward the bayou, somehow managing to escape the notice of the dozing dogs.

Before she'd gotten past the big house, she met Callie cradling her schoolbooks as she came up the path from the main road. Callie was frowning and muttering to herself.

"You look glum," Abby called out. "What's the problem?"

"Book report due tomorrow," Callie complained. "That means I'm going to have to sit in my room all day and night reading and writing."

"Oh, too bad. I was hoping we could go out on the bayou again this afternoon."

Callie shook her head. "No, I've still gotta get through the dumb old *Scarlet Letter*."

Abby grinned. "You mean you haven't read it yet?"

Callie ground her foot in the dirt. "Well, I read the first chapter."

"Callie, you may find that once you're into it, you like it better than you think."

The twelve-year-old grunted, obviously unconvinced. "If you want to go to the swamp, maybe Jimmy can take you out. Anyway, you're welcome to use the boat but you'd better check the gas."

After offering a few more words of sympathy, Abby left Callie and headed on down through the field to the bayou. When she got there, she asked around for Jimmy. She found the Cajun sitting on a chair on his rickety front porch, nursing a beer and a woeful expression.

When she asked if he could take her out, he politely told her in his fractured English, "Sorry, can't today." He pointed to his sock-clad feet. "Dropped an oil can on it, and the ol' lady," he said, gesturing with his head toward a portly woman hanging up some wash, "gonna take me into the doc's t' have it looked at." He leaned over and rubbed his toes. "If you want to use the boat, it's all gassed up. Filled 'er this morning. See those fellas over there." He pointed at a motley quartet of T-shirted fishermen standing around trading jokes at the end of a broken-down pier. "Maybe one a' them can take ya out."

By the time Abby got down to the dock, three of the men had taken off in pickup trucks and the one who was left told her he couldn't help her out because he had to go to town. Soon he, too, took off in a rusty van. In frustration, Abby glanced back at Jimmy's porch. Like everyone else, he'd disappeared, probably already on the way to the doctor's. Now what would she do?

Abby walked down to where the little aqua boat was tied. Her curiosity was fully aroused and was urging her toward the water. There was no guarantee she'd get another chance. Abby stooped to examine *The Pursuit*'s motor. She'd had some experience piloting a friend's runabout back in Annapolis and this motor didn't look all that different from that one. What's more, yesterday she'd kept careful watch on the way back from Aunt Hat's and had a pretty good idea where to find the place they called Devil's Fork. If she remembered correctly it really wasn't that far and she had plenty of time to get there and back before dinner.

Feeling like an adventurer, she stepped into *The Pirate's Pursuit*, started the motor and threw off the line. A few minutes later, she was gliding across the serene green waters of the bayou. The late-afternoon sun struck diamonds from the smooth surface, and the Spanish moss trailing from the cyprus cast deep mysterious shadows.

A little breeze played with Abby's hair and she smiled with anticipation. The trip took longer than she'd calculated, however, and several times she began to worry that she'd lost her way. Little fears ate at her. What if she couldn't find her way back?

She looked at the sun. As long as it didn't go down before she was ready to leave, she was sure she'd be all right. Several minutes passed and the bayou began to seem more and more deserted. She hadn't seen any boats lately and even the birds seemed to have flown away.

She was almost ready to give up and turn back when she rounded a bend and saw the twisted trio of cyprus that marked the spot Callie had pointed out to her. Abby straightened with excitement and reached with one hand for the binoculars while she maneuvered the tiller with the other. After a few minutes she brought the boat up against one of the cyprus roots and looped the bowline around it. There was no way of stepping onto shore without getting wet, so she kicked off her shoes. After checking the water for alligators and seeing none, Abby scrambled over the side of *The Pursuit*.

Wet to her calves, she waded toward shore. The mud seemed to suck at her feet like a living thing and she was grateful when her toes finally found a purchase in more solid ground. Gnats flew up in a cloud and swarmed around her head.

She paused to take her bearings. The chimney she'd spied from the boat rose from a jumble of roots and branches twenty yards away. Gingerly Abby picked a path toward it. She was so busy slapping at bugs that she almost stumbled over the stone foundations of the ancient ruin. Pushing aside a network of vines, she knelt to examine the remains.

The stones, although no longer supporting a shelter for humans, had become the home of myriad swamp creatures. As Abby shoved aside greenery with a stick, she discovered nests of termites, ants, centipedes, spiders and even snakes. Regretting that she wasn't wearing shoes, she placed her feet carefully and began to search inch by inch. After an hour, she had new respect for archaeologists. She was tired, her back ached, and for all her efforts, her examination of the site had yielded nothing more than a few bits of broken crockery, some glass and a half a dozen rusted nails.

Wiping at her sweaty brow and brushing a spiderweb from her hair, she found a precarious but, happily, insect-free perch on a large piece of broken foundation and sat down. However, after a few minutes its rough edges made her squirm with discomfort. Giving up, she stood and prodded a pile of loose stones with the stick and peered into a crack between two large rocks. Another shard of pottery caught her eye and she pried it loose and lifted it. It was a broken cup of some kind with something rolling around inside.

She pulled the object out, wiped it against her shorts and held it up to the fading light. "Oh," she exclaimed, wiping her find some more and holding it up again. It was a piece of chain with a figure of some sort dangling from the end. She rubbed it with her thumb and inspected it some more. Though the ornament was badly corroded, she could see that it had once been handsome. It wasn't likely to have belonged to the owner of such a humble shack.

Abby's heart began to dance wildly. Dare she even think it? She closed her hand around the chain. Could this have belonged to Lydia? A necklace of hers, maybe? Abby shook her head. It was highly unlikely it had anything to do with the Forbes-Stewart drama, she argued with herself. Yet...

Taking one last look at her discovery she carefully zipped it into the little purse she wore hooked to her belt. She'd take it home, polish it up and see what it looked like. If nothing else, the piece would make an interesting souvenir of her little trek out here.

Then she shot another look at the lowering sun and consulted her watch. "My word, it's getting late," she muttered. She'd searched over the entire foundation so she was certain that if there was a ruby or cipher disk here, it would take a better detective than her to find it, or at least more time than she had today. Giving the site a regretful look, she headed back toward her little boat.

But when she approached the spot where she'd come ashore, she spied a dark shape swimming a few feet from land. A water rat.

Anxious to get away from the sinister-looking creature, Abby backed off. She was no more than thirty feet from the water and squinting to figure out the shortest path through the next labyrinth of bayou growth, when the solid earth seemed to melt beneath her. Before she knew it, Abby was knee-high in muck.

With a cry of disgust, she tried to lift her legs and walk out of it but her efforts only made her sink in deeper. A chill of terror swept over her. Quicksand. Callie had said something about quicksand here.

Desperately, Abby reached out for something to grab hold of, searching for anything that might serve as an anchor. As the quicksand closed around her waist, her fingers found and seized the exposed end of a root and she clung to it with all her strength. But how long would she be able to hold on to it, she wondered? The sun was going down, shadows lengthened around her, and the swamp closed in.

Chapter Nine

Carter squinted out over the shadowy water. Darkness usually fell early on the bayou. The overhanging screen of branches blocked out the last rays of the setting sun, turning the wetlands into a place of mystery and danger.

Carter rarely went out into the swamp at night. It was just too easy to damage a boat on a hidden log or to make a wrong turn and lose your bearings. But tonight he had a strong reason for breaking his rule—Abby.

When Callie had first suggested that Abby might have gone into the swamp with Jimmy, Carter hadn't been worried. Until he'd met Jimmy who was on his way back from the doctor's, and he'd realized that Abby might be in trouble.

He'd hurried to check back at Abby's cottage and found it still empty, and went rushing from there down to the landing. When he'd found Callie's boat gone, and no one around, Carter's fears began to take on a shape he didn't like.

He asked Callie if she had any idea where Abby might have gone.

Straddling her bike, Callie rested one foot on a pedal. "Maybe she went back to Aunt Hat's."

"Aunt Hat's?"

"Yeah, we went there yesterday. We took Aunt Hat some gingerbread and lemonade."

"Hmmm, first I've heard of it. Why would Abby want to go back there, though?"

Callie shrugged. "She liked Aunt Hat, and she was real interested in the swamp."

Carter narrowed his eyes. "What was it about the swamp that interested her?"

"Well..." Callie thought. "She wanted to know about how Aunt Hat lived in the swamp. And then she wanted to know about Devil's Fork, you know where that old chimney is. She thought maybe Lydia Stewart might have stayed there when she ran away. Abby's real interested in that old story."

"Devil's Fork?" Now Carter really was alarmed. "Do you think she went there today?"

"Dunno," Callie said. "I guess she might have."

Carter scowled and looked out at the dark water. "I'm going to go out and look for her."

"Can I come?" Callie asked eagerly.

"Seems to me I remember hearing something about your having a book report due," Carter had replied. "You get home and tell your Aunt Mary Lou I'll be late for dinner. I'm going to borrow a boat from Jimmy."

Fifteen minutes later Carter switched on the lantern Jimmy had lent him and swept it over the dusky landscape. He hoped this was a wild-goose chase and that he'd find Abby had made her own way safely back at The Prize. Of course, if she was safe she would probably be amused by his being so worried about her that he'd gone chasing out into the swamp at night. It certainly mocked the cool facade he'd assumed for her benefit yesterday. After all, she'd made it very clear that his overtures were unwelcome. He had his pride. He was still smarting from having made a fool of himself once.

But what if she *was* out here someplace by herself? Even most of the natives avoided the bayou at night. The natural dangers were bad enough—the gators, snakes, and treacherous terrain. A woman alone in the swamp might run into other problems. Misfits sometimes hung out in these gloomy, isolated spots. Even Aunt Hat kept a loaded shotgun by her door.

At the very least Abby might be lost. An image of her frightened, desperately trying to find her way through an insect-riddled maze made him widen the arc of his torch and peer anxiously around the perimeter of its beam. As he directed it into the dark recesses of the shore, animals scurried away and birds took to the air, squawking eerie protests. A dank odor rose from the water and he heard a splash. Aiming his light toward it, he caught sight of a dark snout disappearing below the surface.

Beyond it the beam fell on the skeleton of the old Number Five oil derrick. Devil's Fork was just around the bend. Again Carter hoped that Callie was wrong and that Abby had not ventured ashore at that spot. There were too many dangers. He thought about the quicksand, the swamp rats and the water moccasins. No, he hoped she was nowhere near that place. But just in case, he nosed the bow of Jimmy's little boat in that direction.

TEARS STREAKED ABBY'S FACE, but she dared not brush them away. She was too afraid to loosen her grip on the tree root that was all that stood between her and an unimaginable choking death. Her arms ached, and her fingers had lost all sensation.

How long had she been struggling to hold on here, she wondered—three hours, four hours? Or had it been merely minutes? No matter. She felt as if she'd been balancing on the brink of death for an eternity. Trying to walk out of the gritty muck that held her prisoner hadn't worked. It had only made her sink deeper, and now she was up to her neck.

Could she swim out of it, Abby wondered. But she was afraid to let go of the tree root long enough to find out. More tears oozed out of her eyes and she whimpered in terror. It was so dark, and this place seemed so remote. Was there any chance of someone finding her? If only I'd left a note, she thought, cursing her foolishness.

Something large and brittle with wings landed in her hair and made a crackling sound. Abby screamed and shook her head violently. Without thinking, she let go of her anchor with one hand and swatted at the huge insect. Instantly she sank to her chin. Spitting out mud, she lunged back at the tree root and held on for dear life despite the pain that shot through her deadened arms.

Her heart thrumped, and she let out horrified little gasps. If she sank below the mud, would anyone ever find her body, she wondered. For that matter, might not there already be bodies floating at her feet, animals that had stumbled into this morass and never found their way out? Or—she shuddered—even people?

At the thought, Abby thrashed wildly, stirring up waves of gunk that threatened to choke her. Spitting out more evil-tasting mud, she forced herself to take a deep breath. Be calm, be calm, she told herself. Getting hysterical would only make things worse. If she could just hold on until morning, someone was bound to miss her and come out looking. Weren't they?

It was then that Abby heard the putput of a motor. She turned her head toward the sound. "Oh, please, please," she implored whoever was out there, "see my boat and help me." But it was so dark. *The Pursuit* probably blended right in with the shoreline.

"Help, help!" she cried out. But the words only came out in croaks.

Suddenly a beam of light shone through the trees, and she heard her name echo out over the water. Now, with her heart thudding, she strained her eyes and tried to yell louder.

"Help! Oh, please, help!"

The light swung past her once more and then went out, as did the sound of the motor. Abby tried to see through the darkness but it was as inky as pitch. Had her would-be rescuer floated on past without hearing her?

But then the light reappeared and Abby knew that he was still there. Once again she began to yell, half sobbing as she cried out again and again.

"Abby? Abby, is that you? I'm coming, don't worry."

Over the jabber of crickets, Carter's deep masculine voice resonated through the night.

"Carter, I'm over here!"

The beam wavered up and down and then from side to side. "Keep talking, Abby, so I can find you."

"I'm here, I'm here," Abby sniffled. "Oh, Carter, thank God! I'm so frightened! It's been so awful!"

The light flooded her quicksand prison, and she blinked, dazzled.

"Abby!"

The rustle of brush told her that Carter was close. But it was a moment before her eyes had adjusted enough to see that he had stopped in a patch of grass just beyond the root to which she clung. Abby stared up at him, her gaze traveling from his sneakered feet, to his legs, to the belt around his trim middle. Beyond that his torso was lost in the glare of the light. Still, what she saw of him looked solid and absolutely wonderful.

"Hold still, Abby," he told her as he dropped to his haunches so that she could see his face in the halo of the beam. "Now listen to me. The worse thing you can do is panic and thrash around. Try to relax."

There was no way Abby could relax. But she took a shuddering breath and did her best. When she was still, he went on. "I want you to try to move your body up horizontally and float."

"Float?" Abby asked incredulously.

"Yes, you can do it. You can't drown in this stuff if you lie on your back. You'll float, I promise you, and it'll be a lot easier for me to get you out."

Abby swallowed. Even though her mind told her he was probably right, she was so frightened and distraught that it was hard for her to do what he asked. She just couldn't make herself believe what Carter suggested would work. But she knew she had to try.

"That's it," Carter coached as she slowly rolled onto her back. As her body rose to the surface, Abby felt a thrill of elation. She really could float in the quicksand. Nevertheless, she kept her grip firmly on the root for insurance.

"Good, Abby, just stay like that until I go fetch a paddle to pull you out with."

Though it couldn't have been more than a few minutes, it seemed like a long time before he returned. While she waited Abby lay on her back, staring up through the trees at the stars and trying to take deep, calming breaths. Again, the rustle of the brush warned her when he was near.

"Okay," he said, "now I'm going to put the paddle out alongside you. Grab on to the end of it, and I'll pull you free."

Abby could feel the quicksand ripple as Carter slid the wooden paddle across its surface. When it touched her, she gingerly removed one hand from the root and reached for the oar. Then, quickly, she grabbed with her other hand.

"Great! Hold on now, Abby," Carter encouraged. Slowly and steadily he began to pull her in, and she felt her body flow through the soupy muck toward him. A moment later his arms were around her shoulders, pulling her onto solid ground.

"Got you!" he cried as he drew her free.

Shivering from nervous exhaustion, Abby's knees buckled and she collapsed at his feet. She couldn't keep herself from sobbing.

"It's all right now, Abby. You're safe." Ignoring the gritty paste coating her body, Carter knelt and took her in his arms. "It's okay, it's okay," he murmured, stroking her shoulders and then her mud-caked hair.

"Oh, I was so frightened," she babbled. "I didn't think anyone would ever find me."

She was lucky that someone had, Carter thought. But this wasn't the time to tell her that. She'd had a very narrow escape, and he couldn't blame her for being close to hysteria. "Let's get you out of here and back to civilization," Carter said. He started to help her to her feet, but Abby sagged in his arms.

"Oh, Carter, I don't think I can walk."

"Of course you can't. That was thoughtless of me." Bending, he scooped her up and, juggling the torch, carried her to the shore where he'd beached the boat.

Gently he set her on the bank. Then he took two plastic jugs of water out of the boat. "I'm sure Jimmy won't mind if we use up his drinking water in a good cause," he said. By the light of the torch, which he'd set down next to Abby, he eyed her mud-daubed form. "At least we can wash your face and hair. And you're probably pretty thirsty, I'd imagine."

"Oh, yes. I've been drinking dirt cocktails," she joked weakly, and then grimaced.

"Well, here's a chaser," he said, holding the jug of water to her lips. It was warm and stale, but compared to what she'd been swallowing, it tasted like ambrosia.

When she'd drunk her fill, Carter lifted the container and tipped it over her head. As the clean liquid spilled over her, his fingers combed gently through her hair, working out some of the mud.

Abby closed her eyes and sat very still, luxuriating in the careful strokes of his fingers. It was so wonderful to feel the muck sliding away from her ears, neck and shoulders. But as Carter emptied the second jug over her and she felt the water dripping down past her shoulders and into the V between her breasts, she became aware that her top was molded to her bosom as if she'd gone from a mud-wrestling competition to a wet T-shirt contest.

Self-consciously, she tugged the shirt away from her body. Though he must have noticed and realized what was going through her mind, Carter said nothing and directed the stream of water to her legs.

"There's another jug on the boat, but I think we'd better keep that for drinking. Are you okay to move now?"

Abby nodded. "I'm really sorry about this, Carter. I feel like a fool."

"Are you always this thorough when you research a travel article?" he commented dryly. He helped her to her feet and guided her into the boat.

For a moment Abby considered telling him the real reason why she'd been poking around Devil's Fork, but she thought better of it. Instead she answered lightly, "Well, it's a good idea to know what to avoid as well as what to recommend in a travel article."

"By that logic you'd have to hurl yourself into Mount Vesuvius before you could visit Pompeii."

While Abby tried to think of a rejoinder, Carter pushed off from the shore and started the motor. As they cruised back, the night breeze blowing on Abby's damp body chilled her. By the time they got to the landing her teeth were chattering.

"I hope you're not going to get sick from this," Carter said as he took an old blanket out of the back of his Jeep and wrapped her in it. "I think the best thing we can do is take you back to your cabin and get you warmed and cleaned up."

"Clean and warm again. That sounds so lovely!"

While Abby waited in the passenger seat with the blanket clutched around her, Carter went up to Jimmy's house to thank him for the use of his boat. As the two men talked, Abby watched Carter through the windshield. The man had saved her life, she thought. She'd acted stupidly, and he'd had every right to lecture her. Instead he'd treated her with care and concern. He'd been gallant, and gentlemanly and tender.

Carter drove her to her cabin. On the way neither of them spoke, but in the intimate enclosure of the car, it was almost as if they could hear each other's thoughts. Abby knew that Carter was remembering the kiss they'd shared, just as she was. As he steered his Jeep, her gaze fell on his tanned hands with their capable, well-shaped fingers. Even now she could feel the way those fingers had massaged the dirt from her hair. Unconsciously a little sound escaped from her.

Carter turned and glanced at her through the shadows. "Something wrong?"

"No, just cold and tired."

"A hot bath and some brandy will fix you up."

Abby shivered and drew the blanket tighter. "Carter, I really am sorry about all of this," she apologized once again. "I feel so stupid."

"Well, if it makes you feel any better," he said as he pulled into the parking lot close to the cabins and turned off the engine. "I, too, have taken a dip in quicksand."

"You did?"

He propped an elbow on the seat back and turned toward her. "Not intentionally, of course." He smiled. "When I was about twelve my buddy Dan Hill and I dared each other to leap across a pit of quicksand in the bayou. Dan, who had much longer legs than I did, made it. I didn't."

"What happened?"

Carter chuckled. "Dan stood there and laughed, of course. Naturally I yelled and thrashed in the goo, which only made me sink deeper and made Dan bray even louder."

"He wasn't going to just stand there and let you drown, was he?"

Carter grinned and shook his head at the memory. "No, just as I was going down for the third time Dan kindly thrust a stick in the direction of my nose so I could free myself." Carter got out and went around to Abby's side and opened her door.

"Something like the way you helped me," Abby said.

"Yes, in retrospect, that little episode came in handy. I'd had some practice with quicksand search-and-rescue techniques," Carter joked as he helped her out of the Jeep. "So when I found you tonight I put that old memory to work."

Carter took her elbow and they walked down the path toward the cabin. He looked at her dubiously. "Do you still have your key?"

"Yes, as a matter of fact I do, at least I hope I do," Abby said, reaching in under the blanket and checking the belt at her waist. She sighed with relief. Although its zipper was clogged with dirt, the small purse was still securely in place.

After she'd extracted the key, she gave it to Carter who unlocked the door. He held it open for her and then followed her in. "Just sit down and relax," he told Abby. "I'll go run you some bathwater."

"Thank you, Carter." Still clutching the blanket around her, Abby perched on the edge of a chair while he went into the next room and turned on the tap.

"What about *The Pursuit*?" Abby called out over the sound of the running water.

Carter ducked his dark head around the door. "Don't worry about it, Abby. Jimmy can pick it up tomorrow. The only thing that matters now is that you're all right." He smiled at her reassuringly. "All set in there. Anything more I can do before I go up to the house and get some brandy?"

Abby shook her head. "You've gone out of your way enough already."

"Well," he said, resting his hands on his lean hips while he looked down at her, "A shot of brandy will help you sleep. There's a bottle of good stuff up at the house. I'll bring it down so you can have some when you finish your bath."

After he left, Abby dropped the blanket and hurried into the invitingly steamy bathroom. She smiled, pleased and surprised by Carter's thoughtfulness. At the side of the tub he'd laid out a thick terry-cloth towel. He'd also taken the trouble to pour some scented oil into the water. She took a deep breath. The room smelled of jasmine.

After closing the bathroom door, Abby stripped off her filthy clothes. Even her underwear was gritty. Dropping the offending garments in a pile, she stepped into the little corner shower to wash her hair and sluice off the worst of the dirt. When she was finished, she came out and lowered herself into the clean, fragrant tub water.

With a sigh of pleasure, she stretched out her aching limbs and let her arms float. Though she'd always enjoyed baths, she'd never before appreciated one quite the way she did tonight. Abby picked a shell-shaped bar of soap from the porcelain dish on the tiled ledge and began to work lather over her skin. When she was satisfied she was clean she luxuriated for a few minutes more, her ears cocked for the sound of Carter's return.

He was right about the brandy, she reflected. Though she was very tired, she wasn't ready to go to sleep yet. She needed to talk to someone—to him. She needed to see Carter's face again and hear his voice, though she wasn't yet ready to acknowledge the reason why.

When Abby finally heard the outer door click, a little twinge of excitement made her sit up. Quickly she pushed the drain lever down and let the water gurgle out. As she stood on the bath mat, drying her flushed body, she could hear Carter moving around on the other side of the door. It gave her a strange, quivery sensation to think of him so close while she was naked and vulnerable.

After wrapping the towel around her hair, she grabbed the terry-cloth robe off the hook on the door and slipped it over her damp shoulders. Her muscles were cramping from their long ordeal and every little movement of her arms was becoming more and more of an effort.

As she gingerly tied the belt, she reflected that once again she'd be having a tête-à-tête with Carter while she was in nightclothes. For some reason the prospect didn't bother her nearly as much as it had the other times. After removing the towel from her hair, she glanced at herself in the steamy mirror.

She studied her face. Freshly scrubbed, it looked pale. Yet if she put on lipstick or eye makeup, Carter was bound to think she was doing it for his benefit. And he'd be right, she suddenly realized. Instead of reaching for her cosmetic kit, she picked up a small bottle of lotion and rubbed some of the creamy substance into her skin. Then she opened the door.

Carter sat in a padded rocker, his long legs up on the matching footstool. A decanter and two brandy snifters were arranged on a small table beside him. He'd tuned the small FM radio on the bureau to a classical music station. The subtle strains of a Chopin étude were filtering through the warmly lit room.

"How nice," Abby said as she crossed over to the bureau and picked up her comb. "Classy room service you have around here."

"Only the best for my guests," Carter murmured, his appreciative gaze traveling over her as she awkwardly lifted the comb to her damp locks.

Carter got to his feet. "What's wrong?"

"I'm a little stiff from all that hanging on I did back in the swamp."

"Here," he said, coming over to her, "let me help."

Carter took the comb from her and put it into the breast pocket of his chambray shirt. Then he led her over to the footstool. Gently placing his palms on her shoulders, he eased her down onto its needlepoint seat. He poured a generous brandy and handed it to her. "You sip this, and I'll take care of your hair."

Not quite sure what he had in mind, Abby cradled the globe-shaped glass between her palms and looked up at him questioningly.

Slipping in behind her, he seated himself back in the rocker and then, with his calves on either side of the footstool, he leaned forward, took the comb out of his pocket and began to untangle the strands of her wet hair.

The touch of his fingers and the heat from his strong, healthy body affected Abby profoundly. As he ministered to her, she almost wanted to curl up like a cat and purr with pleasure. "This is really very superior room service, indeed," she said. She glanced up and saw the bed just a few feet away. Quickly she dropped her gaze.

"That's because you're a very special guest."

Abby sipped her brandy. As the deep golden liquid trickled down her throat, it seemed to send a fiery thread through her body. Already she was beginning to feel light-headed. The sensual strokes of Carter's fingers as he combed through her damp locks intensified the giddy feeling.

She sat there sipping the brandy while he continued his soothing, mesmerizing attentions. Around them the Chopin melody wove an intimate spell. As the warmth of the brandy seeped through her veins, Abby began to feel almost as if she were floating in a haze of warm shadows. And at the center of that warmth and comfort was Carter.

"Ummm, that feels so good." She almost moaned.

For a moment his fingers stopped, their tips just brushing her silky hair. Then he placed the comb on the edge of the table and leaned forward to fill a brandy snifter for himself.

As his arm brushed her back, she half turned to look up at him. Their gazes met and held.

"When I think how I would have felt if I hadn't found you tonight . . ." His voice was gruff with tension. Without finishing the sentence, he set his glass down and took her almost empty snifter away as well. Then, putting his hands on her shoulders, he turned her body toward his and kissed her hard.

Abby responded to his overture explosively. Eagerly her mouth melded with his and all her restraint of the past nights floated away. She knew there were reasons why she shouldn't be doing this, but tonight she simply couldn't—and wouldn't—consider them.

Under his demanding lips, her mouth parted and their tongues met. At the same time, she forgot the ache in her arms and lifted them to encircle the tanned column of his neck. As the kiss went on, Carter gathered her up and drew her onto his lap. Their mutual caresses continued, Abby pressing herself against his chest as if she wanted to fuse her body with his.

"Abby," Carter said, dragging his mouth away from hers at last, "if you don't want this, say so now. Because much more, and I won't be able to stop myself."

Abby didn't want to be asked to think. "I do want this," she murmured and sought his lips with hers. Their embrace grew more and more fevered. Carter's fingers roved over her back and down the curve of her hip. At the same time, he tipped her head back and nuzzled the hollow of her throat. With a moan, Abby closed her eyes and arched her back in invitation.

His questing lips moved around to the side of her neck behind her ear and nibbled the sensitive spot. With his free hand, he pushed aside one of the lapels of her loosely belted robe and uncovered a creamy shoulder. His supple fingers kneaded it and then he moved down to drop kisses on it. As his hand found her breast and stroked its silky contour, his mouth went back to Abby's.

Forgetful of anything but the sensations he was arousing in her, she writhed in his embrace, and her body slid down his thighs and half off the chair.

"Oops," he said, and pulled her back. They stared into each other's eyes, half laughing, half-breathless. "I think it's time we relocated," Carter said. "What do you think?"

"Yes," was all Abby could manage. "Oh, yes."

Without another word Carter slipped his arms beneath her back and hips and carried her to the bed. As he lay her down on the coverlet her robe fell away revealing her shapely legs. For a moment Carter stood admiring them. Then he sat down next to her and caressed one of her smooth knees. "You have beautiful legs, Abby. The first time I saw you in shorts I could hardly keep from staring. Now at last I can look my fill."

As he spoke he lifted her left leg and sensously kissed the tender spot at the back of her knee. No one had ever done this to Abby before. It was a wholly new sensation that fairly made her wriggle with pleasure.

"Oh, Carter," she said as he released his grip and she rolled toward him. As they kissed again, her fingers went to the buttons on his shirt and began working them loose. But her excitement combined with the soreness in her fingers made her awkward.

"I'll do that," Carter said, his voice rough with his own intensifying urgency. He drew back long enough to tug his shirt free from the waistband of his pants. Then, quickly, he pulled the garment open, revealing a broad chest sprinkled with curly dark hair. Immediately Abby's fingers twined into his chest hair, and as he stripped the shirt off, she buried her lips in the flexed muscles of his shoulder.

While Carter loosened the belt on her robe, she began unhooking his trousers. A moment later he turned from Abby long enough to remove the rest of his clothes. Abby's robe now lay completely open, revealing the slender lines of her naked body.

With a passionate groan, he slid her arms out of the wrapper and began fondling her breasts and belly. "Abby," he whispered as he slid back up the length of her body, "I haven't got anything with me."

"It's okay, I'm fine," Abby whispered, putting a finger to his lips. Though she hadn't had a lover since her breakup with her ex-fiance six months earlier, she'd continued taking the pill.

The last barrier between her and Carter had fallen. Now as they began kissing again, it was with a fervor that swept every other reservation away. Against her stomach, Abby could feel that Carter was fully aroused. So was she.

"Oh, Abby, I want you so much," Carter said hoarsely as his hands lifted her pelvis up to meet his and he penetrated her. As he filled her, she clung to him.

At first their lovemaking was slow and rhythmic. But the passion of their coupling quickly mounted. Carter's thrusts became more powerful and Abby's response more frenzied.

A moment later she cried out in release, her loins quivering with rapture so intense and fulfilling that when it finally ebbed it left behind a warm glow of satisfaction. It wasn't until Carter felt the crest of her fulfillment that he gave in to his own pleasure. When it was over for both of them, he wrapped his arms around her, kissed her deeply, and they both slipped into a dreamless sleep.

Chapter Ten

"I suppose for propriety's sake I should have left you before dawn," Carter murmured when he woke. "But I don't think I could have."

"I wouldn't have let you," Abby declared, turning to face him. Just the sight of Carter lying beside her warmed and aroused her.

Their lovemaking that morning was slow and sensual. Carter explored each part of Abby, stroking and kissing and murmuring endearments until her whole body was once more aflame. When, finally, they came together, they shared a burst of fiery ecstasy. Afterward, they lay in bed cuddling, Abby's body cocooned against Carter's.

"You're a wonderful lover, Carter," Abby said.

He kissed the lobe of her ear. "You provided the proper inspiration. And the truth is that I've been wanting you ever since I first saw you." He toyed with one of her fingers. "Will you be offended if I ask what happened to break up the engagement you mentioned?"

Abby shook her head. "Gavin and I were colleagues in the history department," Abby began. "For a while it seemed as if we were made for each other. We shared so many interests—not just our field of study, but other things."

"What sort of things?" Carter questioned.

"Oh, we were both mad about bluegrass and country auctions. We both loved eating crabs and sailing on the Chesapeake. One of the things I most admired about Gavin was his community spirit. He even persuaded me to donate time to a soup kitchen for the homeless in Baltimore. And it's one of the best things I've ever done."

"Sounds like quite a guy," Carter said without much enthusiasm. "What went wrong?"

"I don't know," Abby said. "I guess it was a combination of things. Anyhow, when the acid test came, we failed it."

"What acid test?" Carter watched her closely.

"Gavin was offered a job at Wayne State University."

"Oh? That's in Detroit, isn't it?"

"Yes, and that was the problem. Neither of us would compromise. I guess what it all really meant was that what we had together just wasn't strong enough."

Carter nodded. "It was that way between my ex-wife and me."

Abby studied his thoughtful expression. He looked as if he were remembering things that he'd rather forget.

"While we were courting it seemed to both of us that we were perfect for each other. I was a photographer, she was a model. Our physical attraction was very strong. Diana was smart, pretty, and had a lot of personality." He shook his head. "We used to have great conversations about everything from aardvaarks to xylophones. But when it got down to the business of day-to-day living, when we had to compromise and make sacrifices for our marriage, it just didn't work."

"That's right, she was unhappy leaving New York, wasn't she?"

"Diana was never really content with being transplanted. She considered New York City the hub of the universe. During those first years I was traveling for my job, she accompanied me as a model, and things went along fairly smoothly. But after Callie was born and Diana started staying home more, the marriage just stopped working."

Though Carter had always seemed like a very self-sufficient man, there was an air of loneliness about him. "I'm surprised you haven't remarried," Abby said, thinking to herself that this was getting to be a strange conversation to have while lying naked in bed with a man.

"I guess my experience with Diana has made me cautious. If I ever do marry again I want it to be for keeps. I want to have a relationship that's based on all the right things."

"What do you think those are?" Abby asked.

"Love certainly and physical attraction, mutual interests and a shared sense of humor," Carter said, stroking Abby's arm. "But along with that goes respect, trust and honesty. Maybe honesty is the most important thing of all. If you can't be honest with each other, then the relationship has no solid foundation."

Honesty. The word made Abby flinch. Little did Carter know how low her honesty quotient with him was. Was it time to mend that, she wondered. If she didn't tell Carter the truth now, she'd hardly be able to look him in the face.

"Carter," she said.

"Hmmmm?" He twirled a lock of her hair around his forefinger.

"Speaking of honesty, I have a confession to make."

"Oh?" Carter propped himself up on his elbow and traced the line of her chin with his finger. "And what would that be?"

She shot a quick glance at his face and then looked back down at the hem of the sheet, which she was nervously pleating with her hands. "Actually I have other reasons for being here besides the travel article I'm writing."

"Yes, the book, too—right?"

Abby sighed. "Yes, the book." She pulled the sheet up around her breasts and sat up and faced him. "But I haven't been entirely open about the kind of book I'm writing."

Carter eyed her. "You said it was a Civil War novel, didn't you?"

"It's not a novel, exactly."

Frowning slightly, Carter pushed himself up into a sitting position, as well.

"It's a history. My book's about real events. As a matter of fact—" Abby took a deep breath. "My book's about the Lydia Stewart-Byron Forbes affair."

Carter's eyebrows began to rise. "You mean our Lydia Stewart and Byron Forbes?"

"As a historian, I think it's a fascinating tale," Abby hurried on. "Ever since hearing about it, I've wanted to get to the truth of it."

"The truth of it?"

"Yes, I mean to discover what actually happened."

Carter gestured awkwardly. "Well, Prestwood's play gives you a pretty good idea what went on."

Though Abby could hear wariness coming into his tone, she pressed on. "I don't think it does, Carter. I think Prestwood's play is based on a false accusation. I don't believe Lydia Stewart was ever a spy."

Carter stared at her and drew back slightly. "I don't understand what you're saying."

"What I'm saying is that I think Lydia Stewart was framed."

"By whom?" Carter's voice now had a sharp edge.

"I'm not sure. I don't have all the facts yet."

Carter stared at her. "Now let me get this straight," he finally said. "You're not here just to write a travel article about The Prize. You're also here to debunk my family lore and, if that's the case, ruin the pageant as well."

Abby held up a hand. "I'm not writing bad things about your pageant in my travel article. The history is for my book."

"Excuse me, but I don't see how you can give a positive account of the pageant while at the same time you're calling it all nonsense." He scowled at her. "Just what is your interest in all of this, anyhow? I mean, why us, and why now?"

This truth-telling was really not going very well, Abby thought. "Carter," she pleaded, "please understand, this is nothing personal against you or your family. It has to do with my family."

"Your family?"

Once again Abby took a deep breath. "Lydia Stewart was my great-great-great-aunt."

Carter looked stunned. Then, without saying a word, he turned his back to Abby and reached for his shirt. As he pulled it on and then buttoned it, there was a heavy silence.

Abby sat with her hands pressed to the sides of her face, trying to think of a way to set things right. "Carter, I'm sorry. I was only trying to be honest with you," she finally said.

Standing, he pulled on his pants and belted them. "Honest," he said, turning toward her. "Now that's an interesting word coming from you. You've been deceiving me from the moment we met, haven't you?"

"Carter..."

Swiftly he put on his shoes and socks. Then he strode over to the door. Pausing and giving Abby a look that made her want to weep, he said, "You're still my guest, and I intend to treat you with courtesy. But clearly, spending the night with each other was a mistake for both of us." He shook his head. "Now that I think about it, though, you do your great-great-great-aunt proud."

FOR A LONG TIME Abby huddled in bed. Tears leaked down her cheeks. She'd really botched this, and right now she felt like packing up and leaving.

Abby got up, ran a hand through her hair and sighed. For several minutes she stood, trying to sort out what she should do.

Tempted though she was by the idea of slinking away, she simply couldn't. She was a professional who had a contract to do an article on The Prize and its festival. What's more, she had an obligation to her father, and to herself, to get the true story. Yet it all went back to the same old thing. She didn't want to hurt Callie, Mary Lou or Carter.

Carter...how was she going to even face him at breakfast? "Oh," she groaned out loud. Everyone had probably heard about her swamp expedition from Callie. What was she going to tell them about that episode now?

While she showered and changed, Abby fretted over the web of problems that she'd woven. She decided she would go to breakfast, try to do a little more research in the library and then play it by ear from there. Maybe she'd find what she needed in Byron's journal, or one of the other books in the library.

"Well, there's the intrepid adventuress," Ordell called out. "Callie and Carter have just been telling us all about your solo expedition."

Despite herself, Abby flushed. Just what had Callie and Carter been telling them?

"Dad says you had some problems getting out of the swamp last night," Callie said after she'd downed the last of a tall glass of milk.

"You could say that," Abby answered cautiously. She shot a look at Carter who seemed interested only in the piece of coffee cake he was munching.

Without looking up, he said, "Even old-timers like me get lost in the swamp from time to time. It's no big deal."

"Well, she certainly doesn't look the worse for wear to me," Ordell commented.

Abby felt relief well up at Carter's gently offered alibi. As Callie gathered her books, said goodbye and went off to school, Abby slipped into her seat and spread a napkin on her lap.

Ordell handed her a plate of crisp bacon. "Don't suppose you stumbled on any interesting eateries, or perhaps a buried pot of pirate treasure?"

"I hate to break in and interrupt your story, dear," Mary Lou said to Abby. Then she held up a finger and addressed the group. "But speaking of treasure, I have a problem. Months ago I agreed to hold a treasure hunt here for the local Boy Scout troop. I had forgotten all about it, but when the scoutmaster called this morning to confirm everything I nearly dropped my teeth. I hate to disappoint the boys but I just don't know how I can be here this afternoon."

"I'd be more than happy to fill in for you," Joanna said, "but Ordell and I are committed to meet with the New Orleans tourism board today."

Abby, knowing what was coming, shrank into her seat. She felt like an unprepared student who didn't want to be called on by the teacher. But as Mary Lou continued to fuss over her problem, Abby had second thoughts. Her guilt about taking advantage of Mary Lou's hospitality was eating away at her. Maybe this was a chance to partly repay her hostess for her kindness. Not only that, but it would provide a way to fill out the day and keep out of Carter's way. "I'll be glad to help out," Abby piped up. "Just tell me what to do."

"Oh, you sweetheart," Mary Lou cried, "I'm sure you'll be just wonderful with the children. And I'll be eternally grateful to you. And so will Carter. He wasn't too happy this morning when I told him he would have to run the treasure hunt all alone."

Abby blinked and then shot Carter a surreptitious look. So instead of avoiding him, she'd put herself in a position where they'd have to spend the afternoon together. Carter was concentrating on his plate. He didn't look any happier about the prospect of working together than she was.

"Hello y'all," Prestwood called from the door.

Mary Lou gave him a smile, "Prestwood, pull up a chair and have some breakfast. Maria," she went on, addressing the young woman who was restocking the serving table, "please get Mr. Matthews some coffee."

"Thanks, coffee would be great." Prestwood settled his lanky form into one of the Hepplewhite chairs. "No breakfast, though. Carter and I have to go over the pictures he took for my latest brochure, and then I have to get them to the printer's."

Just then a car horn sounded outside.

"Up, up, Joanna," Ordell said, wiping his mouth and rising. "There's our ride. I hope you ladies and gentlemen will excuse us."

Joanna took another sip of coffee, wiped her own mouth and then pushed her chair back from the table. "Duty calls," she said, smiling at the others.

"You'll be back in time for dinner, won't you?" Mary Lou asked.

"With bells on my napkin," Ordell tossed over his shoulder.

A brief silence fell after the two food experts and their driver departed. But Mary Lou soon filled it by starting to explain what Abby would be doing that afternoon. Meanwhile, much to Abby's relief, Carter and Prestwood took their leave.

Soon after that, Abby said goodbye to her distracted hostess and sought the quiet of the library to continue her research.

She went immediately to Byron's journal. But after opening the closely written old book, she found it impossible to concentrate. As much as she wanted to delve into Byron's personal account, her mind kept shifting to her rift with Carter and the uncomfortable situation scheduled for this afternoon.

Twice Abby thought she heard footsteps in the corridor. But no one came in.

At last she got up and walked out into the empty hall. A telephone sat on a small table by the door. A phone call back to Baltimore was long overdue, Abby realized. She checked her watch. Her father ought to be just coming in from his morning aerobics class. Using her telephone credit card she dialed his number, and he picked it up on the first ring.

"Good timing, I just came in the door," Peter Heatherington exclaimed. He grunted. "Boy, the old muscles sure got a workout this morning!"

Abby grinned. It was her theory that her father liked his seniors aerobics class as much for the leotarded ladies in it as for the muscle tone it provided.

"Anyhow, Abigirl, what have you been up to? I've been waiting with bated breath for your latest report from the Rebel front."

Abby looked from right to left to make sure she was alone and then lowered her voice. "I did get into the swamp and took a look around. Unfortunately, I didn't find anything at the ruins of the cabin where Lydia stayed overnight during her escape. But," she rushed on, I've come across a journal—one that Byron Forbes kept—and he wrote about Lydia. I think it's very possible that something may come of that."

"From the horse's mouth, huh?"

"How about you, Dad? What did you discover? Were you able to find any information on Jerome Matthews?"

"Nope, the well at the university library was dry. But tomorrow I'm going to the Library of Congress to research my American Heritage article. You know, the one on eighteenth century hand tools. Maybe I'll uncover something on our boy there."

"I hope so," Abby said with a sigh. "I'm not getting very far here at all. And with the pageant only a few days off, I'm going to run out of excuses for staying soon."

"Don't give up yet," Peter encouraged. "If Christopher Columbus had turned back when his crew told him there was no hope, all our globes might still be flat."

"Anything else new up there?" Abby questioned. "How are Antony and Cleopatra doing?"

"Pampered as ever. When they're not lolling around looking imperious, they're scarfing up that gourmet feline food you feed them. I think they eat better than I do."

Abby laughed and they chatted on about the cats' antics. However, a subtle click stopped her midsentence. "Did you hear that?" she said to her father.

"That click, you mean? Sounds like someone hung up an extension. You got any Confederate spies lurking around there?"

Abby frowned. Probably someone, possibly the maid, had just picked up the phone and hung it up again when they realized it was in use, she told herself. But what if someone had been purposely listening in on her private conversation? And if that was the case, who might it have been? Abby said goodbye quickly then hung up and headed into the library.

A RAUCOUS GAGGLE of Boy Scouts poured out of the van that had just pulled up in front of the main house. As Abby walked up the road she could see Carter, casually dressed in blue jeans and a striped sport shirt, shaking hands with the driver. Callie, school books still slung over her shoulder, stood by his side.

"Abby, ready for the treasure hunt?" Callie called. After dumping her books on the ground, she hurried over. "Aunt Mary Lou hid the toy pirate sword and even we don't know where it is."

"Well, that should make for a challenge," Abby said, putting an arm around the youngster's shoulder. As Mary Lou had explained, the afternoon's activities would consist of games to win clues. The Scouts would be divided into three teams. The team that collected enough clues to guess where the "treasure" had been secreted would win a pizza party and passes to a free movie.

As the two walked up to meet Carter and the boys, Abby pasted a smile on her face; Carter did the same thing. Looking at them, Abby thought, no one would imagine that there was anything wrong.

Politely he introduced Abby to the driver, who then said goodbye. When they were alone with the milling Scouts, Carter got their attention simply by raising his hand. "Now boys," he said with a grin, "here's how the game works..."

After he'd explained the rules, they started their first game out on the lawn, a rowdy round of musical chairs punctuated by much laughter and good-natured shoving. After the winner had collected his clue, they went on to a boisterous croquet tournament that produced several new clues.

When they weren't catching errant balls, Abby, Carter and Callie offered suggestions and shouted encouragement.

"C'mon Baton Rouge Rogues!" Abby cried.

"Way to go, Louisiana Leaping Lizards," Carter cheered. In the infectious camaraderie of the contest, the morning's ill feelings began to melt away like ice cubes on a sunny day. Grinning, Carter turned to Abby. "You swing a mean mallet," he said.

"We play croquet in Maryland," she answered, smiling. If he could make the effort to put unpleasantness behind them, she was more than happy to do the same. "We even have a few old plantation houses. Nothing as beautiful as this, though," she added, glancing appreciatively around at the green manicured grounds of The Prize. It really was beautiful, she thought. "It's amazing how quickly this place has come to seem like home to me," she went on. The words slipped out before she had time to consider how Carter might react to them.

He looked at her, an odd expression in his fine, dark eyes. Then his gaze swept over the sun-drenched landscape. "Even though the Mogul's ruby is long gone, as far as I'm concerned, this place is, and always has been, the real treasure."

Once again, Abby was moved by his love for the land. And it seemed as if each day she spent at The Prize made her empathize with it more deeply. The place really did get into your blood.

Just then Callie came running up. "My team, the Swamp Rats, just scored," she exclaimed. "We get the clue."

"Okay." Abby opened the shoe box Mary Lou had given her and one of the "Rats" stuck in a pudgy paw and pulled out a folded piece of paper.

The next game involved a timed search for clues.

"All right, guys," Carter said, holding up a stopwatch. "You've got ten minutes to locate five clues." He drew an envelope out of his pocket. "My Aunt Mary Lou has left a hint that should start you out in the right direction." With a flourish, he opened the envelope and read what was written on the flap. "It says, 'Go west, young man, but stay east of the crepe myrtles.' "

For a moment the boys stood around scratching their heads. "What do you think it means?" one of them said.

Another held up a finger. "I know." He took out a compass. "The clues are west of the house—that way." He pointed. With a yell, all of the boys scattered out on a run. Smiling, Callie, Carter and Abby followed them.

Callie turned to Abby and playfully tapped her on the shoulder. "My Rats are going to decimate your Rogues."

"You think so, huh? Well, don't underestimate my Rogues. They're a crafty group."

"But nothing compared to the Lizards," Carter interjected.

Callie waved him away. "Nah, everyone knows Rats eat Lizards!" Cackling, she raced off to join her teammates.

When she was out of earshot, Carter turned to Abby.

For a moment Abby lost track of her surroundings. All she could see was Carter, and all she could feel and remember was his kiss. At the same time, his gaze dropped to her lips. Abby's hand started to go out toward him. But then she remembered the harsh words between them that morning and the Boy Scouts who were within view, and her hand fell back down to her sides. She sensed more than saw that Carter had done the same thing.

"Hey, Dad and Abby," Callie called from the other side of an old magnolia.

They looked over and saw her standing next to a low wall of stone.

"What is it, Callie?" Carter shouted back.

"Come on over and take a look at this."

"What is that she's standing by?" Abby asked Carter as they broke into a jog.

"Just the foundation of the old schoolhouse," Carter replied.

"The one where Jerome Matthews taught?"

"The same."

Abby's interest quickened. She had forgotten there was anything left of the building.

Callie had climbed to the top of the ruined wall and was walking around the edge of it peering down.

"Look at all these holes, Dad."

Carter rested his hands on the stone and leaned over. "My God," he exclaimed. "Looks as though a gopher's been at work around here."

Abby eyed the spot herself. On the other side of the wall the ground looked like Swiss cheese. Someone had methodically dug at least two dozen holes. Some were small, and some were quite large, almost like animal tunnels. Only whoever had done it hadn't been an animal. In the freshly turned dirt Abby could see marks that had obviously been left by a shovel.

Chapter Eleven

Carter stood shaking his head. "This is very strange. Who could have done it?" He turned to his daughter. "Do you have any idea?"

Callie shrugged and poked her stick at one of the pits. "I don't know but they couldn't have been dug more than a day or so ago."

"Yes," Abby agreed. "The dirt appears pretty fresh."

"I was playing around here last week," Callie volunteered. "There weren't any holes then except for the one I dug with Beau Bradley," she said, naming a school friend.

"What were you and Beau digging for?" Carter asked. He swung his leg over the wall and began walking from hole to hole, pushing at their rims with the toe of his shoe.

"We were just playing pirates, you know, digging for buried treasure."

"Find any?" Abby asked.

"Nah, nothing much." Callie picked up a stone and sailed it over the wall. "An old dish, some broken pieces of pottery and a marble."

"Which of these did you dig?" Carter asked.

Callie pointed at a corner. "We were playing over there."

"Do you think Beau came back and did more digging?" Abby queried.

"I suppose maybe he could have," Callie agreed. "That must be it."

They lingered at the spot a few more minutes and then left to rejoin the boys. The five clues had been found and the Rats won the day when they discovered the toy sword planted in a pot of camellias.

After the prizes were awarded and the boys had been treated to cookies and lemonade, Carter, Abby and Callie, flanked by Barney and Goldie, stood on the driveway in front of the house waving as the boisterous group was driven away.

Once the van was out of sight, Callie started a game of fetch with the two dogs. For a while Abby and Carter joined in. Then Carter checked his watch and looked at Abby.

"Care to join me on the veranda for a mint julep before dinner? I don't know about you, but I could use a spell of quiet."

Abby looked at him uncertainly. From the warmth in his dark eyes, she could see that Carter wanted to mend their fences. Since Abby wanted the same thing, she nodded. "That sounds like a wonderful idea."

While she took a seat on one of the wicker rocking chairs and settled down to watch Callie and the dogs, Carter went inside. A few minutes later he reappeared carrying a tray with a frosty pitcher and two glasses with ice and sprigs of mint.

"Maybe we should toast the Rats and their success," Abby said.

Carter grinned and lifted his glass. "To the Rats, to their success, and to their departure."

They both chuckled and sipped their refreshing drinks.

Then Carter settled back in his chair and turned toward Abby. "This afternoon was fun. I didn't expect to enjoy it, but I did."

"Yes," she agreed. "It really was fun—even if the Rogues and the Lizards did lose."

For a moment Carter rotated his glass between his palms. Then he glanced up and gave her a serious look. "Abby, I've been thinking."

"Yes?"

"About this morning. I don't know why I was so upset to find out who you are and what you're doing. I hate to admit it, but I guess I felt threatened." He took another sip and then went on. "I know you're down here doing what you think is right—you're just looking for the truth."

"Oh, yes, Carter," Abby said earnestly. "Believe me, I don't want to do anything that would hurt you or your family. I just need to find out what really happened." She gazed out at Callie who was playing tug-of-war with Barney over a stick. "You must know that I think the world of Callie and that I really like your aunt Mary Lou."

Carter cocked his head. "And me? How do you feel about me?"

Abby swirled the liquid around in her glass and studied it. She was picturing herself as she'd been the night before, entwined in Carter's strong arms. Feeling her cheeks go warm, she lifted her eyes to meet his. "I think you must know how I feel about you."

"No, I'm confused, Abby. Tell me."

The question threw Abby off balance. Given her circumstances and the fact that Carter hadn't made any declarations to her, how should she answer? "I think you're one of the most interesting and exciting men I've ever met," she admitted.

"Nothing more?" Carter asked.

Abby tilted her chin toward him. "And just what do you think of me, sir?"

Carter took her hand and brought it to his lips. "You, Miss Heatherington, are very beautiful and very desirable." He leaned toward her and touched her lips lightly with his. His kiss tasted of mint and cool bourbon. She knew that the fleeting kiss would have quickly developed into a longer and more passionate caress had they been somewhere private.

Reluctantly Carter drew back but continued to clasp her hand. "Anyhow," he said with a smile, "I find, much to my surprise, I'm delighted to meet and kiss the lady descended from my great-great grandfather's nemesis." Once again he raised her fingers to his lips and this time kissed each tip. "Now I know why Byron was so smitten with Lydia."

A car door slammed and a voice cried out, "Yoo hoo, I'm back." Mary Lou toddled around the corner loaded down with a stack of costume boxes. "Don't get up," she said, dumping the boxes on the porch with a thump as Carter let go of Abby's hand and began to raise himself out of his chair. She waggled her hand at him. "Sit down, sit down." Carter settled back into the seat.

"Well," Mary Lou said, scrutinizing her nephew and his guest, "I do declare you two don't look the worse for wear. I gather the Boy Scouts didn't pull the house down."

Mary Lou checked the time on her antique-gold pendant watch. "Ooh, it's later than I realized. Dinner is at seven sharp at The Ruby tonight, and *pshеww*," she exclaimed, tugging at her neckline. "I declare I'm just sweatin' like a prizefighter. I'd love to join y'all for a drink, but I just have to get under the shower this instant."

When she was gone, Abby stood. "A shower sounds like a good idea to me, too. I think I'll head on back to my cabin."

"I'll walk with you," Carter said. "I want to check something at the studio. Just let me carry this tray back into the kitchen."

A moment after Carter had disappeared inside with their empty glasses, Abby found a paper napkin he'd left on the porch. She followed him with the idea of tossing it into the kitchen trash, but in the hallway she paused and frowned down at the table where Callie's and Mary Lou's candid instant camera shots of their party had been displayed. The two Abby had wanted were missing. She wondered for a moment whether Carter might have taken them.

"Something wrong?" Carter asked as he came striding down the corridor.

"Uh, no, nothing. I was just looking for somewhere to toss this." Abby held up the napkin. She decided not to bother him with questions about the photos. It really wasn't important. Carter threw the napkin into a trash can, then took her arm as they stepped back onto the porch. They had no sooner descended the porch steps than Goldie, Barney and Callie fell in alongside them.

"I bet my yucky old costume is in one of the boxes Aunt Mary Lou's brought home," Callie pouted. "Now I'll have to get pins stuck in me again."

As Callie rattled on with more complaints about having to wear a big dress with long skirts, Abby squinted into the setting sun. Something was sitting in front of her door, but she couldn't make out what it was. As they got closer she could see it looked like some sort of a ball.

"Speaking of pins," Abby said, reaching down to pick it up. "Does anyone know what this is?"

"Don't touch it," Callie yelled and knocked Abby's hand away. "It's voodoo," she breathed. "Someone's trying to curse you!"

Carter pushed past them, picked up the object and held it in his open palm. Abby leaned over and stared at it. A cold chill rippled down her spine. It appeared to be a wax ball with straight pins stuck in it. What's more, she realized with a shudder, there was some hair embedded in the thing.

Carter pulled out a strand and held it to the light. "It's reddish brown."

"Just like Abby's," Callie whispered. "Someone must have got hold of your hair."

"Uhhh," Abby shuddered. "But how could someone get my hair? I don't remember anybody pulling it out," she said trying to make light of the creepy feeling crawling up her spine, "and I don't think I shed that much."

"Hmmm," Carter said, twisting the strange little ball around in his hand, "your brush."

"My brush!" Abby recoiled and then pulled out her key, opened her door and ran over to the bureau. Gingerly she lifted her brush and then her comb. They were clean. Her hand went to her hair and she remembered the night when she'd pulled out a tangle. She didn't remember throwing it away. What had happened to it?

"This is really spooky," Callie whispered. She and Carter were staring down at the immaculate brush and comb.

"I'll have a talk with the cleaning people," Carter said. "Meanwhile, let's forget this. Intelligent people know that voodoo is just nonsense."

"Yes," Abby agreed. But she could see the look of concern on his face and it wasn't reassuring.

"I'll take care of this," Carter said as he gave her shoulder a brief squeeze. "Don't worry." Then, carrying the offending object away with him, he and Callie headed back toward the house.

Voodoo was once again the topic of conversation that night at dinner. As the group sat in the candlelit restaurant enjoying a jambalaya, Carter frowned at Callie who'd brought the subject up. But once she'd described the wax ball Abby had found on her front porch, interest in other topics melted away.

"I saw something like that when I was in Haiti ten years back," Ordell volunteered. "It seemed the chefs of two competing gourmet restaurants were brawling over a woman. Both gentlemen in question wanted to be her one and only and neither would back off. The older of the two Romeos purchased a hexing charm from a local bokar—that's someone who works black magic," Ordell explained.

"What happened?" Abby asked, none too happily.

"When the victim's stews started tasting like reheated mud and he lost customers, he blamed it on the gris-gris and did the only thing he could. He went to another bokar and bought an equally potent gris-gris against his rival. The last I heard the cuisine at both restaurants tasted like dog food and they were at a standoff."

"That's it," Callie shouted. "We have to go back to Aunt Hat's and get a good gris-gris for Abby."

Abby blanched. The idea of returning to the swamp did not appeal to her in the least.

Joanna, noting the distress on Abby's face, reached over and patted her hand. "Such foolishness, dear. Someone's just trying to frighten you. Ignore it. After all, you're going to be leaving in a few days."

"I wouldn't dismiss it quite so casually," Prestwood said, putting down his wineglass. "Some very strange things have happened in connection with voodoo." He turned to his sister. "Remember that story about Grace LeBouef's hair falling out?"

"I'll say," Elaine said, pulling her chair closer and resting her elbows on the table. "Grace LeBouef had an all-out argument with Clara her cleaning lady and refused to pay her. Clara left in a huff and went straight to the voodoo woman for a hex. Now Grace had forgotten in the meantime that Clara had a key. Unbeknownst to Grace, Clara snuck in one night and tucked gris-gris all over the house. All of a sudden Grace started getting all kinds of strange ailments. Her hair fell out, she got a twitch in her eye, a toenail went black, her nose started to run like Niagara Falls. She was really racking up doctor's bills."

"And Grace, I conjecture, found herself another practitioner of the art who undid the spell?" Ordell said.

"Y'all are exactly right," Elaine answered. "He cleansed the house and scattered his own gris-gris about."

Carter, who had been fidgeting in his seat, broke in with "This is absurd. It's all folklore." He turned to Abby. "Joanna is right. Whoever did this is just trying to scare you."

"What I don't understand," Joanna interjected, "is why? Why in the world would anyone want to hurt our sweet little Abby?"

"Undoubtedly pure jealousy," Ordell said.

"That has to be it," Mary Lou agreed. "Now let's change the subject before it ruins dessert."

After dinner they returned to the house and Abby joined Joanna and Ordell out on the porch where they'd started a game of checkers. Around the porch light a halo of moths fluttered. The fragrance of fresh mown grass and verbena scented the air. Abby, nervous about going back to her cabin, perched on the white porch railing and watched the good-natured duel.

"Another lovely evening," Joanna said as she jumped two of Ordell's red men.

"Easy for you to say," the plump food writer harumphed as he surrendered his pieces.

"Oh, you've been in culinary heaven since you've been down here, admit it," Joanna chided as Ordell drummed his fingers on the table, considering his next move. While she waited Joanna turned to Abby. "And it's obvious that you love this place."

"You're right, I do." She glanced up at the house and then out at the moonlit garden. "But how is it so obvious?"

Joanna gave her a teasing look. "Oh, it's the way you get along so well with Callie, the way your eyes glowed when you looked out at the lawns just now. And then there's the way you and the master of The Prize gaze at each other."

Abby wrapped her arms around the porch post and leaned back like a child on a merry-go-round. "Now what do you mean by that?"

"C'mon now," Ordell chortled. "We've seen you two making goo-goo eyes." He swooped down on a checker. "Take that, woman!" he exclaimed as he jumped one of Joanna's kings. "Ha, ha! You were so busy with your matchmaking that you weren't paying attention."

"I was so paying attention," Joanna retorted. "I just tossed a man your way to keep you in a good humor."

Swiftly she moved a piece to block one of Ordell's kings and then turned back to Abby. "Are you sure you really want to go back north when the pageant is over?" Joanna asked.

"What else would I do?"

"I suspect our host might have some suggestions," Ordell piped up slyly as he slid another checker forward.

Joanna chuckled. "Don't the Forbes men have a way of losing their hearts to Baltimore ladies and vice versa?"

Abby sighed. Now that she'd told Carter her true identity, there was really no reason to hide it from anyone else, she thought. "I'm afraid there's a little more to it than that," she began.

The checker game came to a halt as Abby confessed her relationship with Lydia and the true purpose of her visit.

"The plot really does thicken," Ordell exclaimed.

Joanna put a finger to her chin and tapped lightly. "Goodness, do you think the gris-gris you found has anything to do with all this?"

Abby shrugged. "Maybe. I just don't know. I must have made an enemy somehow. But who? And why?"

"Well, you're a stranger who's interfering with a very popular local legend."

"Yes, but only Carter knows what I'm doing."

Ordell shook his head. "Not his M.O. The man's got too much class."

Abby blanched. It hadn't even occurred to her that Carter might have planted the horrible little wax ball.

"No, it's not Carter. It's someone else," Joanna said firmly. "But remember, dear, you're far from home but you're not alone. You've got a pair of allies."

Ordell rubbed his hands together. "Tracking down the culprit in this little drama shouldn't be any more difficult than my search for the mystery ingredient in Doc Wannabee's secret Bogota stew. Did I ever tell you about that?"

"No," both women said in unison.

Ordell was in the middle of describing his trek into the jungles of South America to track down the elusive Dr. Wannabee and his wondrous recipe when the screen door creaked and Carter came out onto the porch.

"Don't stop for me," he said when Ordell broke his narrative. Casually Carter leaned against a post and watched the little threesome. Ordell had thrown himself into the story, acting it out complete with dramatic gestures, voices, and even animal calls. As Carter listened in, however, he gradually tuned Ordell out and focused all his attention on Abby's moonlit profile.

She looked so lovely sitting there laughing at the older man's absurd tall tales. Already, Carter had grown to love her high spirits and the sound of her laughter. But he loved looking at her even more. The way her hair curled against her creamy cheek made him want to reach out and touch her skin. The little lift of her mouth as she smiled warmed him. Even the soft sweep of her eyelashes pleasured his gaze.

Abby's hand pushed aside an errant curl and he remembered the touch of her long delicate fingers on his flesh. How would it be when she left and took all that with her? he wondered. She'd brought a new spark of life to the plantation—and to him.

It was at that moment Carter finally admitted to himself he didn't want Abby to leave. The realization shook him, and for several minutes he stood frozen while he absorbed the implications. Despite all his resolutions, in the space of just a few short days she had touched his heart—and Callie's.

Yet the irony of getting so seriously involved with a woman who was not only a northerner like his ex-wife but one who was Lydia Stewart's descendant as well... Carter raked an agitated hand through his hair. To make matters worse, Abby had been snooping around trying to clear Lydia's name. What might all that lead to, he asked himself. Byron's love affair with Lydia had been a disaster, and this could very well be history repeating itself.

Meanwhile Ordell had finished his story and was taking bows to the two women's enthusiastic applause.

"Bravo," Carter said when the clapping finally subsided. "I'd love to stay for an encore, but I've got some prints to get done before the pageant." With a last regretful glance at Abby, he stepped off the porch and walked away into the darkness.

After Carter had gone, Ordell took a look at the checkerboard, hopscotched a piece halfway around it and swallowed up the rest of Joanna's men.

Joanna's jaw dropped. Then she put her hands on her hips. "How did you do that?"

Ordell pointed to his head. "Brilliant strategy. A quality I share with the great conquerors, Caesar, Alexander..."

"And Attila the Hun," Joanna completed the sentence. "Abby, you play with this man. He's impossible."

The checker tournament went on for another hour as the two took turns on either side of the board. Finally, however, the hour grew late. They put the checkers back into the box, folded up the game and strolled back to their cabins.

"Remember," Joanna said to Abby just before they parted for the evening. "We're with you. If there's anything we can do to help, just let us know."

Smiling with gratitude, Abby turned toward her own cabin and strolled down the last twenty yards of gravel path that led to it. As she climbed the steps she looked around with some trepidation and was much relieved to see nothing unusual waiting for her on the doormat. Inside, she flicked on the light, looked around and, when she found nothing amiss, went into the bathroom.

After brushing her teeth, she turned the radio on and picked up one of the tourist magazines stacked on the bureau. Flipping it open, she sat down on the bed and reached over to prop up her pillow against the headboard.

As she moved the pillow, her hand encountered an odd shape beneath the case. Letting out a little scream, she yanked her hand back as if it were on fire. Then with trembling fingers she turned the pillow on its side and watched in horror as a muslin bag tied with a rough cord slithered out.

For several seconds Abby simply stared at it. It was like the bag that Callie had worn around her neck the first night at dinner, so Abby recognized that this must be another gris-gris. What was inside, she wondered with a little shiver. She didn't want to touch it let alone open it, but curiosity got the better of her and she gingerly undid the fastening. Then, using the open magazine for a container, she dumped out the contents.

An unpleasant mixture tumbled out. Bits of hair that she recognized as her own, ashes of some sort, small chunks of bone, and torn fragments of a photograph. Involuntarily Abby recoiled. But she wanted to know whose image lay on that photograph. Using a nail file she retrieved from her purse, Abby pieced several of the bits together and as the picture took form she shuddered again. It was one of the photographs that had been missing, the one Mary Lou had taken of her that first night. Abby grimaced as she recalled her romantic notion that Carter might have taken it to keep for himself.

As she stared at it in horror, she crossed her arms over her chest and began to shiver. Suddenly she couldn't stand to look at the whole horrible mess another minute, and shut the magazine up over it. It was at that moment that she heard the eerie noise outside her window.

An unearthly wailing pierced the night, as if a demon had escaped from hell and was calling to its kind. With a horrified little exclamation, Abby leaped off the bed, pushed the lace curtain aside and peered through the window. Dark shadows moved like ghosts on the path leading past her cabin. Abby clutched at her chest.

The shapes moved closer and she sighed with relief as she recognized them.

"Ssssh, Barney," she heard Carter say as he took the old hound by the collar and started to urge him past Abby's cabin.

Such relief flooded through Abby at the sight of Carter that she ran to the door, pulled it open and called to him.

"Sorry if Barney woke you," Carter said, still holding the dog firmly. "He may be an old dog, but every once in a while his hunting instincts surface and he starts howling at everything, including the moon."

Framed in the light of the doorway, Abby put a hand over her heart and sagged. "So that horrible noise was only Barney. Thank goodness!"

Carter approached closer and regarded Abby. "Are you okay?"

Abby shook her head. "No, I don't think I am. Oh, Carter, I just found another one of those awful things in my pillowcase."

"Damn!" Releasing Barney, he strode onto the porch and took Abby into his arms. For several minutes they stood there while he stroked her hair and murmured comforting words. When she finally drew back he said, "Show me what you found, Abby."

Nodding, she led him inside and over to the bed. "It was a gris-gris, and I opened it up to see what was inside. After that I couldn't stand the sight of it," she said, pointing at the magazine. "It's shut up in there."

Carter rubbed her shoulder. Then, releasing her, he sat on the coverlet and carefully opened the magazine. Frowning, he gazed down at the bizarre collection of oddments. "Is that your picture?" he asked, pointing at the torn fragments of paper.

"Yes."

He shook his head. "I'd love to know who's doing this so I could wring his neck," he said between his teeth. Carter stood, went over to the wastebasket and looked inside. "Good, it's empty," he said, removing the plastic liner. Then he tipped the contents of the magazine into the bag and picked up the muslin and string and tossed it in after. "I'll take care of this."

"What do you think I should do?" Abby said.

He turned to face her, concern written on every line of his handsome face. "Obviously this person is trying to scare you, or he's making some sort of a sick joke. Truthfully I don't think you're in any kind of danger. But I'd be more comfortable if you took a room in the big house. There's one at the opposite end of the hall from mine." For the first time since he'd entered the cabin, a smile began to light Carter's eyes. "Aunt Mary Lou's room is in between, so she can play chaperon."

Abby smiled tremulously. "I don't know that a chaperon is what I really want." She knew for certain that it wasn't what she wanted tonight. Right now she ached to have Carter's arms around her again.

Her longings must have been reflected in her eyes because Carter read them instantly. Putting the bag on the chair, he reached for Abby and gathered her into his arms. "Well, I'm absolutely certain that a chaperon isn't my heart's desire," he murmured hoarsely.

"And what is?"

He tipped her face up to his and searched it. "After this morning I tried to tell myself that we should cool things."

"That's what I was doing, too," Abby admitted.

"Didn't work very well for me," Carter added, brushing her lips with his.

Abby clung to his strength. The fear and horror of the past few minutes were transmuting themselves into another powerful emotion. "Me, neither," she whispered, pressing herself against his broad chest.

"Good," Carter said huskily and lifted her into his arms. With a quick stride, he carried her to the bed and laid her down on it. He, too, seemed galvanized by the strong emotions of the moment.

Carter's mouth went to her temple and then to her ear. "I want to stay with you tonight and keep you safe. I want to be part of you," he whispered.

"Oh, yes, Carter," Abby whispered back as her hands cupped around the back of his neck and her fingers traced the deep hollow sculpted there. "Please, please stay with me."

With a groan, Carter slipped the straps of her sundress down over her arms and buried his lips between the V of her breasts. Then he raised himself up on his elbows and stared down at her with burning eyes. "Oh, Abby, the spell you've cast over me is much more potent than any voodoo charm. You've bewitched me, Abby Heatherington."

Abby drew his head back to hers. "Then let me weave this spell a little stronger," she whispered back as she once again pressed her body against his.

Chapter Twelve

Ordell balanced a suitcase in one hand and swatted at a fly dive-bombing his head. "Pesky kamikaze insect!" he muttered as he trudged past a group of workmen busily setting up a platform on the lawn for the pageant.

Behind him Abby lugged her camera bag, train case and a portfolio stuffed with her notebook and the tourist brochures she'd collected on the trip. "You managing okay?" she shouted to Ordell, who'd volunteered to play porter.

To save Abby embarrassment Carter had left her cabin at sunrise, early enough to avoid running into Joanna who was usually up at dawn taking her constitutional. Before he'd left, though, he'd made Abby promise to move into the main house that morning.

The room Mary Lou had provided was a high-ceilinged guest chamber with a view of the garden. "Well, you certainly ought to be comfortable here," Ordell said, dropping Abby's suitcase on the crocheted coverlet. He glanced around at the trellises of roses on the wallpaper and the matching swags with their apple-green trim. "This should confuse that voodoo varmint, or at least make things inconvenient for him—or her."

"I certainly hope so," Abby said, rubbing her forearms.

"By the way, I spoke to Prestwood a little while ago," Ordell said. "Since Carter and Mary Lou are going to be tied up at one of those endless meetings about the pageant festivities, Prestwood thought it would be nice for the three of us to join him at Lilyvale for dinner this evening."

"Oh, that sounds like a good idea."

"I did have a bit of worry," Ordell went on, "about what kind of fare skinny-shanks Elaine might produce." With his hands he drew Elaine's figure in air as if she were shaped like a stick. "So, to insure that we'll eat well, I've agreed to do the cooking and Joanna's agreed to be my sous chef. And I can promise," he declared, holding up an exclamatory forefinger, "that dinner will rank among your happiest gustatory memories."

"I don't doubt it," Abby laughed.

After Ordell left her room, Abby spent a half hour unpacking and arranging her toiletries and clothes. She was just unfolding a blouse when she heard the phone ring and a moment later Maria knocked and poked her head in the door.

"Telephone for you, Ms. Heatherington. You can take it right out in the hall. Or, if you want some privacy, you can use Miss Forbes's study. I'll hang up when you get on the line."

"Thank you, Maria." Abby dropped the blouse on the bed and hurried to the sunny little room where Mary Lou's pageant materials were stacked in every corner and on every available surface. When Abby picked up the receiver, her father's hearty voice boomed down the line as if he were in the same room and not a thousand miles away.

"Sherlock Holmes reporting in," Peter Heatherington sang out. "How's Nancy Drew doing?"

Abby waited until she heard Maria click off. No way did she want to be overheard like last time. "I thought I at least ranked with Mata Hari," Abby retorted. "But if you're talking about my progress as a secret agent, I'm not doing terribly well." Quickly she filled her father in on the voodoo charms she'd found in her cabin and explained that she was in the process of moving her mission headquarters to the main house.

Considerably sobered by her news, Peter said, "Listen, honey, I don't like the sound of that. I want you to be very careful. Especially since I have a tidbit to add to your info."

"Oh?" Abby shifted the receiver into her other hand and settled back into the leather wing chair. "I'm all ears."

"My little expedition to the Library of Congress really paid off," Peter Heatherington began. "You owe me, Abigirl—I think a gourmet feast at Tio Pepe's at the very least," he said, naming a popular, and expensive, Baltimore eatery.

Abby laughed. "We'll see how good your information is."

"I spent quite a bit of time, but it was worth it because I struck gold. Your boy Jerome Matthews, it turns out, was not all he was cracked up to be. Or maybe I should say that he was more."

"How's that?" Abby twisted the phone cord over her forefinger.

"I poked into some obscure memoires of Captain Osgood B. Thompson, a Northern officer in charge of a certain spy network—one called Operation Slate."

"Operation Slate?" All the name conjured up was a bunch of rocks.

"Slate, as in blackboard. Slate it seems was a code name for a double-agent operation run by none other than our favorite Louisiana schoolmaster."

"You mean—" Abby drew a breath.

"That's right, our boy Jerome Matthews. He came to The Prize of India as a northern spy."

"But he was the one who accused Lydia!"

"Think about it. Lydia was the perfect scapegoat. By accusing her, he ensured that the spotlight would never be turned on him. Very clever, and very ruthless. But no one ever hired a spy because he was a nice guy."

Abby was speechless. This news changed everything. "Are you certain of this?" she whispered into the phone. "Jerome Matthews died a Confederate hero at Vicksburg."

"Well, this memoir was written within five years of the war, and as far as I can tell Thompson had no reason to want to discredit Matthews. In fact, it's obvious from the way Thompson writes about the man that he considered Matthews an ace and the pillar of his operation."

"But nobody down here seems to know that."

"Probably no reason why they should. Thompson's memoirs were written for his family and were never widely disseminated. It was persistence abetted by luck that brought me to them."

Abby sat up very straight. "I wonder—" She thought for a moment. "I wonder if it was Matthews who stole the ruby and the cipher disk."

"Don't know about the ruby, but the disk would certainly have been one of his objectives. And it's more than likely he did take it, given the fact that he intercepted Confederate transmissions about troop movements. Perhaps you need to look into Jerome's activities after the ruby disappeared. Any evidence of sudden wealth—you know, buying a fancy house or whatever—might point to payoffs from the North, or to his part in the disappearance of the ruby," Abby's father went on.

For the next few minutes, Abby and her father talked about his discovery. After he rang off, she replaced the receiver in its cradle and sat for a few moments sorting through this new breakthrough.

Now she was very glad that she'd be going to Lilyvale for dinner. Maybe under the guise of historic interest, she could ask Elaine and Prestwood more questions about their ancestor. But was there anything in the meantime that she might do to answer some of the questions racing through her mind? She doubted there'd be anything in the Forbes's library. She thought back to the archives in Baton Rouge. There were other accounts of Lydia's trial there that she hadn't read through. Perhaps one of these might tell her more about Jerome Matthews's actions.

THAT AFTERNOON in Baton Rouge, Abby closed yet another book of yellowed records, sat back in the hard wooden chair and blew a wayward tendril of hair off her forehead. She'd spent a good three hours wading through documents. Her eyes felt as if they were about to fall out, and all for nothing. Though she'd uncovered some interesting facts, which might be useful when she came to writing her book, she hadn't learned anything significant about the increasingly mysterious Jerome Matthews.

Shutting her eyes, Abby tried to think. Had Lydia written anything about Jerome that might confirm what Peter Heatherington had discovered? Suddenly Abby's eyes flew open. Lydia's diary! It and the history book with Byron's picture were still hidden on top of the armoire in the cabin. In her haste to move out that morning, she'd forgotten to take them with her. Leaping up, Abby returned the volumes she'd been studying to the librarian and hurried out to the stationwagon she'd borrowed from Mary Lou.

All the way back to The Prize she fretted. What if someone else had come for the pageant and was staying in the room? What if the maid had decided to do a thorough cleaning and had discovered the diary and given it to Mary Lou or Carter? Abby hadn't told Carter about the diary and didn't feel ready to show it to him yet.

As soon as she pulled into the driveway, Abby leaped out and hurried down the gravel path toward the cottage. Luckily she'd not returned the key yet. She was only a few yards away from the cabin's door when Callie materialized from a connecting path.

"Oh, Abby, I've been looking for you. I want you to see Sugar's new kittens," the ponytailed girl said. "They're in the old barn."

Abby stopped and draped her arm across Callie's shoulder. "I'd love to see them. I just need to get a book that I left in the cabin. I forgot to take it with me when I switched rooms this morning. Why don't you wait out here, and I'll be right with you."

"Okay," Callie agreed happily and sat down on the edge of the stoop.

Before entering, Abby knocked to make sure no one was staying in the cabin. When she didn't get an answer she unlocked the door and stepped in. Making a beeline for the armoire, she reached up on tiptoe. Her hand encountered the leather binding on Lydia's diary right away and with a little sigh of relief Abby pulled it and the history book down and stuffed them into her satchel.

Then she turned to take a last look around in case she'd forgotten anything else. It was then that she saw what was dangling in front of the mirror. Abby screamed.

"Abby, what is it?" Callie cried, rushing in. Her gaze went from Abby's white face to the dead chicken hanging on a string in front of the mirror. "Omigosh, more voodoo!" Callie stared at the suspended fowl in awe. Then, grabbing Abby's hand, she pulled her around. "This is really serious. We've got to talk to Aunt Hat! She'll know what to do."

Abby couldn't stand the sight of the limp bird another minute. "Let's get out of here," she cried, pulling Callie out of the cabin. Outside she stood on the porch, breathing deeply. "Let me think for a moment." Going out to see Aunt Hat might be a good idea, Abby thought, rubbing her forehead. If nothing else, the old conjure woman might be able to shed some light on what was going on.

But then she remembered Ordell's dinner arrangements. "You're right, we'll go to Aunt Hat's," she told Callie. "But first I have to find Ordell or Joanna."

Ten minutes later Abby came across the culinary duo photographing plants in the herb garden. Quickly she explained about finding the chicken and what she planned to do.

"Excellent idea," Ordell commented. "But it's unfortunate that you'll miss my gourmet feast. I shall have to save you a doggie bag."

"Don't worry about a thing," Joanna chimed in, adjusting the angle of a mint leaf and then studying the effect through her viewfinder. "Ordell and I will be undercover agents for you tonight. If there's anything to be discovered at Lilyvale, you can count on us."

Hurriedly she told them what she'd found out about Jerome Matthews, and she cautioned them to be careful.

After hiding the diary and history in her new room, Abby met Callie down by the landing and together they set off for Aunt Hat's shack.

It was late in the afternoon when they arrived and the bearded cypress were already casting long shadows on the dark green water. Though Aunt Hat hadn't known they'd be coming, her sharp ears had apparently picked up the drone of their motor. Just as they rounded the bend she came down to the dock to greet them.

"Lordy, I just cooked up a whole batch of red beans and rice. The feeling in my bones just told me I was gonna get some company."

Callie jumped off the boat. "Aunt Hat," she said in a rush, "somebody's doing voodoo against Abby. You have to help us out!"

"What's this about, child," Aunt Hat exclaimed, turning to Abby. "Somebody putting a hex on you?"

While they walked up to the house, Abby told the little old woman all that had happened.

Scowling, Aunt Hat shook her head. "That's bad, real bad. I'll have to fix you up with a gris-gris that'll keep you safe."

Inside the shack Aunt Hat went right to work. Abby and Callie took seats at the table and watched the little woman bustle about. Humming, she took jars down from her shelves and dumped mysterious bits and pieces out of them onto a muslin cloth.

While she mixed and sorted, Callie, kneeling on the chair and leaning over the table, watched every move. Meanwhile Abby asked the questions she'd hoped Aunt Hat could answer. To her disappointment, though, the old lady had no idea who might be behind the disturbing mischief at The Prize.

"There's lots of folks round about that knows how to set spells," Aunt Hat said as she sprinkled a gray powder out of a green tin onto the unappealing mixture and then began to tie it all up in the little muslin bag she'd prepared. "And then there's folks who dabbles in hoodoo but don't know what they're about." The scornful expression on Aunt Hat's wrinkled face was that of the professional disdaining the amateur. "You wear this around your neck," she said, slipping the stringed bag over Abby's head. "You'll be good and safe."

"Now we both have protection," Callie added, grinning as she pulled her own gris-gris from beneath her T-shirt.

Abby fingered the little bag Aunt Hat had given her and said politely, "I feel safer already." However, that was true only because she felt she was with friends who were concerned about her.

Aunt Hat's golden brown face glowed with pleasure, and she folded her hands over her stomach. "And now, to fix you up really right, I'll give you some eats."

The spicy smell coming from the big kettle on the stove had long ago started Abby's mouth watering. After she and Callie set the table with a charming hodgepodge of mismatched cutlery and plates, Aunt Hat put a round green metal trivet on the red checked plastic cloth and placed the steaming pot on it.

"Now eat up hearty," Aunt Hat enjoined as she dished up generous portions.

Abby and Callie, who'd both worked up good appetites, cleaned their plates, washing the tasty mixture down with cool tea Aunt Hat had made earlier by placing herbs in a jar of water and letting it brew in the sun.

Abby patted her stomach. "That was delicious," she said as she rose to help Callie clean up before they left. Callie had already picked the pot up off the trivet and carried it outside to wash it in the wooden tub Aunt Hat used as a sink. "What an unusual trivet," Abby said, lifting the heavy metal disk and turning it over to examine more closely.

Aunt Hat nodded and smiled. "Callie brought that out to me a couple of weeks back. I like it real well."

Abby rubbed a finger over the fine engraving masked by layers of greenish corrosion on the piece. "Have you thought of polishing this?" she murmured.

"No, I don't hold with such fancy stuff. It's fine the way it is." Callie came in to collect more dishes and Aunt Hat addressed her. "Where'd you find that metal thing, honey?"

Abby held the trivet up so that Callie could see it.

"Oh, that? That was the dish I was telling you about, the one buried by the old schoolhouse."

Abby's hand tightened on the metal disk. "You mean you dug it up around the foundations of the old school?"

"Yep. It's a funny old thing, isn't it? You should have heard the fuss Elaine made over it."

"Elaine? When did she see it?"

"I ran into her on the way back to the house. She was just leaving after getting her costume fitted. She even tried to buy it off me." Callie made a face. "But I don't like her so I wouldn't sell to her. She was fit to be tied."

Abby's eyes narrowed. "Mind if I take this out into the light?" she asked, already moving toward the door. Abby stepped into the fading sunlight and stared at the object in her hands. As she gazed at it, a tide of excitement flooded through her and her hands began to tremble. This was no ordinary dish. And Elaine must have realized that, or why would she have tried so hard to buy it?

Abby clutched the metal object to her chest. What she held, she realized, was a cipher disk—one that hadn't been seen for over a century—the one that had doomed Lydia Stewart's love—and life. She was sure of it, this had to be the missing decoding device that had belonged to Byron Forbes.

"Something wrong?" Aunt Hat asked, peering over Abby's shoulder.

With great care Abby handed the disk back to the old woman. "It's very interesting," she said, controlling her excitement. "I've never seen anything quite like it before."

Aunt Hat rubbed the round object against her apron. "Yes, it works real fine." She took it back inside the shack.

As Abby watched her go, her mind raced. Was the fact that the disk had been buried in the schoolyard proof that Lydia Stewart was innocent? Could it be the proof she needed that Jerome Matthews had stolen and buried the disk? Surely Callie's having dug it up in the foundation of the schoolhouse indicated that. But no, it wasn't irrefutable evidence.

She turned to Callie, who was rinsing the last of the dishes in the tub. "Does anyone know that you've given that trivet to Aunt Hat?"

Callie shook her head. "Don't think so."

Abby nodded and decided to drop the subject. For her to try to buy or borrow the disk from Aunt Hat would only raise questions she didn't want to have to answer yet. And if she did manage to persuade the old lady to give it up, where could she put it that would be safer than out here in the swamp? For now, perhaps, it was best to let sleeping dogs lie.

Abby cast a worried glance at the dimming light. Already a slice of the moon was visible. "We'd better get going."

Callie squinted up at the lavender sky. "Yeah, it's getting pretty late. My dad will be mad if I'm not home by dark."

After finishing the dishes and thanking Aunt Hat, they set off. But before they reached the landing, the sky had turned to purple and the stars had begun to appear.

As they edged closer to the dock a dark silhouette came into view. "Uh-oh, that's Dad," Callie said. "I'm gonna catch it."

From the hands-on-hip pose of the tall masculine figure standing on the end of the pier, Abby could tell that Carter was irritated. His annoyance became even more evident when the little motorboat nosed up against a wooden piling and Callie threw a line over it.

"Do you know what time it is, young lady?" Carter pointed at his watch. "Aunt Mary Lou was so worried she sent me out of the meeting to look for you."

Callie and Abby stepped out of the boat. "I'm sorry, Dad," Callie said as she steadied herself on the pier. "You and Aunt Mary Lou weren't around when we left, and I forgot about leaving a note."

"Where have you been and what have you been doing so late?"

Abby placed a hand on Carter's arm. "It's my fault, Carter. We left in such a hurry that I didn't think to check to make sure you knew where we were going."

"Dad, we had to go see Aunt Hat," Callie insisted. "Something terrible happened this afternoon. Abby found a dead chicken on her mirror."

Carter's face darkened. "When was this?"

After Callie explained the reason for their expedition into the swamp, he drove the two of them back to the house and sent Callie inside to let Mary Lou know she was okay. When Carter and Abby were finally alone, he turned to her and said stiffly, "Callie wasn't the only one I was worried about, and that shouldn't surprise you after what happened last time you disappeared into the bayou. Next time something like this happens, please let me know before you go running off to the swamp."

All during the drive back to the house Abby had sensed that Carter was angry at her as well as at Callie. Now, put off by his cold tone, she said, "I'm sorry if you were worried. Believe me, I would have talked to you first if you'd been around."

Carter ran a hand through his hair. "Look, Abby, I've been thinking about all that's been happening. I don't know who's behind this voodoo stuff, and I don't like it. But today I got something in the mail that I'd like you to see."

"All right," Abby said a little warily. "What is it?"

Carter took her to his office and switched on a light above his desk. Then he picked a white envelope off the top of a pile of papers and handed it to her. "Notice the Baltimore postmark," he said.

Abby examined it. The envelope had been mailed two days earlier. Inside there was a typed, unsigned letter. Warily Abby unfolded it.

"Beware of the female spy you've let into your house," it read. "She's a known character assassin who is writing a book accusing Byron Forbes of being a Yankee spy who acted in consort with Lydia Stewart to betray Louisiana and the glorious Confederacy."

Abby's mouth dropped open and she reread it just to be sure of what it really said. "This is a lie," she declared flatly. "Surely you don't take an anonymous letter like this seriously."

"I don't know what to make of it," Carter replied wearily. "It was obviously sent by somebody who knows you and knows that you came down here. What's more, it jibes with what you've told me. You claim you're trying to prove Lydia Stewart was framed. But if she was innocent, then someone else's reputation will have to be blackened."

"Carter..." Abby began to protest.

But he had turned away. "Since you've come here, there have been so many deceptions that I don't know what to believe, Abby." He shook his head and thrust the note back into the envelope. "But for now, I've got a meeting I've got to be at." And with that he left her.

ABBY PACED back and forth on the veranda. The moonlight etched a lacy pattern through the live oaks and crickets filled the air with night sounds. As she took a deep breath she noted the sweet fragrance of magnolia and reflected that she'd never again be able to smell that scent without thinking of The Prize.

For the past half hour Abby had been replaying the conversation she'd had with Carter. The more she thought about it, the more disturbed she became. Who on earth could have sent that anonymous letter, and if Carter cared anything for her, how could he take it seriously?

Once again she mentally ran through a list of her friends and acquaintances in Baltimore. Other than her father, there wasn't anyone there she'd discussed Lydia Stewart with. Her father certainly hadn't sent the letter and, knowing him, she was certain he wouldn't have mentioned the matter to anyone else, either. So, who could have written the thing? Too bad Joanna and Ordell weren't back from Lilyvale. She could sure use a sounding board now.

Abby paced the length of the veranda again. Though she'd had a tiring day, she was far too restless to consider going to bed early. In her hand she held the flashlight she'd carried down from her bedroom. Deep in thought, she unconsciously flicked it on and off. Then, the decision made, she stepped off the porch and started up the path.

The foundations of the old schoolhouse were on a gentle rise. As Abby climbed toward them, she turned the flashlight on again and swept the beam across the stones. Her shoes squelched in the dewy grass, and she could feel the moisture seeping through to her toes.

Ignoring the discomfort, she came up to the foundation, rested a hand on one of the stones and shone her light at the pitted earth she and Carter had discovered yesterday. Since she now knew the cipher disk had come from here, she wondered if the ruby could have been buried there as well. Would that account for all these holes? Had someone been digging around trying to find the Forbes's lost treasure?

Abby swung her legs over the low stone wall and went down on one knee to examine one of the pits. It was then that she was pushed from behind. She lost her balance and sprawled forward. A wet tongue licked her face and a cold nose nudged her ear. Clutching at her galloping heart, Abby gasped with relief. "Oh, Barney, you big, silly, old hound. You scared me."

Abby sat up, patted the old dog's head and then brushed the dirt from her legs. "Have you been following me?"

In answer, Barney sat down and began to pant.

"Actually he followed me following you," a voice said out of the darkness.

Tensing, Abby whirled around. A shaft of light from a few feet above the foundations blinded her.

"Who's there?" Her hand grabbed at the flashlight and she flicked it on toward the beam shining in her eyes.

As abruptly as it had appeared, the opposing light veered away and suddenly she saw Prestwood throwing one long leg over the wall. As he came up to her, she got to her feet and said, "Prestwood, you startled me."

His tall shadow loomed over her. "Sorry. I just dropped off Joanna and Ordell. Elaine and I were about to join Carter, Mary Lou and the others for the pageant meeting when I saw a light out here and thought I'd better come investigate. What are you doing here this time of night?"

Abby tried to think of a rational explanation. "It was too early to go to bed, so I decided to take a walk. Carter and I were here the other day, so I thought I'd come back and take another look."

"In the dark? You must have a mighty strong interest in schoolhouses."

"Well, I am a teacher." Even to Abby's ears her explanation sounded lame.

Prestwood's flashlight beam skimmed over the pitted terrain. "What are all these holes?" He turned and faced her. "Have you been doing some archaeology?"

"No, but someone else has," Abby replied.

"Who?" He continued to skip his light around like a giant erratic firefly.

"I have no idea, but it's an interesting question, isn't it?"

Prestwood eyed her and the silence between them lengthened. "I hear that you're having more troubles with voodoo," he finally said.

"Yes." Abby sighed.

"Sounds like someone around here just doesn't like you."

"I can't imagine why. I haven't done anything to anyone," Abby said, though that wasn't quite the truth.

"Well, I can't imagine, either," Prestwood retorted, "but let me give you a friendly suggestion. From what I hear, you've been asking a lot of questions about the story my pageant play is based on. Maybe your problems come from stirring up local legends. People around here tend to be very protective of that sort of thing. If I were you I'd sit back and enjoy the pageant. Then I'd go home and forget all this nonsense."

Abby didn't answer. Maybe Prestwood was right, she thought. Maybe that was exactly what she should do.

Chapter Thirteen

Though Abby was not anxious for his company, Prestwood insisted on walking her back to the house. The conversation between them was strained, and Abby was relieved when they reached the veranda.

Just as their feet hit the steps, something stirred in the bushes.

"What was that?" Prestwood stopped and looked around suspiciously.

"I don't know. It might have been one of the dogs."

Prestwood squinted into the darkness and then shrugged. "You're probably right. Callie's animals are everywhere you turn. Anyhow, I'd better get into that meeting. Are you coming inside?"

"No," Abby said, sinking into a rocker. "I think I'll just sit out here for a while longer and enjoy the lovely evening."

"Well, good night then."

"Good night, Prestwood."

The screen door shut with a whine and Abby leaned back and closed her eyes while she rocked gently.

"Psst," a voice came from the darkness. Abby sat up in her rocker and peered into the shadows.

"Pssst, Abby!"

"Who's there?" she whispered back.

She was greeted with a chorus of "Shhhhhhh." Then, with a loud rustle, as if a large animal were trying to be stealthy in the boxwood, Ordell emerged on tiptoe followed by a giggling Joanna.

"Hush, woman," Ordell warned over his shoulder. Then he beckoned to Abby. Smiling, she came down off the porch to join her two friends.

"What's going on?"

"Shhhhhh! Don't talk until we get farther away from prying ears," Ordell commanded. Linking arms with each lady, he guided them into a deserted gazebo in the far reaches of the garden.

"What in the world..." Abby murmured, half laughing as she sat down on one of the gazebo's wooden benches.

"We have to tell you about our evening at Lilyvale," Joanna whispered. "What a scoop!"

"Except for the dinner I cooked..."

"We cooked," Joanna interjected.

"Ahem, I stand corrected. Except for the dinner we cooked, nothing remarkable happened until after coffee and my *Crème Brulé* was served. No sooner had the last spoonful of my perfect creamy custard slipped down Elaine's and Prestwood's throats when they excused themselves to put together some materials they needed for the meeting." Ordell gestured with his head toward The Prize. Abby's gaze followed and through a lighted window she saw Prestwood, Elaine and Carter huddled together in front of a writing desk.

Abby looked back at Ordell. "All right, then what?"

"As I was saying," Ordell continued. "As it was the maid's night off, Joanna and I volunteered to help with the cleanup."

"This is the interesting part," Joanna broke in. "We'd used the small saucepan for the caramel sauce, and when I went to put it away I couldn't remember where it had been stored." Joanna pantomimed opening a cabinet. Then she sat back with a satisfied grin, her hands crossed over her stomach. "And that's when we found it."

Abby blinked and looked from one food writer to the other. "What's it?"

"The evidence," Ordell pronounced darkly. "Joanna was rooting through that cupboard when she pulled out none other than a pot caked with a hardened green crust."

Abby shrugged. "I thought Elaine was a better housekeeper than that."

"I doubt the lady's into cleaning," Ordell said. "After all, she's got a maid."

"Then maybe she needs to have a talk with her or get a better dishwasher."

Joanna waved her hands in frustration. "Stop it, you two. You're getting off the track. The green stuff in the pot wasn't cruddy food, it was wax."

"Wax?"

"As in voodoo balls," Ordell put in. "Don't you get it? We've found the culprit. Elaine is the one who's been decorating your room with dead chickens and wax balls."

"Elaine?" Abby sat back. "But why?"

"Ah, the earlier part of the evening explained her motives," Ordell said, holding up a finger.

"Oh?"

"Yes, it seems our Elaine has a major crush on Carter Forbes and views you as a rival," Joanna explained.

"She's using voodoo to get you to go away," Ordell said.

"Or, at the very least, she's trying to scare you with it so you'll choose to go away," Joanna added.

Abby stood and began to pace the gazebo, thinking about this. Then she stopped and told Ordell and Joanna about finding the cipher disk at Aunt Hat's.

When she had finished her revelations, Ordell rubbed his chin. "That does put a whole new dimension on our mystery. I agree with you. The same person who stole the cipher disk probably made off with the ruby as well. It is likely that both objects were buried in the same spot. The thief wouldn't have wanted to risk being caught with them. The question is, who's got the ruby now?"

They all sat down to think. For several minutes, except for the hoot of an owl, all was quiet.

"Well, we know that Prestwood has one ruby," Joanna finally said. "We saw it on that purple cushion of his."

"Yes, but that's just glass," Abby said.

"Or at least, that's what Prestwood tells us." Ordell looked at Joanna and then at Abby. "You don't suppose, do you..."

"That it's the real ruby!" Abby exclaimed. "It couldn't be. Could it?"

The three friends stared at one another.

"There's only one way to find out," Joanna said. "We have to go back and check."

"When?" Abby asked.

"Now," Ordell declared. "We know they're all busy up there in that meeting. Now is the perfect time for us to strike."

Abby nodded. "Let's do it."

They took Ordell's rental car and left it hidden down the road from the old mansion. Then, staying in the shadows, the trio cut through a field and up into the alley of live oaks that led to Lilyvale's main entrance. Splitting up, the three looked through all the first-floor windows to make sure the house was empty. After testing the doors, which were all locked, Ordell got out his Swiss army knife and pried at the screen of an open window. After a few minutes he was able to get it open. With a boost from Ordell and Joanna, Abby climbed through and then came around to open the back door for the others.

"Now I know the excitement of a life of crime," Ordell murmured as he tiptoed into the kitchen. "I feel like a regular cat burglar."

"And you do move with such feline grace," Joanna teased.

"Meow," the portly food writer answered as he led the way into the dark dining room.

His reply was answered by a real meow as a thin tabby with glowing eyes sauntered in, leaped up onto the table and regarded them suspiciously.

"I'm glad you're not a watch kitty," Ordell said to the cat as he reached out to pet its striped head.

The cat hissed and Ordell yanked his hand back. "Hmmm, perhaps I've made a mistake and you *are* guarding the house."

"Well, if he is, he's not doing a very good job of it," Joanna muttered impatiently. "Can we turn on the light?"

"Better stick with my flashlight," Abby said, switching it on and running a stream of light over the walls.

"The ruby's over here on the sideboard," Joanna told her.

When Abby swept her beam in that direction, it picked out the silk cushion with the large red gem resting on its center. Gingerly the three of them approached the stone and examined it in the halo of light.

"How do you tell whether or not a ruby is genuine?" Joanna murmured.

"Good question," Ordell replied and reached out to pick it up. At that moment the cat sprang off the table and darted between his feet. Caught by surprise, Ordell staggered, lost his grip on the gem and the red stone went flying across the room where it shattered against a marble pedestal.

"Well, that's one test," Abby said. "Now we know it was glass."

"Just great," Joanna exclaimed, covering her eyes and shaking her head. "How are we ever going to explain this to Prestwood?"

"Very simple, we're not even going to try," said Ordell. "We're going to leave and let the cat take the heat for us. After all, that inhospitable little creature is the one at fault."

The decision was made for them when they heard the sound of a car's engine outside. Instantly Abby turned off her flash. Joanna ran to the window. "My God, there're two cars coming."

"Let's beat it," Ordell said.

"Definitely," agreed Abby.

They scrambled out of the dark dining room toward the hall. But without any light to guide them, they stumbled over one another.

"Ouch!" Ordell cried as Joanna dug her heel into his in-sole. "Are you trying to cripple me, woman?"

"Sorry, but you take up an awful lot of this hall!"

"Yeowww," the cat shrieked. Abby had stepped on his tail.

"Dratted animal," Ordell complained.

"So much for a quiet getaway," Joanna hissed as they slipped into the kitchen and headed through the rear door. Outside they paused on the gallery to take their bearings.

"I hear voices over there," Ordell said, pointing to his left. "Let's go thisaway."

The three grabbed hands and set off to go around the other side of the house. But a few paces later, the two women were pulled up short by Ordell.

"I wonder what's going on over there," he said. "I hear raised voices."

"And not happy raised voices, from the sounds of it," said Joanna.

They all stood still, listening. "It's Carter and Prestwood," Abby exclaimed. "But I can't make out what they're saying."

Ordell shrugged. "I guess their pageant-planning meeting didn't go smoothly."

"That doesn't bode well for tomorrow," Joanna whispered. "But maybe we'd better get out of here before they go into the house and find the broken ruby. Then we'll really hear some shouting."

Abby and Ordell agreed that it was best to leave, and together the three scurried down the moonlit alley toward the road and the place where they'd hidden their car.

"ELAINE, GO INSIDE. Carter and I have business to discuss," Prestwood was saying in a strained voice.

Elaine looked from her brother to Carter and then nodded tightly. "I'll fix us some cocoa."

"None for me," Carter said.

When Elaine had disappeared through the door, the two men faced each other. "I think you owe me an explanation," Carter said to his neighbor. "Just what exactly were you doing up in Abby's room?"

Prestwood threw up his hands. "Look, Carter, I'm sorry. I was just trying to keep a promise to Elaine."

"I don't understand. You excuse yourself to use the bathroom, and when I go upstairs to get a book from the library I find you coming out of Abby's door. When I go inside I find this." With an expression of distaste, he took a small bag out of his pocket and thrust it at Prestwood.

"What has putting this thing in Abby's room got to do with a promise to Elaine?"

Prestwood took the gris-gris and tucked it into his jacket. He sighed. "Look, you know how Elaine is."

"No, I don't. Why don't you explain how she is," Carter retorted with an icy edge sharpening his voice.

"She's crazy about you, Carter. She always has been, ever since we were kids. You know that!" Prestwood ran an agitated hand through his thinning hair.

"So?"

"Don't you see? I know you've never given my sister any reason to think it, but when Diana left, Elaine believed she might have a chance with you. Then Abby came along. Well, it's obvious that you've a thing for her. And from the looks she gives you, I would guess it's mutual."

Carter stood with his hands on his hips. "Go on, I'm listening."

Prestwood shook his head. "So where does that leave Elaine? She sees you slipping away from her all over again, and she's upset."

Carter took a breath and looked up at the sky. "I've always thought of Elaine as a friend and neighbor, but never anything more."

"I know, I know. That's obvious. It's just Elaine who can't see that."

"So why are you encouraging her to imagine things that aren't true, and what's the purpose of all this voodoo stuff?"

Prestwood wove his fingers together and locked them tightly. "Elaine found a conjure woman to put together a go-away charm. She was hoping it might make Abby go back home to Baltimore. She made me promise to try to put it in Abby's room."

"And you went along with it?" Carter asked in disgust.

Prestwood threw up his hands again. "I'm her brother and I feel sorry for her. Of course I know it's all nonsense, but I thought I'd humor her. I never meant to jeopardize our friendship. I just wanted to make my sister feel better. I really am sorry, Carter."

But Carter didn't look mollified. The moonlight revealed clearly that his handsome features wore a grim expression. "I can't believe that you would harass a guest of mine like this."

"It was a complete lapse of judgment on my part," Prestwood apologized. "I guess between the pageant and the election, and the business problems I've been having lately I wasn't thinking too clearly."

"That's an understatement," Carter snapped. "What about that dead chicken Abby found hanging from her mirror?"

"Dead chicken?" Prestwood looked shocked. "I swear I don't know anything about that. And I can't believe that my sister would have anything to do with it, either. But I promise you I'll talk to Elaine tonight."

"Do that," Carter said in a clipped tone.

At that moment the woman they were discussing appeared in the doorway and looked imploringly at her brother. "I'll be in in a minute, Elaine," Prestwood said. The two men watched her as she hesitated a moment and then disappeared back into the house. When she was gone, Prestwood said, "It won't happen again, Carter."

Without answering, Carter turned on his heel, got back into his car and drove away.

After his automobile sped off, Elaine opened a window and stuck her head out. "Is he gone?"

"Yes, what is it?"

"The ruby." Elaine's thin face was pale. "I think we've got a problem."

CARTER PULLED HIS CAR into The Prize's driveway, parked it, killed the lights and then sat. What was going on, he wondered. The situation was getting more and more bizarre. First Abby's astonishing revelation about her "mission," then out of the blue the accusatory letter. And all this voodoo stuff—with Prestwood, of all people, involved in it!

Carter rubbed his forehead. "I hope everything goes smoothly tomorrow," he muttered under his breath. He and his family, not to mention the whole community, had invested so much time and energy in this pageant. Mary Lou would be heartbroken if anything marred the day. The success of the new restaurant, The Ruby—as well as his hopes of giving up his business travel to stay home with Callie—depended on it.

But even if the pageant went well, what about after it was over? Abby planned to leave the next day. Carter groaned.

ABBY LAY WIDE AWAKE, her pillow propped against the headboard. She knew it was going to be a sleepless night. The situation at The Prize was becoming so complicated that she no longer seemed able to grasp it all. Bits and pieces of recent events flitted through her mind like whirling autumn leaves and left her feeling confused and distressed.

Since coming to the plantation she'd managed to alienate her host, make someone so angry that they were willing to work voodoo against her, and very nearly drown herself in quicksand. Then there was that incredible letter from Baltimore. The very thought of someone she knew penning such a poisonous missive and sending it to Carter gave her the shivers. Now, as if all that weren't bad enough, with the help of her friends she'd succeeded in destroying the main prop of the pageant.

Abby squeezed her eyes tightly shut and put a protective hand over them. It was bad enough that she was trying to debunk the legend that everyone here put such stock in, but to physically smash a facsimile of their ruby and probably ruin the centerpiece of the pageant, the play—Carter would never forgive her. And she couldn't blame him.

Carter! Even though her eyes were closed, his dark gaze seemed to stare accusingly at her. And in her imagination, his face seemed to blend into that of his ancestor, Lydia's love, Byron Forbes. Now Lydia wasn't the only woman from the North who'd lost her heart to a dashing master of The Prize of India. For the first time Abby acknowledged to herself that she truly loved Carter.

It seemed so incredible. A little over a week ago she hadn't known Carter, or Callie or Joanna or Ordell for that matter. Carter had just been a name on a list, a means to an end. But then she'd stood in the moonlight with him on the deck of the *Mississippi Queen*. And then she had felt the magic of his lips on hers as they embraced in her cabin at The Prize. And now Carter was the center of her world. She thought about him constantly, longed for his touch, even ached for the sight of him.

Yet, whether she cleared Lydia's name or not in a day's time she'd be on a plane heading north and all of this, which seemed so familiar and so dear to her heart, would be no more than a memory. Abby flinched at the thought. It was terrible to think that Carter would remember her as a snoop who'd made nothing but trouble for him. And yet it was true. From the start she'd been dishonest with him as well as with Callie and Mary Lou.

And now...Abby thought of the shattered ruby. The least she could do, she told herself, was own up to Carter about how it happened and offer to replace it—if not for this year's pageant, then for the next. Though it was certainly ironic to think that she'd be providing a prop for a play that painted her own great-great-great-aunt as a traitor. She'd talk to him in the morning.

THE NEXT MORNING Callie fidgeted impatiently.

"Hold still," Mary Lou demanded as she placed the last pin into the full skirt of the girl's costume. She'd already donned her own hoop-skirted outfit. With a sea of blue moire billowing around her, Mary Lou was finding that working around Callie's equally elaborate skirt was like maneuvering ships in a tight harbor.

"We go onstage only forty minutes from now, and the front yard is swarming with strangers," Mary Lou fretted. "Why, just look at them all," she exclaimed, picking up her hoop and sidling over to the window to glance out.

Knots of people strolled on The Prize's manicured lawns sucking on lemon ices and drinking frothy cups of café au lait that one of the pageant committee members had brewed over an open fire. Craftspeople strolled among the tourists selling their wares. Gaily decorated booths, set up in a semicircle at the far edge of the property, displayed everything from handwoven cloth to straw hats, hand-forged wrought iron, household items and paintings. One even displayed Carter's plantation photographs. Next to it another, decorated in red-white-and-blue bunting and Confederate flags, touted Prestwood Matthews's candidacy for State Senator.

Catching sight of it, Mary Lou raised her eyebrows. "That Prestwood doesn't miss a trick." Then her gaze swept the crowds heading toward the platform beyond the gardens where Prestwood's play would be performed. "Thank the Lord, my committee seems to have everything under control," she muttered as she turned back to Callie. "Now let's see if we can do our parts."

Abby, who'd been standing in the doorway watching all of this, knocked softly and then entered the sun-filled parlor. "Oh, Mary Lou, you look like something out of *Gone With the Wind*."

Mary Lou patted her bouffant hairdo and looked pleased. "Why thank you, dear."

"And don't you look beautiful, too," Abby went on, turning to Callie. "I feel distinctly underdressed," she added, glancing down at her own simple flowered sundress.

The girl only made a face. "I wish I was wearing what you have on. I'll be glad when this darn play is over. I'm gonna roast in this thing," she added, plucking the heavy folds of the yellow satin skirt.

"Well, I'm ready to break a leg," Elaine declared as she swept into the room, a vision of antebellum chic in her elaborate costume.

Abby took in the long green gown draped over Elaine's angular body and then glanced up at Lydia's portrait. She couldn't help but observe that the dress had looked much better on the soft curves of her ancestor.

"Is Carter around?" Abby asked. "I need to talk to him about something."

"I would guess he'd be upstairs getting dressed," Elaine said, eyeing Abby with faint disapproval. "Maybe you can catch him after the play. Right now I'm sure he's focused on the pageant and doesn't want to be distracted."

"That's true, dear," Mary Lou seconded. "There's so much going on here, it's hard to think about anything else right now."

Abby decided not to press the matter. But she knew she had to talk to Carter, and it couldn't wait. A few minutes later she excused herself and slipped upstairs.

She'd never been to Carter's room, but she knew where it was. Goldie was asleep by the door when Abby knocked. Yawning, the dog stood and stretched out her front legs. Then she ambled over to the other side of the hall and, with a groan, sank next to the wall.

"Sorry, Goldie," Abby said, patting the dog's smooth head.

Just then Carter opened his door and looked out. "Yes?" he asked with a lift of his eyebrows.

For a moment Abby was speechless. Though Carter wore the cream-colored breeches that were part of his costume, he hadn't yet donned the frilly shirt that went with them. He was naked from the waist up. Though Abby had seen him with less on, somehow the impact of his virile, broad-chested physique was even greater now.

Abby swallowed. "Carter," she began, "I know you're awfully busy, but I need to speak with you about something."

His gaze swept over her. "I'm running a little late. Can it wait until after the pageant?"

Abby shifted uneasily. Despite her decision the night before, it had taken a while for her to get up the nerve to confess her guilt about the ruby—especially with that accusing letter still hanging over her head.

"Carter, what I have to tell you affects the pageant, and I'm afraid it can't wait."

Carter sighed and opened the door. All night Abby had been on his mind. He'd tried to sort things out, but had kept coming up with the same confusing set of facts. Now, as he gazed down at Abby, one of those facts struck him a fresh blow. The sight of this woman aroused emotions in him that he was beginning to fear had the power to tear him apart. Despite everything, he wanted so much to take her into his arms and run his hands through her soft curls. Yet, at the same time, he was angry—angry because it was beginning to look more and more as if his feelings for her were destined to give him nothing but pain.

"Look, I know you believe Lydia Stewart is innocent, but the play's going on just as it was written. It's too late to change the script now. Anyhow, I've got to get dressed," he said gruffly.

Hurt by his curtness but determined to make her confession, Abby squared her shoulders. "Then I'll talk to you while you're putting your costume on."

Carter shrugged and then stood aside so that she could walk past him into his room. As he headed over to a wooden valet and picked up his shirt, Abby took a second to glance around.

His sleeping quarters were decorated with masculine elegance. A large mahogany armoire dominated one antique white wall, and a matching four-poster bed took up most of another. Wooden shutters framed the windows. Notes of pattern and color came from Oriental rugs on the polished wood floor. On the bureau, stacks of books and magazines competed with photographs of Callie for space. Abby's eyes widened when she saw her own image in one of the instant camera shots that Mary Lou had taken. The candid photo, propped up against a framed picture of Callie, showed Abby laughing as Goldie jumped up to lick her face.

It was ridiculous, but for a moment Abby remembered the torn photograph that had been placed in the gris-gris she'd found in her pillowcase. So, Carter *had* taken the other. A tiny doubt crept into her mind. But surely Carter could have had nothing to do with the voodoo. He must have appropriated this snapshot because he wanted a memento—something to remember her by. The thought was flattering and gave her courage.

"Carter," she began, turning toward him as he buttoned the pearl studs on his shirt. Halfway up his chest his long fingers stilled as she told him what had happened to the ruby the night before.

"You, Ordell and Joanna snuck into Lilyvale and broke the ruby," he exhaled incredulously.

Abby nodded. "And there's something else," she went on, determined to make a clean breast. But just then there was a knock on the half-open door.

Dressed in the stiff black frock coat of a nineteenth-century schoolmaster, Prestwood strolled into the room. After doing a double take when he saw Abby, he recovered, greeted her evenly and then turned to Carter.

"Mary Lou asked me to check to make sure you know you're supposed to be down at the platform in fifteen minutes."

"I'll be ready," Carter answered. "There's no problem, is there?"

"Not that I know of. Everything's going smoothly."

Carter's eyes narrowed. "What about the ruby? Have you got it?"

Nervously Abby waited, expecting Prestwood to produce the shattered pieces of red glass she'd seen on the floor of the dining room at Lilyvale the night before. Instead he merely smiled, reached into his pocket and withdrew a cloth bag.

"Safe and sound in here," he said.

Carter gazed at him. "Safe and sound?"

"Of course." Prestwood opened the drawstring on the bag, reached in and pulled out a glowing red gem. "See?" he said, holding it up. Rays of sunlight from the window struck the crimson jewel and refracted brilliantly. "The jeweler did a good job, don't you think?"

"I certainly do," Carter murmured, shooting Abby a puzzled look.

Abby's mouth hung open and all she could do was shrug and shake her head.

"My other purpose for coming," Prestwood added, eyeing Abby guardedly, "was to let you know that I talked to Elaine and straightened things out."

"Good," Carter replied.

"Well," Prestwood said, popping the ruby into the bag and tucking it back into his frock coat pocket, "I'll see you in a few minutes."

Carter finished dressing without speaking. As he knotted the string tie at his collar and slipped on his gray coat, Abby broke the silence.

"I can't imagine how the ruby got fixed."

"Maybe you imagined breaking it." Carter went to his bureau, picked up a brush and ran it through his ebony hair.

Abby shook her head. "No, Carter, that was not my imagination. I have witnesses, remember?"

"Then where do you think Prestwood got the ruby he showed us just now?"

"Maybe he dug it up from the foundation in the old schoolhouse," Abby blurted out.

Carter dropped his silver-handled brush and swiveled around. "Schoolhouse? What are you talking about?"

Abby placed a hand on the carved bedpost to steady herself. "Carter, I said there was more I needed to tell you. Those holes we saw the other day—I've discovered that Callie dug up the cipher disk from one of them. She didn't know what it was and gave it to Aunt Hat."

"What?" Carter took a step forward.

Abby held up her hand and hurried on. "There's more. I think the ruby may have been buried there as well and that whoever dug the rest of those holes was looking for it. Perhaps they found it. Perhaps what Prestwood showed us just now was the real Prize of India."

Chapter Fourteen

"You're joking!" Carter exclaimed.

"No," Abby shot back, "I'm not joking. I'm telling you what I really think."

Carter stared at her. Then slowly he began to shake his head. "If that were the real ruby, Prestwood wouldn't risk carrying it around in his pocket."

"But since the prop was broken, where did he get the stone he just showed us?" Abby demanded stubbornly.

Carter threw up his hands. "I don't know. Maybe he had two copies made up at the same time."

"A backup ruby?"

"It's possible, and much more likely than what you're suggesting. Frankly I don't believe Prestwood would stoop to thievery, and even if he had, he surely wouldn't be so foolish as to flaunt the evidence."

"It does seem strange," Abby agreed. "But this play is important to him. He's proud of having written it, and it's an opportunity for great visibility for someone who's running for office. But think about it—putting the show on without the main prop would be a disaster. So what does he do on such short notice? He pulls out the real thing. I'm sure he thinks that no one would ever suspect him of using the true ruby instead of a fake."

"And there's something else," Abby added. She'd began to pace back and forth excitedly in front of Carter. "I hadn't told you this, but yesterday I had a call from my father. He's uncovered something at the Library of Congress, something that makes all of this—" Abby waved her hands expressively "—seem more plausible." Stopping, she faced Carter and told him what her father had learned about Jerome Matthews being a double agent for the North.

Before Carter could react to her words, Maria the maid poked her head in the door. "Miss Mary Lou sent me up to tell you curtain's about to go up," she said.

"My public awaits," Carter murmured dryly. "We'll talk about this later, Abby," he said, reaching for the wide-brimmed hat that completed his outfit. Putting it on he added, "I do hope we can straighten this whole mess out, but it can't be done in the next thirty seconds."

"I leave tomorrow, Carter," she said.

Their eyes locked. "I know that all too well, Abby." With that, Carter strode out the door leaving Abby staring after him in frustration.

For a brief moment she stood rooted to the spot, listening to Carter's footsteps as he hurried down the broad staircase. When she heard the front door close behind him, she clasped her hands, took a deep breath and then walked out of the room to follow him down to the site of the performance.

Outside, throngs of festival goers streamed through the gardens to the back lawn where the open platform, its eight-foot base draped with Confederate buntings, stood.

"Yoo hoo, Abby, over here," Joanna called out.

On a little hillock above the heads of the crowd Abby could see Joanna's halo of permed curls and next to her she caught a flash of Ordell's white linen suit. Abby began to weave her way toward her friends.

"Phew, getting warm already," Ordell commented, fanning himself with his broad-brimmed hat.

"Don't you look pretty," Joanna cried, casting an admiring eye over Abby's trim figure revealed to advantage in her pink sundress. "But then you always do. All ready for the big show?"

Abby struggled for an appropriate reply. But Joanna caught the strained expression on her face. Placing an arm on Abby's shoulder, the older woman said, "Oh, how thoughtless of me. Of course you aren't ready to see this play. It's going to be full of nasty things about your aunt."

"It's all right," Abby answered. "I'm prepared."

But when the performance finally began, Abby found that she wasn't nearly as prepared as she'd claimed. Around her, the crowd was in a merry mood. Children holding balloons milled around adults clad in blue jeans, shorts and T-shirts. The crowd talked and laughed among themselves until Carter, tall dark and dashing, made his entrance. Then they cheered and clapped.

"That man is a handsome creature," Joanna whispered with admiration in her eyes.

"Hnmm," Ordell commented, "it's uncanny how closely he resembles that portrait of Byron Forbes hanging in the dining room. It's almost as if old Byron himself has been reincarnated."

As she stood gazing at the platform, Abby was having the identical sensation. Seeing Carter up there in his period garb was eerie. A chill crept up her spine, much like the one she'd experienced the first time she'd opened that history book and seen the picture of Byron Forbes gazing out at her.

The same wasn't true when Elaine swept onstage, however. To Abby's eyes she seemed like a parody of the real Lydia Stewart. And as she mouthed the simpering lines Prestwood had written, Abby felt sick. Suddenly she was no longer able to watch. She touched Joanna's and Ordell's shoulders and leaned in between them. "I'm sorry. This just isn't for me. I think I'll go back up to the house and start my packing."

Joanna regarded her with concerned eyes. "Are you all right, dear?"

"I'm fine, really," Abby reassured. With that, she threaded her way through the thick crowd of spectators and headed past the gardens and up the gravel path to the big house.

Inside the mansion it was quiet and cool, a welcome respite from the heat and confusion outdoors. With a sigh, Abby got herself a glass of lemonade from the kitchen and walked up the stairs sipping it. At her door, she paused and reflected that by this time tomorrow she'd be leaving. The realization gave her a sinking feeling.

Instead of going into her room, she veered off to go downstairs to the library. This would probably be her last chance to look through the family documents she'd been studying on and off for the past few days.

Retrieving Byron's closely written diary and another book or two, including the family bible from the dusty collection, she climbed back down the ladder and set them on the carved oak table. Because Byron's antique script was so difficult to read, she hadn't made much progress with the journal. Even now, though she tried to concentrate, the noises from the visitors outside distracted her.

Giving up, she closed the volume and opened up the large Bible. Idly her eyes scanned the entries on the Forbes family tree inscribed on the inside cover. It started with the first Forbes, the famous pirate who'd settled down and married someone named Luisa Fontaine. They'd had a large family, but in those days, with cholera and smallpox, only two sons and one daughter had survived to adulthood.

With her finger, Abby traced through the generations, trying to imagine what each had been like. Her gaze drifted down past Byron's birth entry to Carter's father and then to Carter himself. But suddenly, her attention darted back up the map of births and deaths.

"Victor," she exclaimed. "Byron Victor Forbes. Byron V. Forbes. V." Suddenly bits of information began to click together. In her diary Lydia had written about the mysterious V. V. had been her rescuer, the person who'd ensured her escape from certain hanging and arranged her passage to safety in the North. All along V. had been Byron himself! Abby sat back and took a deep breath. So, despite the accusations and the war itself, Byron had never stopped loving Lydia.

The realization sent excitement surging through Abby. This gave Lydia's story a different twist and Abby reevaluated her picture of Lydia's life after the war was over. Obviously, because of the ill feeling that persisted toward her in the South, she and Byron had never been able to officially consummate their love. But it had still burned brightly between them. And somehow Abby knew that that had sustained her aunt, even in her darkest days.

A new idea came into Abby's mind. Jumping up, she shut the books, put them away and hurried to her room. From the pocket of her suitcase, where she'd hidden it away, she pulled out the tissue in which she'd wrapped the ornament she'd found at Devil's Fork.

After rubbing it clean to uncover the elaborate pattern, she carried it downstairs to the dining room where Byron's full-length portrait hung. It had seemed the wildest of chances, but when she walked up to the painting and studied the watch chain hanging from Byron's vest pocket she gave a little cry. There it was, the same unique gold ornament. He must have lost it in the swamp the night Lydia had stayed at the cabin at Devil's Fork. Byron had spent a last night with his beloved in the swamp. His had been the knock on the door that had interrupted Lydia's writing.

Her heart pounding, Abby glanced at her watch, pocketed the ornament and rushed to the window. From her vantage point, she could only see the edge of the stage. But she guessed it must be close to intermission. Perhaps, if she hurried, she could tell Carter about her discovery before the second act.

The show was just about to go on again when she caught Carter in back of the raised platform and breathlessly told him the news, while dangling the watch fob in front of him. As other actors and stagehands scurried around with last-minute preparations for the play's final act, he took the piece into his hand and stood musing over it.

"I know what this is," he murmured. "I recognize it from the portrait in the dining room. When he was an undergraduate my great-great-grandfather belonged to a secret society of scholars at the University of Virginia. This was given to him when he was inducted. We never knew what had happened to it."

He weighed the small gold object in his palm and then looked into Abby's eyes. "I've been doing some thinking about all this myself," he said at last. "It's hard to explain, but when I was onstage a few minutes back, I almost felt as if I had really stepped into Bryon's shoes."

"Watching you out there, I felt the same," Abby admitted. She didn't tell him that seeing Elaine portraying Lydia and listening to her speak those bogus lines had been so upsetting she'd had to leave.

"It should have been you in that green dress," Carter said unexpectedly. His intense, dark gaze continued to hold hers. "I know how Byron must have felt about Lydia. If it had been you, I would have defended you to the death, and, yes, I would have helped you escape—even though it would have broken my heart to know I was losing you forever."

"But Lydia wouldn't have betrayed Byron," Abby declared with absolute certainty. "She didn't steal the ruby."

Carter nodded. "I've been thinking about that, too. Zack Darwin is here. He's a local jeweler. After the performance I'll borrow the prop and ask him to take a look at it. I still can't believe there's any chance it's the lost ruby, but at least we'll do our best to clear that question up."

"Great!" Abby exclaimed. "That'll set both our minds at ease."

"Curtain time!" Prestwood called, appearing around the edge of a rack of costumes.

He smiled at Abby, but as she caught his guarded expression a lump rose in her throat. Was there any chance he'd overheard their conversation, she wondered. If he had, he showed no sign. "How we doing so far?" he asked.

"Great," she assured him, even though she hadn't actually seen more than a few minutes of the first act.

Meanwhile the actors had begun climbing the makeshift wooden steps to the stage. Smiling, Abby told Carter to break a leg.

"Thanks," he answered and reached out to give her hand a brief squeeze. The touch of his flesh on hers sent a warm glow through her and gave her hope that their problems might yet be straightened out.

With a lighter step, Abby went around in front of the stage to watch. The final act of the play with its condemnation of Lydia set her teeth on edge—all the more so now because she had a good idea of what had really happened. But she was so excited about the prospect of rediscovering the real ruby that she tuned out the words and settled down to enjoy watching Carter perform.

"Well, it was interesting, but I don't think Prestwood will be picking up any Pulitzers this year," Ordell muttered as he finished clapping after the last bows. He wiped his sweaty brow with a fresh white handkerchief.

"Nor a Nobel, either," Joanna agreed. "What do you think, Abby?"

"I think he may have to rewrite a few lines before he hits Broadway," she murmured with suppressed excitement. She placed her hands on Joanna's shoulders and quickly filled her friends in on the new information she'd uncovered.

"Given what we've just seen and what you've told us, I'd say Prestwood had better do some major revisions on his version of history," Ordell responded.

"Yes, indeed," Joanna agreed. "I'd like to be around to see Prestwood's face when the jeweler looks at the stone."

"I'll wager Prestwood's face will be as red as the ruby itself. I wonder if he'll enjoy revising his play from a jail cell?" Ordell asked.

"Jail!" Abby hadn't even thought about that. But surely Prestwood hadn't really done anything criminal, she told herself. She'd had no wish to get anyone into serious trouble. She had just wanted to set the record straight.

After Ordell and Joanna strolled off to roam through the food booths, gathering more local color for their articles, Abby headed back toward the stage.

Behind it, confusion reigned. Carter and a short thin man seemed to be facing off against a flushed and irate-looking Prestwood.

"The ruby is missing," Carter snapped as Abby came up to them. "Prestwood doesn't know what's happened to it."

"Maybe one of the prop people took it," Elaine volunteered. "I don't understand all the fuss. It's only a silly piece of glass."

Prestwood turned to his sister. "Yes, but if it's gone we're going to have to pay for another reproduction when we put the play on again next year." He turned back to the other men. "My sister's probably right. The ruby's most likely mixed up with the other props. We're bound to run across it in the next couple of days."

"I don't want to wait for that," Carter retorted crisply. "Let's find the propman and go through his stuff now."

"But we're supposed to be up at the house this very minute for a cast picture," Elaine protested.

"You go on ahead," Prestwood told his sister. "We'll be along in a couple of minutes." After she left, he, Carter, Zack and Abby found Alan the propman and had him open his box of stage materials.

"Damn!" Prestwood exclaimed, frowning down at the jumbled assortment. "Will you look at that!" Reaching in, he pulled out a piece of broken red glass. "This is my fault. I should have warned everyone to handle the ruby more carefully."

"Gee, it was fine when I put it in there," Alan said, his freckled face flushed. The ruby had been the teenager's responsibility, and he looked upset. "I had it sitting on top. But I guess it must have fallen through and somebody put something heavy on it."

Abby plucked at Carter's sleeve and then whispered, "Maybe this is a piece of the ruby we broke last night."

"Maybe," Carter replied sotto voce, "but there's nothing I can do about it now." Then he declared in a normal voice, "We have to get over to the house for the shoot." He took out a gold pocket watch from his vest and checked it. "We were due over there ten minutes ago, and we can't keep the press waiting any longer. Mary Lou's probably having fits as it is."

Abby nodded sympathetically and agreed to meet Carter later. Then she looked up and saw that Prestwood had been watching their whispered exchange closely. Zack was talking to him, but obviously Prestwood's attention was focused on them—and he looked worried.

After the men had left Abby wandered around thinking about this new development. She decided she needed to talk it over with Ordell and Joanna. But the first person she met was Callie, back to her normal attire of jeans and T-shirt.

"Did you see me?" the girl cried, rushing up as soon as she spotted Abby.

"I sure did. You were wonderful," Abby told her. "But why are you out of costume and not at that photo shoot?"

Callie waved her hand dismissively. "I couldn't stand that dress a minute longer. And there's so much going on at the house, I don't think anyone will notice I'm not there. Not everyone's there for the pictures, anyhow. Elaine isn't."

"She isn't?" Abby frowned. "But she's Lydia, one of the principals. Why would she miss a photo opportunity?" Abby asked, remembering that Elaine had made a point of wanting to go up to the house early for the shoot.

Callie shrugged. "I don't know."

"Did she say anything to you about not being there?"

"Nah, nothing important." Callie's gaze wandered to a trio of strolling musicians and then to a booth selling barbecued turkey legs. "Boy, am I hungry."

Abby persisted. "Did you talk to Elaine after the play?"

"Yeah," the girl admitted. "I met her when she was walking up to the house."

"What did you talk about?"

"Oh, she was just asking me again about that plate I gave to Aunt Hat. You know, the one I dug up in the schoolyard."

Abby grabbed Callie by the shoulders. "Did you tell her you gave it to Aunt Hat?"

Startled by the urgency in Abby's demeanor, the girl nodded dumbly. "Yeah, I figured it didn't really matter if she knew. But she acted real funny about it—all upset. Then she went rushing off."

"Where?" Abby demanded.

"Dunno. Maybe she wanted to get changed. Those dresses are hot." Callie shrugged again and Abby let go of her shoulders and stepped back. Once again, her mind raced. Besides the vanished ruby, the cipher disk was the only other piece of evidence of Jerome Matthews's duplicity that remained. What if Elaine knew that and had gone into the swamp to take it away from Aunt Hat?"

"Listen, I think you really should go back to the house for those pictures. Mary Lou will be very disappointed if you don't."

Callie rubbed her foot in the dirt and looked resigned. "I suppose."

"Do you mind if I borrow your boat?" Abby went on.

Callie's eyes lit up. "Sure. Are you going into the swamp? Can I come?"

"Not this time," Abby said, laying a restraining hand on the child's arm. "Mary Lou and your father put a lot of work into this pageant. Right now pleasing them is more important than anything else."

Reluctantly Callie acquiesced and started to straggle back toward the house. Abby turned and took a quick look around. Now that the play was over, the milling crowd had thickened. Strolling fiddlers peppered the air with lively music. A peddler holding a rainbow of helium balloons sang out over the steady hum of voices. Across the way, the sign emblazoned with Prestwood's campaign slogan, touting three generations of service and loyalty to the South, stirred in the faint breeze. In front of it a young man handed out bumper stickers and brochures.

The sun, at its height, beat down on the heads of the fair goers, some of whom sported large straw hats and parasols to counteract its effect. As Abby wiped a bead of perspiration from her forehead, she wished she'd thought to bring an umbrella. Then, in the distance, she spotted Ordell and Joanna taking pictures of each other in front of an old-fashioned loom set up at a craft stand. Abby hurried toward them.

"Are you sure it's wise to go into the swamp by yourself?" Joanna protested when Abby told them what she intended to do.

"By now I really know the way," Abby replied. "And I won't rest easy until I'm sure that Aunt Hat and the disk are all right."

"I don't see Elaine as the violent type," Ordell pointed out.

"No, I don't, either, but still..." Abby left the sentence unfinished and gave each of her friends a quick peck on the cheek before turning away.

When she was out of sight, Ordell and Joanna looked at each other. "This worries me," Joanna said. "Let's keep our eyes open."

"Most definitely," Ordell agreed. "What's more, I think it might be wise to station ourselves strategically so that we can monitor the 'traffic' on that path to the dock." The two set off for the booths at the far end of the lawn.

They were just about to plunk down money for cool beers when Ordell nudged his colleague. "Look, look!" He gestured with his head toward the path.

"Prestwood and Elaine!" Joanna hissed. "Hmmm, and they look like they're up to no-good."

"What do you say to our following them?"

Linking her arm with his, Joanna replied, "I say 'Lay on, MacDuff.'"

Behind them Barney shook the sleep from his eyes in the shadows of the live oak where he'd been napping. As the two food writers set off surreptitiously, he followed in their wake.

Chapter Fifteen

The light from the sun was green as it filtered through the dense canopy of leaves in the bayou. Nervously Abby swung the tiller and headed *The Pirate's Pursuit* down the twisting branch of dark water that led to Aunt Hat's.

Despite her brave words to Joanna and Ordell, Abby was frightened about being in the swamp alone. As the boat putted past Devil's Fork, she shuddered. Vividly she recalled the horror of sinking into its smothering pit of quicksand with no one to hear her terrified cries.

As she approached Aunt Hat's cabin, she grew increasingly apprehensive. What if Elaine had gotten there ahead of her? What if she had already taken the cipher disk away from the old woman and pitched it into the murky water? It would sink into the muck and be lost forever. And even if Aunt Hat had resisted Elaine's request, Abby still wasn't looking forward to the inevitable confrontation that would occur when she and Elaine met.

But, to her relief, there was no sign of a visitor at Aunt Hat's rickety dock. As Abby guided *The Pursuit* toward it, the old woman came tripping down the hill from her cabin, her dark features wreathed in a welcoming smile. She was wearing her "special spyglass" around her neck.

"Saw you comin'," Aunt Hat said, patting the binoculars. "You ain't all by yourself, are you?"

"Yes, I'm afraid so," Abby replied as she tossed Aunt Hat the line and the older woman looped it over a piling. "Has anyone else been out to see you?"

Aunt Hat shook her head. "Nope. Been right lonely these last couple of days. Didn't expect anyone today, either, with that pageant going on and all." She looked at Abby curiously. "Something special on your mind?"

Abby nodded. "Aunt Hat," she began as the two of them walked up the bank. "There's something I need to talk to you about, something important."

Aunt Hat paused, her sharp eyes surveying Abby. "What is it, child? I'm listening."

When they were inside, Abby explained about the cipher disk. As she spoke, Aunt Hat listened intently, interrupting every now and then to ask a question. Then the old woman went to a cupboard, pulled out the cipher disk, examined it briefly and handed it to Abby.

"Sakes alive, who ever would have guessed this old piece of metal could hold such power? I don't want it 'round here no more. You take it back to Mr. Carter with my blessing. In fact, now that I think on it. Maybe I'll give you some go-away powder to take with you. That'll surely speed it on its journey."

Busily Aunt Hat went to a shelf, took down a canister and dumped white powder from it into a small plastic bag. "You take a care now," she said, handing it to Abby. "If any enemies come round, you just throw this in their path. That ought to keep you safe."

Accepting the offering, Abby thanked the old woman and carefully tucked the bag into her pocket next to the good gris-gris she'd received on her last visit.

Together they walked back down to the boat, and Abby worried the whole way that Elaine might appear around the bend in the river at any moment. But, except for the birds and a pesky buzzing fly, the bayou was quiet. At the dock

Abby and Aunt Hat hugged each other and said goodbye. Abby was just about to pull away when Aunt Hat cried, "Wait! Wait!" Removing the binoculars from around her neck, she thrust them across the gap of water into Abby's hands. "I just got a feelin' in my bones that you might want these," she said. "And I've learned to trust these old rickety bones."

"Oh, I can't take your special spyglass," Abby protested.

The old woman waved away her objection. "Callie can get 'em back to me when you're through using 'em."

Gratefully Abby accepted the binoculars and hung them around her own neck. Then, with a last wave at her elderly friend, she ventured back out into the swamp.

It was very still out on the water. Heat seemed to shimmer through the thick greenery, and not a breeze stirred. Except for an occasional stinging gnat, even the insects seemed to have settled for an afternoon siesta. As the boat chugged along, Abby looked around nervously. If anybody was out here looking for her, they'd have no trouble finding her. In the eerie silence the boat's motor reverberated like a giant buzz saw.

Now, as Abby approached the turn at Devil's Fork, her forbodings welled up once again. In the distance the twisted shapes of the cypress trees that marked the spot loomed like specters. As if she were hypnotized, Abby found herself lifting Aunt Hat's spyglass to take a closer look. No sooner had the trees come into focus when she let the binoculars drop. Memories of her futile struggles to free herself from the quicksand rushed over her. Despite the heat, a cold sweat broke out on her brow, and she shivered.

It was then that she heard the sound of another motor in the distance. Snatching the binoculars up again, Abby peered through them. Beyond the screen of cypress she could see another boat heading up the bayou to round Devil's Fork. Focusing the binoculars more tightly, Abby made out two figures. One of them was a tall, thin woman in a yellow dress.

"Elaine and Prestwood," she gasped. It would have been bad enough to encounter Elaine alone, but now with Prestwood . . . Her heart beating wildly, Abby turned the rudder hard and aimed her little boat toward the Fork where she hoped to hide among the bearded cypress that grew so densely there.

As she slipped in among the cypresses, she knew the others had to have heard her motor. But maybe, with luck, they would dismiss the noise as having come from a fisherman's craft. By grabbing on to branches, Abby concealed the boat more securely among the jungle of roots. Quickly she cut the motor and looped a line around a stump. Then, holding her breath, she sat very still and waited. Tensely she prayed that they'd pass by without seeing her.

But as the sound of their motor came closer, Abby's original fears about Elaine going out to Aunt Hat's resurfaced. What might happen to Aunt Hat if Prestwood and Elaine thought she still had the disk and was hiding it from them? Surely they wouldn't hurt the old woman, Abby told herself. But how could she be certain?

Abby's fears for Aunt Hat were short-lived because, at that moment, she lifted the binoculars to her eyes and realized that the Matthews's boat was not going to continue down the bayou. Instead it had veered toward her and Elaine was pointing directly at her hiding place.

As soon as she realized that they must have seen her, Abby felt trapped. Now that she was in among the roots, she couldn't easily extricate the boat. Elaine and Prestwood would be on her before she was able to move it very far. Her only alternative was to get out of the boat and try to hide the cipher disk. Grabbing the precious antique device, she kicked off her shoes and scrambled over the side. In the water, Abby hesitated and reached over the boat's side. Her fingers closed around Aunt Hat's go-away powder. A person never knew. Maybe this voodoo stuff worked.

"IT DIDN'T TAKE YOU LONG to get back out of that dress," Carter commented as Callie strolled by him in her jeans and an old T-shirt. She was munching a turkey leg that she'd gotten from one of the booths. At her heels, Goldie followed. The retriever's tongue lolled out in the hopes of Callie dropping a sliver of meat in her path.

"Good riddance," Callie murmured between bites.

Carter reached out and tousled his daughter's hair. "I know what you mean. I was glad to get out of my costume, too," Carter agreed. "Seems nobody dressed for comfort back then."

Callie eyed her father's twill Bermuda shorts and cotton knit shirt. "Now you look like my dad again," she said.

Carter glanced around at the crowd. "Seen any of our guests?" he asked.

"Not lately," Callie answered, concentrating on her drumstick instead of looking her father in the eye.

Carter cocked his head. "Callie?" he said, eyeing her with suspicion. "Something going on that I should know about?"

"No, at least I don't think so," the girl admitted.

"You don't think so?"

"Well..." Much to Goldie's disappointment, Callie tossed the bone into a garbage can and wiped her hands on her crumpled napkin. "Something funny did happen a little earlier," she conceded.

"Go on."

The twelve-year-old picked at a stray piece of turkey stuck in her teeth.

"Callie?"

The girl sighed. "Well, Abby borrowed my boat."

Carter rolled his eyes. "Not again! What did she do that for? Don't tell me she went back to the swamp."

Under Carter's prodding, Callie described her last conversation with Abby, including Abby's questions about Elaine.

When he'd heard enough, Carter put his hands on his hips and shook his head. He looked around at the crowd. "Everything's under control here. I guess I'd better venture out to where it's not under control."

Callie brightened. "Can me and Goldie come?"

Carter thought for a moment. "Sure, you can help me look."

"WHERE DO YOU THINK THEY WENT?" Joanna said, shifting from side to side as she tried to see around Ordell's bulk. At the prow of the dinghy they'd commandeered, he sat with one hand shading his eyes, peering out at the water like General MacArthur preparing to storm the beaches at Guam. By his side, Barney perched, panting noisily.

"I think I saw them go thataway," Ordell replied, pointing to the right where the river branched.

"We'd know for sure if you hadn't stopped to buy sodas from that Cajun down by the dock," Joanna scolded. She pushed the tiller and aimed the boat in the direction of Ordell's raised finger.

"Joanna, when the sun's been beating down on us for hours you will get down on your knees to thank me for this bottle of lukewarm orangeade—not to mention this poor fur-covered creature who may well owe his life to my forethought," he added patting the top of Barney's head.

Joanna snorted. "We'll see about that. And why in the world you let him jump into this boat with us, I'll never know. I only hope those two up ahead aren't giving Abby any trouble."

"Don't worry. Abby's got grit. If they're besieging her, she'll hold out until we can come to her rescue." With that Ordell raised an arm high above his head and shouted, "Man the propeller, full steam ahead!"

"Aye, aye, sir," Joanna answered, and pushed the throttle up.

GINGERLY, Abby crept up on the bank. Testing the sand as she went along, she searched for a place to put the disk. Hiding it under a rock in the foundation of the old cabin was tempting. But Abby was afraid that would be the first place the Matthews would look.

As their motor ground closer, Abby's already thumping pulse quickened and perspiration dampened the strands of hair that had fallen across her forehead. Reluctantly she moved beyond the foundation toward the spot where she'd encountered the quicksand. At least this time she knew where it was. For a long moment, she stood staring at the deceptively innocent-looking patch of soft earth and her breath snagged raggedly in her throat.

Clutching the cipher disk, she wrapped her arms protectively around her chest and turned away. There had to be someplace where she could hide the Civil War code breaker. Abby's desperate gaze fell on what looked like a hollow tree stump. The sound of the approaching motor was suddenly stilled, and Abby knew in moments her pursuers would find her. Quickly she thrust the disk under the dried leaves that filled the hollowed-out core of the stump.

She was trying to force the metal disk out of sight when she heard the crack and rustle of feet climbing up through the thick growth on the bank. With one last frantic flick of her hand, Abby sent leaves scattering across the disk and moved away.

"Ah-ha, so there you are," Prestwood said, emerging from the greenery, the lower half of his linen slacks black with mud. "We thought we saw you in here."

"Yes," Elaine chimed in, eyeing Abby's wet sundress, which was plastered to her dirtied knees. Elaine, who'd also had to wade up onto the bank, was equally bedraggled. Brown water had stained the yellow of her gathered skirt. "What in the world are you doing?" she asked Abby. "Don't you know this is a dangerous spot? I've even heard there's quicksand around here somewhere."

Abby tried to think of a plausible excuse. "I just wanted to come out and have a look at this old foundation," she managed to say. "There was a cabin on this spot a hundred years ago, and I thought it might be useful to see it for my book."

"Oh, really?" Elaine replied skeptically.

For a moment the three of them stood looking at one another in dumb silence, as if this were merely an awkward social occasion.

Meanwhile Prestwood's gaze swept over Abby. He was looking for the cipher disk, she thought, her hands clenching into fists at her sides. At last, he cleared his throat. "Elaine has heard an interesting little story. I wonder if you know anything about it. It concerns a certain plate that Callie gave Aunt Hat."

"Oh?" Abby shook her head and shrugged.

"It's not really valuable," Prestwood went on, "but it has a certain sentimental importance, and my sister and I are most anxious to find out what happened to it."

Elaine touched her brother's shoulder. "We're just wasting time. She doesn't have it. The voodoo woman's probably still got it."

"Maybe," Prestwood murmured, his eyes not leaving Abby's face. "But I think not."

Through the canopy of leaves, the sun beat down on Abby's head. The simmering humidity and all the tension, combined to make Abby start to feel slightly sick. A bug nipped at the tender place behind her knee and she swatted it. All the while her frightened gaze never left Prestwood's. She didn't want him to go to Aunt Hat's, but she didn't want him to ask her any more questions, either.

"Are you sure you haven't seen this object?" he pressed. "It's about so big," he said, shaping a circle with his hands. "It wouldn't look like much, just a dirty old metal dish with raised writing on it."

Once again, Abby shrugged.

"Whew, it's nasty around here," Elaine complained, swooshing away a cloud of gnats. "I hate this place. I feel as if I'm about to pass out from heat prostration." She looked around, and then to Abby's horror, she walked over to the stump where the disk was hidden and plopped her bony form down on it. For a moment she shifted around trying to make herself comfortable. "I suppose this thing is just alive with creepy crawlies," she muttered. The thought seemed to galvanize her. She stood to peer down into the leaves and check for ants and spiders.

Abby's heart felt as if it were about to jump out of her chest.

"Oh, my," Elaine exclaimed, stirring the leaves with a stick she'd picked up from the ground. "What have we here?"

Prestwood turned his attention from Abby to his sister. "What are you babbling on about?"

With a triumphant smile, Elaine lifted the cipher disk and then held it out, balanced on her palm as if it were a crown jewel. "I do believe I've solved the mystery."

Grinning, Prestwood reached out for the disk. But before it went into his fingers, Abby thrust herself between them, yanked the disk away from Elaine and started to run.

"Oh, no, you don't!" Prestwood grabbed hold of Abby's skirt and sent her sprawling to the ground. "I'll take that," he said, seizing one edge of the disk.

Abby rolled over and yanked it out of his grasp only to have Elaine plunge down next to her. "You give that back. That's ours!" she screamed, clawing at Abby's arms.

The three of them rolled around on the boggy ground struggling for possession of the disk. Three pairs of hands clutched at the flat piece of metal, pulling it in one direction and then another. Abby felt her skirt rip as Elaine dug her foot into the gauzy material. Modesty be damned, Abby thought as she clung to her prize.

Just then a wet nose was thrust into Abby's ear and she felt the rough swipe of a warm, damp tongue. Startled, Abby screeched and would have let go of the disk except that Elaine's and Prestwood's hands, in their fervor to wrest away the treasure, were clamped on to hers.

"My God, what is that?" Elaine cried, rearing back.

In answer, Barney, muddy and practically unrecognizable let out a snarl and barked furiously, sending Elaine sprawling on the ground.

"Unhand that woman, you varmint!" Ordell cried out to Prestwood. Relief swept through Abby as she looked up to see Ordell come crashing through the brush, brandishing a large stick. In his wake Joanna came charging out of the greenery, wielding an even larger club and looking grimly determined.

With violent force, Prestwood tore the disk from Abby's grasp and started to push himself to his feet. In desperation, Abby thrust her hand into her pocket and pulled out the plastic bag of Aunt Hat's go-away powder. It had already come open in the melee. Abby scooped up the loose white dust and hurled it into Prestwood's face.

"Arrrhh!" He dropped the disk and staggered back, grabbing at his eyes.

Before Abby could retrieve the fallen disk, Ordell swooped in and with an agility that belied his corpulent figure, he seized the coveted object and ran off with it like a quarterback about to make a touchdown—right toward the quicksand.

"No, no, Ordell, no!" Abby cried out, holding up a hand. "There's quicksand that way!"

"Oh, my God," Joanna exclaimed and, still holding her stick, sprinted after him. At Joanna's cry, Barney's ears perked up. Forgetting his hostage, the big dog abandoned Elaine to join in the chase. Abby followed close behind the galloping canine with Elaine and then a cursing Prestwood at her heels.

But when Abby's bare feet hit a root, she stumbled and Prestwood bolted past her and his sister. A moment later he'd outdistanced Joanna as well and reached out to collar Ordell as their feet hit a suspicious-looking patch of soft earth.

With some animal sixth sense, Barney planted his forepaws and came to a skidding stop just at the edge of the dangerous bog. But neither Ordell not Prestwood were so prescient. Before either of them could stop, they were knee-deep in the sucking mud. For a moment, they both continued to run, unmindful of their lack of progress. Then, as they sank to their thighs, a look of horrified recognition broke out on both their faces.

Ordell let out a squawk, and tried to turn back. But the twisting motion and his weight, only dragged him down further. Now he and Prestwood were facing each other at little more than an arm's length.

Prestwood flailed out at Ordell. "Give me that disk!" he snarled.

"Not on your life, camel breath!" Ordell waved the disk over his head and then behind him, keeping it out of Prestwood's reach.

"Camel breath!" Prestwood's face went an ugly shade of red. "You wallowing water hippo! Keep your fat snout out of other people's business!"

While the two men clawed and shouted at each other, they slipped inches lower. It was as if each epithet embedded them more surely into the slime.

While Abby and Joanna tried to reach Ordell with a stick thrust in his direction, Elaine jumped up and down wringing her hands. "Prestwood, your pocket, your pocket!" she shrieked, making frantic gestures at his jacket. "Your pocket, your pocket!"

Prestwood broke off midinsult. His eyes followed Elaine's finger down to his coat, which was now waist deep in the quicksand. "Damn it to hell!" He reached into a pocket and fished out a small sack. Clenching it in his fist, he held it above his head. "Give me that disk, Blubber Belly," he said sneeringly to his mud-caked companion.

"Never, never!" Ordell waved the disk tantalizingly. "I shall fight to the finish, you bilious Bard. Your play stinks!" The food writer made a grab at Joanna's stick, but missed.

"Stinks!" Elaine screamed. "My brother's play was wonderful. It was that so-called gourmet dinner you cooked for us that stank!" She thrust a frantic hand out to her brother, but he was too far away.

"You two wouldn't know a gourmet meal from pig slop," Ordell retorted indignantly, taking another lunge toward Joanna's pole. "Prestwood's writing would give anybody indigestion."

The maligned playwright sputtered like a misfiring engine, so angry that he couldn't get words out.

"What's he got in his hand, Ordell?" Joanna shouted from the bank.

Abby had been eyeing the sack in Prestwood's fingers with suspicion. "Is that The Prize of India?" she demanded. "Is that the Forbes's ruby you've got, Prestwood?"

"No," Prestwood denied.

But at the same time, Elaine shouted "You'll never get that ruby from us, you nasty Yankee!"

"Ah-ha!" Ordell exclaimed and, using the disk as a weapon, made a violent swipe at Prestwood's upraised hand.

The women all gasped in horror as the bag tumbled into the quicksand. But it floated and a second later Ordell deftly scooped it up with the metal disk like a chef removing an eggshell from batter. Triumphantly he brandished the sack in one raised hand and the disk in the other. "That'll teach you to underestimate a blubber-bellied water hippo!"

"Aargh!" With his arms outstretched, Prestwood lunged at Ordell's throat. The quicksand, however, made it impossible for Prestwood to reach his quarry.

"Ordell, you big oaf, grab the stick," Joanna screamed.

"How can I when my hands are full?" he pointed out. "Here, catch!" He sailed the metal plate like a discus and Joanna and Elaine fell upon it. Barney, who'd been racing back and forth barking, joined the melee.

Ignoring them, Abby picked up the stick and again thrust it out toward the beleaguered food writer. But when Ordell grabbed on to it, she found she didn't have the strength to drag her friend out.

It was then that Goldie suddenly appeared. At the sight of her, Barney barked joyously and the two dogs greeted each other with eager sniffings and tail waggings. After completing this canine ceremony, the two dogs surveyed the scene in front of them. On the ground Joanna and Elaine still grappled for the disk. In the quicksand, Prestwood cursed and tried vainly to swim to safe ground. Ordell, sack clenched in one hand, gripped Abby's stick in the other. Abby, knelt on the bank and held on tight.

"My God, what's going on here!" a deep, masculine voice exclaimed. An instant later, Carter, with Callie behind him, sized up the situation and grabbed the stick from Abby. Slowly he pulled hand over hand until Ordell lay gasping on the bank like a beached whale.

Carter was about to turn his attention to Prestwood when Ordell, slime covered and panting from his ordeal, sat up and undid the sack. "Voila!" he crowed as he withdrew and then held up the brilliant stone inside. "The ruby!"

For a moment everyone, including the tussling women, went still and Callie took the opportunity to run over and yank the cipher disk from Elaine's hands. She scurried away with it and hid behind her father.

Meanwhile, Carter took the jewel from Ordell and held it between his cupped hands. "The Prize of India," he murmured. "It's beyond belief."

"Do you think it's the real thing?" Ordell gasped.

"Let's ask our friend out there," Abby suggested. "He's the one Ordell took it from." She pointed at Prestwood who was glaring at them from his position chest high in the pit of ooze.

"What about it, Prestwood?" Carter shouted, scowling at his neighbor. "What do you know about this?"

"Get me out of this muck before I drown in it," Prestwood growled.

Elaine, who now stood on the bank tearing at her hair, chimed in, "Do something! Do something! Save my brother!"

"Why?" Joanna demanded. "Why should we, after all he's done? Why not just let him sink out of sight?"

"I'd vote for that one," Ordell agreed. He'd taken off his shoes and socks and was vainly trying to scrape mud off them.

Ignoring the others, Carter pocketed the ruby. He picked up the rescue stick and leaned on it as if it were a giant cane.

"Tell me the truth, Prestwood. Did you dig up the ruby in the schoolhouse yard?"

"That's what all those holes were, Daddy," Callie said, "and here's the plate I found."

Carter took the cipher disk from his daughter's hands and looked down at it with an expression of awe. Then he let out a low whistle and murmured, "I never thought I'd live to see this."

"Those two were trying to steal it from Abby when we got here," Joanna interjected. "Who knows what they would have done if Ordell and I hadn't stopped them in time."

Abby shuddered. Carter handed the plate back to Callie and reached to rub Abby's back soothingly. Then he fixed his attention on Prestwood. "Why?" he asked. "Why didn't you give the ruby to me when you found it? It does belong to my family, and it was on my property."

"Get me out of here, and I'll tell you," Prestwood retorted sourly.

"No, you tell me first."

"The hell I will! I'll take my chances in the quicksand. Think of the headlines, Carter, when you let me drown."

Carter shrugged. "If that's the way you want it." He caught Abby's eye and winked to let her know he had no intentions of really leaving Prestwood.

But Elaine hadn't seen Carter's wink. She began to weep and made more futile attempts to push the stick within her brother's reach. "Oh, this is terrible, terrible," she moaned. "It's not really our fault. It's just because the real-estate business has been awful. We could hardly keep our mortgage payments up, and Prestwood was so worried about his campaign . . ."

"Shut up!" Prestwood shouted.

But his distraught sister rambled on. "It would have hurt us so if the truth about our ancestor had come out."

Abby's ears pricked up. "You mean Jerome Matthews?"

Elaine nodded and wiped her nose on the sleeve of her dress.

"Did he take the cipher disk and the ruby?" Abby demanded. "You might as well know that I've already found out he was a spy for the North."

Elaine nodded and, out in the mud, Prestwood groaned.

From his perch on the bank, Ordell *tch-tched*. He turned a cuff inside out and let gook drain from it. "'Three Generations of Service to the South.' Isn't that your campaign slogan, Prestwood?"

"Ah, but what kind of service," Joanna interjected, shaking her head. "The news that his ancestor had been a spy for the North would have made Prestwood into a laughingstock."

"It certainly would have dampened the voters' enthusiasm in these parts," Carter admitted. He took the pole from Elaine and extended it to Prestwood. "Okay, you might as well come on out."

"Wait," Abby said, holding up her hand. "One more question."

Elaine moaned again.

"Where did that nasty letter about me come from, the one with the Baltimore postmark?"

"Good question," Carter agreed. "What about it, Prestwood?"

Prestwood grabbed for the end of the pole. "Oh, all right. I guess it doesn't matter anymore. A friend mailed that letter for me. I wrote it."

"And all that voodoo stuff?"

Prestwood nodded again. "Yes, yes. It was me." As Carter drew Prestwood to safety, his body made ripples in the ooze. "I overheard Abby talking to her father on the telephone. When I realized what she was up to, I wanted to scare her away."

"That was you listening in," Abby blurted.

"Yes, it was me." Prestwood stood on secure ground now, shaking his hands and trying to fling the gook off of him.

Joanna turned to Abby. "Well, my dear, it looks as if you've solved your mystery and, after all these decades, Lydia Stewart is finally off the hook."

"Wow, does that mean I don't have to wear a dress in the pageant next year?" Callie queried.

Carter shook his head. "I don't know what it means," he said. His dark gaze met Abby's and a look of understanding passed between them. "I'm afraid we're going to have a lot of sorting out to do."

Epilogue

"Here's to the bride and groom!" Ordell said, lifting a glass of bubbling champagne and holding it up toward the blue Louisiana sky.

"Yes, here's to Abby and Carter, may they forge a new legend at The Prize of India—a much happier one than we've ever known before!" Joanna exclaimed.

"Here, here!" The guests gathered around the long table beneath the live oaks on the plantation's manicured front lawn cheered enthusiastically.

Carter, handsome in his formal dark suit, smiled at Abby. In her traditional white lace gown and flowing veil held in place with a wreath of white flowers, she was a vision of bridal beauty. For the something new she'd worn the gown, for the something borrowed she'd accepted Joanna's linen hanky, for the something blue she wore a lacy garter, a gift from her husband-to-be. But for the something old, there'd been only one possibility. Her fingers went up to the pearl-drop earrings that once had belonged to Lydia Stewart and she smiled.

"I'd like to drink to good friends, and a wonderful family," Carter added, putting an arm around Callie.

In honor of the day, the twelve-year-old had donned a yellow dress without issuing a single protest. She was obviously delighted with her new stepmother as she raised her glass of pink lemonade and drained it in celebration.

Glowing with happiness, Abby prepared to cut the cake. Lowering her knife to draw it through the creamy white frosting decorated with candied violets and elaborate scrollwork, she hesitated and shook her head.

"Ordell and Joanna, your cake is too beautiful to eat."

"I must admit it would make Michelangelo swoon with envy," Ordell pronounced, "but I assure you it's not merely beautiful. Your taste buds will be driven to a frenzied ecstasy on the first bite."

As usual, Joanna took a playful swat at Ordell. "Ignore him and cut it, Abby," she said, pointing at the cake.

Laughing, Abby lifted the first piece out, put it on a plate and presented it to her groom. Carter, gentleman that he was, took a forkful and fed it to Abby, who returned the favor. Then the bride, with Joanna's help, began serving her guests.

The only two familiar faces that were missing belonged to Elaine and Prestwood Matthews. "I hear Lilyvale's up for sale now," Joanna ventured as she forked up the last piece of her dessert.

"Yes," Mary Lou answered. "Prestwood's not living there anymore, you know, and neither is his sister."

"It was pretty generous of you, Carter, not to press charges against those two," Ordell said, reaching for a second helping. "Hmmm, this cake really is a masterpiece," he muttered under his breath.

"I don't think pressing charges would have served any purpose," Carter replied. "Anyhow, Prestwood's humiliation at the polls was punishment enough. When it came out that he had found Jerome's private papers and had known his ancestor was really the spy responsible for stealing the ruby and cipher disk, his popularity took a serious dip. He did redeem himself partly, though, by giving those papers to the university so that historians can study them."

"I guess some history books will be rewritten," Joanna speculated.

"You can bet on that," Peter Heatherington piped up as he admired Mary Lou's fluttering eyelashes. "Tell me, what's the dynamic duo doing now?"

"Prestwood's selling real estate in Arizona," Callie said.

"And rumor has it," Abby interjected, "that he's going to run for sheriff."

"What irony," Joanna said, rolling her eyes.

"At least he's not writing plays," Ordell commented between bites.

"Elaine's moved to Florida to train to be a nurse," Abby went on. "Actually I think that's going to be a very good change for her. She needed to get out from under her brother's domination."

"Actually things have turned out well for everyone," Carter said, taking Abby's hand and smiling into her eyes. "The ruby and cipher disk are safely ensconced in the Baton Rouge Historical Society museum where they belong. Lydia Stewart's name has been cleared. The pageant play is going to be rewritten by Abby. And," he said squeezing his bride's hand, "as Joanna put it so poetically earlier, Abby and I will be making some history of our own."

An hour later Abby had tossed her bouquet to Mary Lou and changed into a blue linen traveling suit. When she emerged from the guestroom where she'd been staying, her father carried her suitcase down the stairs for her. Just as they were about to walk out the door to the car where Carter stood waiting, Abby put a hand on her father's arm and said, "Hold on just a minute, Dad. I have to say thank-you to someone."

Peter Heatherington cocked his head quizzically and then grinned. "Sure thing."

Abby crossed the marble floor into the parlor where Lydia Stewart's portrait hung. For several minutes she stood gazing up at her ancestor. "If it weren't for you, Lydia, I would never have met and fallen in love with this wonderful man," Abby murmured. "Thank you. I'll be seeing you again when we get back from our honeymoon."

It almost seemed as if Lydia's mouth twitched into the hint of a smile. But that was just an illusion, Abby told herself as she turned away and hurried toward her groom and her new life.

That night on the *Mississippi Queen* Abby and Carter stood outside their cabin on their little private balcony and watched the lights dance along the dark shore. Abby wore the silken peignoir she'd bought for this moment and Carter had a brief silk robe wrapped around his lean torso. As the water lapped beneath them, they kissed passionately.

When they finally drew apart, Abby gazed up at her beloved. "Did you know that Lydia and Byron first kissed in the moonlight, too?"

"And how did you know that?" Carter said, caressing Abby's hair while he dropped little kisses on her throat.

"Lydia's diary," Abby murmured. "Byron was her favorite topic."

Carter nibbled on Abby's ear. "And, pray tell, who do you write about in your diary?"

"I haven't got one."

"Then maybe you'd better get one," Carter whispered. "Because, beautiful lady, I'm going to give you many romantic moments to remember."

"Is that a promise, Mr. Forbes?"

"Absolutely," he said, sweeping her up into his arms and carrying her back into their stateroom. Then, as the paddle wheeler glided up the winding river, they fell into each other's arms to forge a new understanding between North and South.